Her Husband's Murder

Jaime Lynn Hendricks is an author with nearly 20 years' experience in print media and marketing. *His Missing Wife* is her first novel. She lives with her husband in New Jersey.

Also by Jaime Lynn Hendricks

His Missing Wife

Jaime Lynn Hendricks

HER HUSBAND'S MURDER

CANELO

First published in the United States in 2022 by Scarlet, An Imprint of
Penzler Publishers

This edition published in the United Kingdom in 2022 by

Canelo
Unit 9, 5th Floor
Cargo Works, 1–2 Hatfields
London SE1 9PG
United Kingdom

A CIP catalogue record for this book is available from the British Library.

Print ISBN 978 1 80032 556 2
Ebook ISBN 978 1 80032 555 5

Cover design by Lisa Brewster

Cover images © Depositphotos

Look for more great books at www.canelo.co

Printed and bound in Great Britain by Clays Ltd, Elcograf S.p.A.

I

For my husband John, because I couldn't do any of this without you by my side.

Part One

1

The Killer

The Wedding Day, 7:00 p.m.

He really thought he'd be able to get away with it.

So smug.

It happened quickly. At that point in the wedding reception everyone was drunk, bouncing around on the dance floor, and no one was paying attention. They were throwing glitter from the nearby bin, a bunch of adults acting like five-year-olds hopped up on sugar. People were clamoring together to try to be in the live Instagram video, but I watched closely as Trevor's upper lip curled into itself, and his face turned a slight crimson shade. He stopped jumping up and down to Kool and the Gang and loosened his bow tie, but that did nothing to calm the swelled vein in his forehead.

Then *BAM* he hit the ground like a ton of bricks.

At first there was shock, then chaos as his new wife Fiona wailed for his EpiPen in her bag at the sweetheart table. Half of the guests were screaming to revive him, and the other half were trying to give him room to breathe. His anaphylaxis worsened as everyone panicked.

Trevor's leg convulsed, his face flushed, and his lips swelled. I got a small amount of pleasure as he looked

3

at me, though I wasn't sure in his desperate state that he understood that it was *me* who did it. His threats to expose me to my friends, to hurt those I loved, those were things I couldn't take anymore. I mouthed *Fuck you* to him as he clutched his throat, unable to breathe, and his shiny new wedding ring glistened from the overhead disco ball lights. His handsome face looked wretched as he gasped for air— his eyes bloodshot as the oxygen stopped flowing in his veins. No more gasping. He stopped moving altogether.

The EpiPen that Fiona always carried was nowhere to be found. She screamed obscenities to everyone around her, unable to leave Trevor, repeatedly tapping his face and asking him to wake up. The live video was killed, and the DJ had finally cut the music, which made Fiona's pleas seem louder and more desperate.

It was too late by the time the banquet manager found their emergency EpiPen—Trevor stopped breathing minutes ago. The EpiPen plunged into his leg, and then out ten seconds later. Fiona was on the floor, Trevor's head on her dress, and she freaked out when he didn't respond to the injection—crying and flailing her arms in the air.

The five best friends, me included, gathered around an inconsolable Fiona who still hadn't figured it out. There would be no cake cutting, there would be no honeymoon in Paris, no house with a picket fence and no family pets, children, or grandchildren. Not with him, anyway. Fiona was only thirty-two—she was young enough that she'd find someone else and move on with her life. Eventually. She'd been widowed on her wedding day, so she'd have to grieve, but she'd get over it.

While Trevor lay motionless, we were all ushered out of the room, save for Fiona and both their immediate families. On one side were Fiona's mother, Susan, her

Uncle John, and her brother, Jesse, with his boyfriend, Hector. Trevor's parents, Margot and Harrison Vaughn, were on the other side.

In the lobby bar, the five of us shared our disbelief. There were tears and blank faces.

"I can't believe this just happened."

"Poor Fiona."

"Was it the peanut allergy?"

"Why didn't the EpiPen work?"

"What are we all supposed to do now?"

Everyone else came over and clasped hands on our shoulders and lower backs to console us, sad for us that we lost our great friend. *Pfft*. Trevor was the outsider since Fiona met him only a year ago. Our clan resulted in many hookups, as we all came to find out, but only two marriages. Wait—one marriage, since this once never really took off.

We all had a drink—yes, all of us—but it didn't take the edge off as the stretcher rolled in. The medics were locked behind the ballroom doors for about five minutes when we heard screams, as they let the family know that at that point, there was nothing they could do. Trevor was dead, on his wedding day, and how epic that he was already dressed for his funeral. He did look lovely today. What a shame.

My work wasn't done—he might've had a fail-safe plan in place—but for now, I had to try not to sway with the beat of the lounge music playing low in the lobby bar. After all, I was supposed to be mourning, not celebrating.

All heads sunk low and turned away as the stretcher came out, zipped body bag on top. He was lifted into the waiting ambulance by two EMTs. Trevor's distraught parents got into the ambulance with the body to make an official identification and, in all likelihood, schedule an autopsy.

Fiona's mother and Uncle John escorted her out of the ballroom, her makeup streaked all over her face, colors dripping down and staining the front of her white dress like a Monet painting. Her hair had come undone for the second time, having already been redone once after braving the storm outside, and she looked more like the Bride of Frankenstein than the girl who walked down the aisle on the beach only hours ago.

They were taking her up to rest in the honeymoon suite that would never live up to its name.

I assumed detectives would be questioning everyone soon. I wasn't sure how specific these forensic tests could get. It was never my intention to get the hotel staff or the caterers in trouble, but as long as the blame was placed far away from me, well, those were casualties of war.

And a war it was.

2

ETHAN

Two days before the wedding, 9 a.m.

Ethan Pierce couldn't hold his lovely wife's hand as they rushed their luggage through the airport, even though he wanted to. Wheels quickly turned over with a dull thud on the linoleum as he and Emma bopped and weaved their way through LaGuardia. The airport that Thursday morning was filled with the usual suspects: businesspeople and vacationers, foreign and domestic.

The traffic from their apartment in Midtown was ridiculous, as it always was two weeks before Christmas in New York City. The cab had to make its way through Rockefeller Center, where Santas on every corner jingled their bells, some for the children, some for the Salvation Army donations. The tourists who visited the tree crossed against the lights and walked across the streets holding hands, spanning the entire sidewalk, annoying every real New Yorker in a hurry to get around them. The ice that fell overnight didn't help, and there were a rash of accidents on the expressway. Already late to the gate, they couldn't miss their college friend Fiona's wedding in Miami—her wedding to that wretched Trevor Vaughn.

Ethan had put on a happy face whenever Trevor's name was uttered, and pretended they were friends, just like he'd been instructed to do.

Or else.

Or else Trevor would let his beloved wife know what he'd been hiding.

They finally reached gate B42, out of breath, where over two hundred people ambled around the ropes in the boarding section, indicating that no one had gotten on the plane yet. Emma looked at Ethan, and he smirked at her.

"Told you so," he mumbled under his breath, making quite sure that she knew he spoke, but also that she wouldn't understand him.

"*Com licença?*" she asked with a smile, being used to his snark. She was half Portuguese and liked to use her father's native language when trying to make Ethan feel remorse.

"Nothing, darling," he said as his arm slipped around her neck, and he leaned down almost ten inches and kissed her temple underneath her dark hair. She stood on her tippy toes to meet him halfway, her startling green eyes sparkling.

With one arm resting over Emma's shoulders, Ethan felt in his back pocket for his cigarettes with his free hand, comforted by the structure of the box against his palm. Adjusting the New York Rangers hat over his dark hair, his blue eyes scanned the impatient crowd for a familiar face, looking for Dutch, Veejay, or Allie—they were all supposed to meet at the gate. Instead, he saw irritated businesspeople checking their watches, surely missing meetings because of the delay, and the usual zombies scrolling through Instagram on their smartphones, no doubt hashtagging *#stilldelayed #whyihateflying #getmetothebeach.*

8

Finally, he spotted the mess of loose platinum curls and knew he'd found Dutch, chatting up a young flight attendant. Perennially single, the man was like a heat-seeking missile when it came to women. Ethan let out a sigh, thrilled to see Dutch relaxed. Between the mess with their old friend Roger—Dutch's best friend since high school—and the nasty divorce his parents were going through, he'd been a bundle of nerves for the last few months.

They all had. Roger's deception and disloyalty had thrown them for a loop. Ethan took it as a warning to do as he was told—he was positive the information that got Roger banished from their group of friends came from Trevor. Aside from his love for Emma, Ethan had never been so sure of anything in his life.

"Should've known that's what Dutch was doing," Ethan said to Emma with a chuckle. Having forgotten his contacts in the rush of the morning, he squinted at the digital board behind the counter. "The flight is on a short delay, probably from the ice last night. Corrine said that we're lucky to be getting out of town this weekend. It's supposed to be absolutely freezing here, but it's record-breaking heat down in Miami. Lucky us."

Ethan worked in a newsroom for a local New York City channel, and Corrine was their meteorologist. He was waiting to be promoted to a producer, wanting to guide how the stories they covered were perceived. Chaotic as it was at times, he loved his job. He found out about storms and scandals and school closings before anyone else. Speaking of scandals…

His eyes shifted back to Dutch. When the flight attendant had had enough of his charm, she plugged her number into his iPhone and gave him a playful slap. Dutch turned on his heels and tucked his phone into the back of his jeans pocket. With a satisfied smile, he spotted his friends.

"My man!" Dutch said as he approached Ethan and Emma, and high fived both. That was his typical "hello," an act he probably picked up at the youth center where he volunteered with disadvantaged teenagers for the past decade. "Are you ready to be a groomsman?" he asked, all smiles, while holding up his own tuxedo bag.

"Can't wait," Ethan lied and forced a smile— something he'd gotten used to doing whenever the subject of Trevor or the wedding came up.

They were all *Fiona's* friends—not Trevor's. They barely knew him. Ethan didn't know why Dutch and Veejay were so amped up about being groomsmen. Ethan had to be blackmailed into doing it. *Or else.*

"So, where's Veejay?" Ethan asked, scanning the area around Dutch. "Didn't you guys share a cab from down-town?"

Dutch nodded to the left. "Yeah. He's taking a leak or buying a book on aliens or whatever weird shit he reads. And we know Allie will be the last one here. That girl will be late to her own funeral."

"Watch it," Emma said, naturally defending her best friend.

The door to the jetway opened to let the flight attendants and the pilot into the plane, and the single-digit windchill sailed through the waiting area. The door clanked shut behind the employees, but the biting cold lingered. Emma shivered and pulled her cashmere sweater tighter around her shoulders, and Ethan overcompensated.

"Are you okay?" he whispered into her ear, away from Dutch's eyes. "Are both of you okay?" His gaze drifted south.

They had planned to tell everyone that Emma was pregnant once they'd settled into the hotel, even though they were only at the seven-week mark. People were bound to question why she didn't always have a glass of red wine in her hand while on a mini vacation and at the wedding of one of their closest friends.

Ethan rarely shied away from a cocktail. It was a hard habit to grow out of in his twenties, which had caused a couple of breakups with Emma over the last dozen or so years. Now, at thirty-three, he knew it was time to grow up, especially with the baby coming. Emma was obsessed with her niece Bianca in Portugal, even from across the Atlantic, so he couldn't wait to see what kind of mother she'd become. What kind of parents they'd become, together.

She'd always brought him more pleasure than the bottom of a bottle.

No matter what he did while they were apart. No matter what lies he'd told.

3

EMMA

Two days before the wedding, 9:05 a.m.

"The baby is fine, *shhh*," Emma said with a smile, and giving Ethan that look.

He smiled back at her, pulled her close to his chest, and kissed the top of her head, a gesture she loved. She'd always had stars in her eyes when it came to Ethan, since the first time she saw him in her Intro to Humanities class, when she was still an undergrad. Too inexperienced to make the first move, she waited. And waited. It only took him two years to ask her out, but she never looked back.

That was how she'd rationalized her faults. Mistakes were made, but her heart stayed true.

Breaking away from her husband's comforting embrace to scan the crowd, she still didn't see tall, redheaded Allie, who was hard to miss. Emma, a bit of a gossip at heart, was starving for details regarding Allie's recent divorce from Wharton, but Allie had been vague about the reasons. They'd been married just over five years, and Emma never understood why Allie fell for someone twice her age, but it wasn't like Emma had much dating experience herself. Ethan was her first real relationship. Her first *everything*.

Although Emma wasn't as naïve as she'd let on.

Her stomach dropped every time she thought about what Trevor had said to her five months ago, when she found out that he knew about her past. It still made her sick to that day.

It's not just about you, Emma. You'd all turn on each other if this came out.

The worst part was, she knew he was right. Hell, when Roger's secret was exposed right after Fiona and Trevor's engagement five months ago, the whole group stopped talking to him. In Emma's own situation, everyone would be forced to take sides. While Allie would stay camp Emma, even *she* would probably look at her differently. Once this wedding was over, Emma hoped she'd be able to cut the puppet strings Trevor had been using to manipulate her. She was tired of talking about what a *great guy* he was.

"Has Allie given either of you details about the divorce yet?" Emma asked, thankful for the background noise of another flight's boarding, pushing down her jealousy at the people heading to places like Paris, London, and of course, Lisbon.

Dutch shook his head sympathetically. "Nope, she hasn't said anything to me. But old, rich men like Wharton seem to want to upgrade every few years, and Allie's over thirty now." Dutch scoffed. "Poor girl. She's a catch, too."

Dutch had no love lost for his father, another old, rich man, and Emma always wondered why—the divorce was his mother's doing. Dutch had the most privileged of upbringings, with his father being one of the lead real estate developers in New York City.

"I feel so bad for her," Emma said with a frown and a slow, deliberate shake to her head. "I sent her a box of romance books we have coming out. Hopefully, they'll keep her mind occupied." Emma's Ivy League English degree had landed her a job as an associate editor for one of the top publishers in New York. Emma moped. "Do you think Wharton cheated on her?"

She bit her tongue at the slip in front of Dutch. Divorce was almost always about infidelity.

At least Ethan hadn't been unfaithful to Emma. Not really. His dalliances happened when they were broken up. It crushed her to know that he'd slept with other women since they'd met, but *she* broke up with *him* both times. What was he supposed to do, join the priesthood?

They'd met at eighteen, started dating at twenty, and married ten years later. Their first breakup lasted for three months when they were fresh out of college, both figuring out adulthood, and Emma had had enough of Ethan's constant partying and drinking. She took him back when he promised to change. It didn't last, and their next breakup lasted for a full year. It was the darkest period of Emma's life, for so many reasons. That time, Ethan *had* changed, but she couldn't take him back, even though she wanted to.

Trevor found out why. And he'd been dangling it in front of her for the last five months.

Just do what I say, and he'll never know.

That was reason enough for her to play his sadistic game.

Her phone pinged with a text from her sister, Cassandra, who still lived in Portugal. As she usually did when she got any sort of communication from Cassandra, she dropped everything and fixated on her phone.

"What is it? Is everything okay?" Ethan asked.

She stared for a few more seconds before she turned her phone in Ethan's direction.

"Awww," he said, "so cute."

There was Bianca, sitting on Santa's lap, no longer the baby or even the toddler Emma remembered, but now turning into her own little person. Festive for the holidays, she wore a red dress with red and white striped tights and green and black elf shoes. The ribbons on the top of her soft dark hair were red and green with bells attached. While most five-year-olds were terrified of Santa, big and jolly and hiding behind his big fluffy beard, Bianca stared up at him with admiration, like he was a magical being that really would bring her a new teddy bear, or more likely, an iPad. Emma hoped that Bianca was asking for a visit from Auntie Emma. It's all she ever wanted.

"Look at that face!" Emma squealed, fingering the glass on her iPhone like Bianca would feel it.

Ethan pulled her close and kissed her temple. "I hope it's a girl," he whispered, away from Dutch.

Her heart sank.

4

DUTCH

Two days before the wedding, 9:10 a.m.

Dietrich Von Ryan, known to his friends as "Dutch," had paid for everyone's flights in addition to their room upgrades. He felt he had to. No one would be going to this horrendous gathering if it weren't for him, but they didn't know that. They had all refused his offer at first, of course. Despite the hefty number of zeroes in Dutch's bank account, none of his friends had ever leeched off him.

"I can't wait to get on the plane and get some sleep." Dutch bopped his head from left to right as if to put his sore muscles on display and rubbed the back of his neck.

"Trouble sleeping?" Ethan asked sympathetically. "I know you're dealing with a lot."

Dutch pressed his lips together, then nodded his head. "I was up half the night writing my speech for the mayor's fundraiser next week. The one for keeping the million-dollar condos away from East Harlem. My dad's company is trying to develop it." A reformed party boy, Dutch was the antithesis of his powerful, money-grubbing father.

Ethan hesitated before he spoke. "Oh. Right. One of my friends at work is in charge of that profile on your father," he said.

Dutch scoffed. He obviously knew all about the profile. His father always hogged the limelight with pleasure. Except when he had to pay people to keep bad things quiet.

"I'll take a look at it in editing," Ethan continued, "you know, to make sure." His eyebrows raised.

Dutch laughed. "To make sure that the real reason for the divorce stays hidden, or so that my father doesn't come off looking like a dick? Seriously, like he needs more money. How could he do this? No one is going to be able to afford to live there anymore if this goes through." Dutch shook his head. "Easy for him to bark commands from his ivory tower."

Klauss Von Ryan was a renowned New York City developer, and Dutch was the only heir to the Von Ryan fortune, part of which he came into at twenty-five, the balance due at thirty-five. His father was ruthless and bought up poor neighborhoods, displacing the less fortunate in favor of skyscrapers and luxury apartment buildings, Starbucks and artisanal cheese shops.

Dutch's outlook on life had changed over the last decade, since the summer after college graduation—the one that changed his life. Since then, he'd fought against his privilege and had grown to hate gentrification. It was why he'd ditched his obligatory Ivy League finance degree and lobbied against everything his father stood for. He also donated his time as a counselor in the New York City public school system—all five boroughs. He was a big brother, a volunteer basketball coach, and fundraiser. Habitat for Humanity was a twice-a-year trip. He'd been to Africa to build wells, to Mexico to build schools, and to the Middle East to fight for women's rights. His passport

17

had more stamps than the President's. He had nothing but time.

Whatever would keep his mind occupied, he'd do. He couldn't sit still, running away from his checkered past like he was in a marathon. Anything to keep Los Angeles—and what happened to Kelsey—off his mind. And worse, his role in it.

"I declined the interview for my father's profile," Dutch said, shuddering. "They want a few statements on the record. The reporter said he thought I faked my passion helping people. I'm not like *him*," he said as he spoke of his father. "Or her. Who knew, right?" Dutch added, referencing the somewhat newfound information about his mother.

Ethan clapped Dutch on his shoulder. "Sorry. I can't imagine what you're going through."

"That news guy just wants me on camera to talk about the big, bad corporate monster, while I'm a volunteer. The good son. The yin-yang factor." His lips curled and he shrugged.

Dutch winced as he told the fib. The truth was, he didn't want to be on camera if the gotcha moment came. The one he'd been dreading for a decade.

The bad son.

Trevor knew all about it. But Dutch couldn't let his friends in on the fact that he was being blackmailed. *Trevor is so cool*, he'd practiced saying for five months. *Yeah, man, Trevor is an okay guy!* A few more days and the whole ruse would all be over. Hopefully.

In the waiting area, a baby was screaming on a young mother's hip while a little girl ran around in circles as the father tried to catch her. The baby's wail pierced Dutch's eardrums until he thought his head would explode.

Thankfully, that's when he noticed Vee heading toward the gang with an overflowing bag from Hudson Booksellers. Vee was always a calming influence—so much so that Dutch bet the baby would stop screaming just because Vee was nearby.

"Nerd," Dutch said to Vee upon his return. "More books about aliens?"

Vee's hazel eyes glowed against his medium-toned skin. "Science fiction isn't aliens. It's the future." He'd told them he got his beautiful eyes from his mother, whom he hadn't seen since he came to America from India seventeen years ago.

They all loved to play on Vee's nerdiness, Dutch especially. "The future, huh? So, anything that might capture my interest?" he asked, flippantly jamming his index finger into Vee's polybag. "Living on the moon? Flying cars? Beautiful blue women?"

The baby no longer screamed in the background, only soft cooing drifted to his ears. Dutch was right.

"Well, nothing about the Real Housewives or the Kardashians," Vee said with a smirk.

None of his friends had ever let Dutch live down the fact that he'd been photographed at a party in Los Angeles a decade ago with people famous for doing nothing. However, if it was up to Dutch, he'd erase the entire time he'd spent in LA anyway. He hadn't been back since.

The boarding announcement boomed through the waiting area right at that moment, and frustrated passengers swarmed forward in lines, pushing to the front like they'd get a prize for stepping on the plane first. Who could blame them? They were all awaiting palm trees and pink sunsets and fruity drinks garnished with cherries and paper umbrellas instead of the arctic chill that had come to New York.

"Well Mr. Rahna, it looks like you're the angel of time," Dutch said to Vee. He scratched the back of his head, his hair fuzzy beneath his palm. "Let's do this. Three days of fun!"

Fun. His stomach lurched. Fiona was only with that asshole Trevor because of him; because *his* unfortunate circumstance brought Trevor into her life. Fiona thought she'd met him randomly—they all thought so. By the time Dutch found out that Trevor had positioned himself strategically in Dutch's life and, therefore, Fiona's, there was nothing he could do about it. He was already being blackmailed. He couldn't say a thing.

Dutch extended the handle on his roller bag. "First class awaits."

"I'll stay here and wait for Allie," Emma said, then looked at Ethan. "Go ahead and get settled on the plane, babe."

"You sure?" Ethan asked.

"Yeah. Go with Dutch and Vee. She'll only be a few more minutes."

"I'll wait too," Vee said.

"Okay." Ethan kissed Emma's head. "Love you."

Dutch was the best kind of jealous whenever he was around Ethan and Emma—a couple so perfect for each other, they'd never hurt the other. It was a connection he'd longed for, and he felt another pang of regret. He silently picked up his carry-on and went to the front of the line, and Ethan trailed behind him.

Dutch felt lucky to have this time bonding with his closest friends, since it might be his last. If Trevor got his way, Dutch would soon be in handcuffs.

5

VEEJAY

Two days before the wedding, 9:15 a.m.

Veejay Rahna looked at his watch—an old school digital that quickly beeped twice every hour on the hour. "I hope Allie is okay."

Vee had *zero* romantic feelings toward Allie. Just protective ones.

"You and that stupid watch." Emma smirked, because she knew he adored it. Those types of watches were out of style by the time she'd hit kindergarten, but he'd told her that in India they were the hot new thing when he was in high school. Emma looked at her own watch, then checked her phone, breaking into a smile.

"What's that all about?" Vee asked.

Emma's mouth drew hesitantly into a straight line. "Oh. Cassandra texted me Bianca's Christmas pictures."

Vee grabbed the phone from her hand, and she initially resisted giving it up—he felt the tension—but he was dying to see the pictures that made Emma's smile so wide. His eyes adjusted to the small screen. Emma rejected technology and had an older version of the iPhone while Vee got the latest model every release day. It came with his IT job, always on the cutting edge of everything electronic and security.

21

If only he knew *more* about security, he wouldn't be in this mess with Trevor.

"Wow! She got huge!" Vee said. "I haven't seen her since your wedding. Have you?"

Emma frowned. "A couple times. I hate watching her grow up on a screen. They can't make it for Christmas, but they'll be here for New Year's. I can't wait."

Vee knew the feeling. He thought about his own family back in India, whom he hadn't seen for quite some time. Not his choice. He was cast off, the black sheep of the family, for bringing them shame.

"Anyway," Emma continued, tearing the phone from his hand and sliding it into the front of her purse, "Allie is probably held up at security. She already texted me that she was here."

He smiled at his best friend. Vee and Emma were the first to become friends out of the seven of them—wait, the six of them. He still wasn't used to the fact that Roger was banished. Once upon a time, the guys were Vee's fraternity brothers, while Emma, Allie, and Fiona were sorority sisters. When Ethan and Emma started dating at twenty, they became a group, one that held tight to this day. They were his people. The ones closest to him.

Vee had told everyone he grew up in a small village and had gotten a grant to go to college in the states from India, but the truth was, he'd been shipped to the states and attended a private boarding school in Vermont two years prior to college, for reasons he hoped to take to the grave.

Eager to get away from his dreadful mistake, he'd seized the chance to start anew. He was a straight-A student, a lacrosse player, vice president of student counsel, and thought of himself as an all-around nice guy. Pulling an all-nighter? Vee was there with pizza. Needed advice on what color to paint your wall? Vee was there with swatches and a paintbrush. Someone break your heart? Vee was there with beer. Nothing was going to stop him.

Until Trevor found out about what he did, and it was enough to keep him compliant. *What a catch Fiona! Trevor is such a great guy!*

The reality was, he prayed daily that Trevor would drop dead.

6

ALLIE

Two days before the wedding, 9:15 a.m.

Allie Whitton sat in the back seat of the black car as Ahmed unloaded her bags from the trunk. She checked her phone to see if her father had answered her text yet; he hadn't, but he was probably medicated. She always told him when she left to go anywhere, and she always texted him when she landed. She was going to miss that connection. He didn't have long now.

She took off her designer sunglasses, a gift from her ex-husband, and slid them on top of her head, keeping her now-blond hair off her face. Cringing into the compact mirror, she reapplied her lip gloss. Every time she saw her reflection during the last two weeks, she wanted to cry. Allie rubbed a lightened piece of hair between her thumb and forefinger. Its straw-like feel was a far cry from her former thick, shiny hair. She'd ditched her longer, natural red rather forcibly and she hated the change. She supposed she might as well embrace it and see if blonds really *did* have more fun, but it didn't take out the sting.

The last thing Allie wanted to do was celebrate a wedding. She'd planned on leaving Wharton, eventually—it wasn't like theirs was true love. Then last spring there were divorce papers on the breakfast bar when she walked in from her Pilates class, and she knew why.

Caught.

Sometimes the whole situation felt like it happened to someone else, not her. The way it played out was something she could've watched it in a bad Lifetime movie. That would be the name of the movie too: *Caught: The Allie Tanner-Whitton Story*.

She finished one of her packs of homemade trail mix and drank the last few drops of her lemon water, tossing the Ziploc bag and the plastic bottle in an adjacent trash can. Ahmed had offered to carry her bags to the check-in counter. She'd kept his contact info and still used him as her personal driver after the divorce. She was lucky that Wharton also gave her the SoHo penthouse, even though that was by force. She knew how it made her look, but that was her own fault for marrying a fifty-something-year-old when she was only twenty-six.

She had her reasons for that. It didn't matter what she'd told everyone.

Truthfully, she'd hoped to miss the flight. She hated Trevor and couldn't believe that Fiona was actually going to marry that asshole. Even worse, she couldn't believe how much all her friends loved him.

Dutch wanted all of them together in the cabin, so he insisted on paying for everyone's first-class flights, in addition to upgrading all their hotel rooms to suites. The resident social director. Daddy Warbucks himself. Finally free of Wharton Whitton II—God, what a stupid name— Allie still didn't have the courage to make a play for Dutch. He was hot, but she'd known him too long. Fourteen years. He was in brother territory.

After racing through security ("my plane is *boarding*!"), she finally made it to gate B42 and her heart instantly swelled when she saw Emma, her former college room-mate, and Vee, her savior. At a party freshman year, the first night Emma had introduced her to Vee, he'd almost knocked out a guy that got fresh with Allie against her will, and he'd been her guardian angel ever since—he was the nicest person she'd ever met. Aside from Emma, of course. They shared everything.

Almost everything.

"Ems! There you are!" Allie skipped toward her best friend and threw her arms around her.

"Allie! I didn't even recognize you!" Emma said, her eyes wide. "Wow. You're so… blond!"

Allie immediately knew Emma didn't like it. She knew her mannerisms. If Allie excelled in anything, it was how to be fake, so she could spot it from a mile away. Undeterred, she fluffed up her newly lightened locks that made the spray of freckles across her nose even darker. She spun around, and then walked with her nose in the air, hand on her hip, for five steps before she took a hard turn with her neck like she was walking a runway.

"Isn't it fabulous? Rolph did it." Allie smiled as she said it, but the smile didn't reach her eyes.

"They just announced boarding," Emma said. "We wanted to wait for you. Dutch already got on with Ethan."

"I guess chivalry is fucking dead," Allie said with an eye roll. She caught the words as they came out and put her hand over her mouth. "Sorry."

For fourteen years they'd all apologized for swearing in front of Vee. He was used to it, but he didn't curse. Ever.

Looking at Emma and Vee together, Allie always wondered why those two never got together. Sure, Ethan

26

was smart and ambitious and relatively good looking if you didn't count his crooked, badly repaired broken nose from when he allegedly caught a foul ball with his face in high school. A little on the short side (five-eleven) for five foot ten Allie's taste, she had picked up too many shorn pieces of Emma's heart in the past dozen or so years and wondered why Emma always ran back to him.

Like she had a right to judge anyone.

"Hey, how's your father doing?" Emma asked sympathetically and placed a tiny hand on Allie's upper arm.

Allie's face fell, and she shrugged, not wanting to give away all the pain. "He's doing okay, I guess. I mean, what could they do at this point except try to keep him comfortable. I hate seeing him like this. The doctors don't think there's much time left. A couple of months, max."

"I'm so sorry, Allie," Emma said. "Ugh. What a gut punch."

"Yeah." She blinked away the tears. "It just sucks. He's only sixty-three."

To say Allie was close with her father was an understatement. He was a psychotic Yankees fan, and Allie, otherwise not one to be involved with watching sports, would accompany him to a game every year. It was a family tradition to go from Connecticut the weekend after the fourth of July; they'd started when she was about seven years old. They clung to each other out of necessity after her mother died while overseas when Allie was just a teenager. It happened in the fall, and the Yankees had made the playoffs. They'd just lost to the Boston Red Sox in the ALCS when the phone call came. It wasn't a good day for the poor man.

She often wished she could access the many memories that she'd had of her mother, ones she should've paid more attention to, and could just put them on a zip file and pull them off her brain's hard drive whenever she wanted. Click click, *Oh! Right! Mom baked you a homemade cake for your tenth birthday.* Click click, *There it is! The Bon Jovi CD you asked for.* Click click, *Ah, yes, the bottle of perfume that she said you were too young for.*

Click click. It wasn't that easy to remember all the minute details, and she hated thinking that her mother had faded into the background of her youth.

And soon, the same would happen with her father. She'd been making a conscious effort to remember each moment, no matter how small they seemed to be. The feel of his waxy hand when it held hers. The way his eyes wrinkled up when he smiled. The faded smell of his cologne on her shirts when she got home, clinging to her collar from his constant hugs. All she knew was that, before the cancer ate the last part of his insides, she wanted him to live out what little time he had left thinking that his only daughter was perfect.

She was far from it. And Trevor had been threatening her with it for months.

"We're all in first class. We can cut the line you know," Allie reminded them, and began to walk to the front. She'd become a bit of a priss while married to a multimillionaire; she still didn't like to wait. Emma and Vee trailed behind her.

Allie grinned and uttered a happy greeting as she walked past the flight attendant and before she got to row three, she passed Dutch and smiled. She hadn't seen him in over a month.

"Va va va voom!" he exclaimed and stood, high fiving her, then hugged her. "Damn girl, when did you go blond?"

Allie plastered on another fake smile and pretended again that she loved it. "A couple weeks ago. Nice, right?" She flipped her head back and forth before finding her seat.

She glanced at the man in 3A, thankful he was already settled in his seat because she didn't want to have to get up to let him in—once she was comfortable, she didn't like to move. The stranger was about forty and stared blankly ahead at the DirecTV screen before him, some ESPN show, with huge noise canceling earphones on his head. She thought he looked like Princess Leia with those enormous cones on his ears, laughing to herself at how Vee would like that comparison.

She reapplied her lip gloss, then tucked her Chanel under the seat in front of her and adjusted her iPad, so she could lose herself in romantic movies. She preferred the classics. *Breakfast at Tiffany's* was a personal favorite. She closed her eyes just as Holly entered the room for the first time.

Her eyes sprung open at the pilot's announcement of their final descent, and once they'd adjusted to the light, she noticed the iPad was off. She'd missed the entire movie. She packed the iPad into her purse and tucked the tray table back into the arm of the seat. When the plane touched down, Allie immediately turned on her phone, and she was glad to see that her father had texted back while they were in the air.

Her heart tugged and she missed him like he was already
gone. With a small smile, she texted back to let him know
that she landed, and she'd check on him in a bit.

Then reality hit her like a bus. The wedding was
happening, and Trevor was about to be in her life forever.
Divorce happens, she thought gleefully. Still, Fiona was
going to marry that prick.

Not if Allie could help it.

7

EMMA

Two days before the wedding, 1 p.m.

Emma involuntarily clutched her stomach as they stood waiting for all their luggage—plus the men's golf clubs. There was a "golf with the groom" event on Friday while the girls had a spa day, the rehearsal dinner later that night, and the wedding on Saturday. It was all happening so fast.

Her abdomen churned, but she tried not to give it away—not yet. They were having dinner together tonight at the welcome party, so she'd explain why she wasn't drinking at that time. The anxiety closed her throat when she thought about what everyone's reaction would be.

Once everyone had their bags from the carousel and the guys grabbed the clubs from the oversize luggage area, they trotted along to a waiting Hummer limo, thanks again to Dutch. The heat outside was beyond suffocating, and Emma started to sweat. She took off her cashmere sweater, but she still had on a T-shirt and jeans and sneakers and fluffy travel socks with cartoon rabbits on them. She needed to get into the air conditioning and practically clawed her way inside the limo. She immediately ripped off the sneakers and the socks in favor of thin flip-flops she carried in her purse. It wasn't much, but it was a start.

Dutch had assured them the limo would be stocked with chilled champagne, and he passed out crystal stemware to everyone while the driver loaded the bags into the back. When the bottle popped, Vee and Allie cheered, and Emma widened her eyes at Ethan to signal that she couldn't drink. He gave her a reassuring nod, letting her know that a few sips were okay.

"Cheers! Three days of fun!" Dutch said as he downed the champagne.

Emma took a slow sip, which turned into two, which turned into half the glass before she forced herself to put it down. "Sorry. The bubbles don't work with me. My stomach is going to get upset."

Dutch scanned the tubs filled with ice. "I'm sure we can find a wine or a whiskey somewhere," he said as he thumbed through the bottles.

"No, it's okay. I'm saving myself for later. I can't get hammered if I want to be able to function at the party tonight," she lied. "Slow and steady wins the race."

"No worries. We have all weekend to celebrate," Dutch said.

Saved by the bell, Emma's text rang loudly and popped the bubble of tension inside the limo. She took her phone out of her bag and looked at the message. "It's Fiona. She said she and Trevor are at the lobby bar waiting for us with some of their other family and friends. She tracked our flight on her phone, so she knows we landed. She said she can't wait to see all of us."

She'd have to see Trevor again too. Just uttering his name gave her agita.

This time, she was armed with her own secret, one that he didn't know about. She planned to nip this in the bud quickly. *Let's see how he likes being blackmailed.* She hoped he fell for it and would leave her alone. She certainly didn't want to resort to Plan B to shut him up forever—she was a lot of things, but she wasn't a criminal.

Or worse.

"I haven't seen either of them since the summer, when the two of them came up north and he proposed. Has anyone?" Allie asked.

Everyone silently shook their heads *no*.

Emma lied.

8

VEEJAY

Two days before the wedding, 1:30 p.m.

It was impossible not to spot the couple from the check-in counter at the hotel. Fiona glowed as the bride-to-be, with Trevor standing next to his fiancé, one muscled arm around her shoulder, the other hand in his pants pocket, playing the accommodating groom. Relaxed and casual, he wore linen dress slacks and a loose, untucked short-sleeved button-down shirt. He spoke to her uncle, New York's newly elected Democratic US Senator John Hawthorne, a darling of the party, about to start his role that everyone knew was a stepping-stone to the presidency.

They were surrounded by the rest of their friends and family in the lobby bar, the vast open space behind them with floor-to-ceiling windows that enveloped Biscayne Bay. Past the French doors, the pink stone pavers, and the powdery sand, tiny white caps tickled the shoreline. It was such a contrast from Vee's past years in the Northeast. People from New York might get lost in the shuffle here. Who would pay attention to a bunch of loud mouths when they had this to look at? Still, when the five friends entered the lobby, they were an immediate presence, letting Fiona know her oldest friends had arrived.

"My bridal party is here!" she screeched as she ran up to all of them for a group hug. "Oh, I missed you guys so much!"

Veejay noticed she smelled of vanilla, probably from her conditioner. He also felt her shoulder bones during the hug, which was a first. She'd dropped at least twenty pounds since he'd last seen her. The smile was plastered on her face, and Vee could tell she was on a bride high. Emma and Allie looked like college girls again once they got their arms around Fiona. Dutch and Ethan followed with a bear hug and eventually pulled Veejay and the girls back in again.

It was just like old times, but without Roger. Vee couldn't help wondering how he was doing. And Vee's own guilt for not speaking up against Trevor—like Roger did—ate at him like battery acid. Roger's defiance and the subsequent airing of his mistakes is what kept Vee in line. He had no doubt Trevor would do the same to him. He wasn't proud of himself for pretending to be happy about the wedding. In fact, he felt like a bigger fraud than Trevor. How was he supposed to reconcile that? And where was Roger now? Back in Chicago, last Vee'd heard.

"Hey, I'll see you guys in the bar in a bit," Veejay said to the group. "I'm going to unpack and freshen up and change first."

When he got to his room, he had to admit that having Dutch upgrade all of them to suites was going to be the highlight of the weekend. There was a living room and a full bedroom, both with balconies that kept the entire wall as floor-to-ceiling glass, and the sun reflecting off the ocean blinded him.

He dropped his bags and walked to the balcony door, opening it to breathe in the Southern winter, which didn't constrict his chest like the cold up North. When the humidity rushed in, he immediately started to sweat. Shutting the door, he readjusted the temperature to a cool sixty-five on the thermostat.

In the bedroom, he plunked down on top of the palm-tree patterned comforter, in spite of what he'd heard on an exposé about how hotels *never* launder them, and rubbed his temples. All he had to do was get through three days of fake smiles and pray Trevor kept his word. What he really wanted to do was warn Fiona away from such an a-hole—how could she not see it? He knew, of course, it was because Fiona always saw the good in everyone. She was never one to gossip or talk ill of people. She was a kindergarten teacher—before Trevor made her quit— sweet as homemade apple pie.

Trevor seemed nice enough—back then—and everyone else thought he was an okay guy. Vee remembered not long after Trevor was introduced to everyone, when they were still friendly and there were no threats between them, that he had warned Trevor not to mess around with Fiona's heart. He'd said it in his big-brotherly way, the way he spoke to all suitors when it came to his closest friends. "*Or what?*" was the response he got. Looking back, he should've kept his mouth shut. It'd obviously turned Trevor vengeful.

Five months before the wedding, 4 p.m.

When Trevor called Vee to have a beer, alone, a scant month after he'd moved Fiona to Miami, Vee was going to try to give him the benefit of the doubt. His friend loved Trevor; even leaving her teaching job, her friends, her family, and basically her whole life for him. He couldn't be all bad.

When Vee got to the W hotel lobby bar in Midtown, Trevor was already waiting with a half-drunk martini at the steel, silver bar just a few feet away from the plush couches where tourists sat with their luggage, waiting for their rooms to be ready for check in. It was the end of June, and New York City was a huge tourism draw this time of year, since everyone wanted a live look at the Macy's Fourth of July fireworks on the river.

Trevor smiled at Vee. A sneer, really. Vee smiled back genuinely because that was just the type of guy he was. Trevor didn't stand when Vee approached, but stuck out his hand for a shake, which Vee returned. It was more of a rough clasp than a shake, but Vee brushed it off. The chair clattered against the floor as he dragged the back of the metal barstool next to Trevor and sat down.

"Bud Light, please," he said to the bartender after scanning the thin happy hour menu and beer list, then waved at Trevor's drink. "Another?"

Trevor popped a handful of popcorn in his mouth and chewed with his lips slightly parted. Loudly. Apparently on purpose.

"Nah, bro, I'm good. This won't take long."

Bro? Now they were *bros*.

"So, what's up man? How was the flight?" Vee was going to make small talk because he still didn't know what he was doing there.

"It was fine, we got in last night and stayed with her mom. Fiona is having a girls' lunch with her in Westchester today and meeting me here tonight. I came into the city early to have breakfast with John Hawthorne. Her uncle. You know he's going to win the senate seat this fall, right?" He said it like he wanted Vee to be proud of him. Or jealous. "Then I had some other business to attend to here in the city. I've been in meetings all day. Now, I'm left with all this free time, and I just didn't know what to do." He said the last sentence slowly, with purpose, accentuating each word like he was speaking in italics. "So, I caught up on some reading. Pretty interesting stuff."

"Oh yeah? I'm a bit of a book nerd myself. What did you find?"

Trevor shook his head slowly. "Nah, bro, I'm not into that sci-fi shit you read. No spaceships and magical powers. I prefer nonfiction."

Vee didn't miss a beat. "Ah, I get enough of that by watching the news. I like to crack open a book and lose myself in different worlds. Emma just finished editing this—"

"Emma." Trevor interrupted, then stopped right after he said her name. Another handful of popcorn disappeared. "She's smoking hot, that one. You two are pretty close, huh?"

What a terrible thing to say when he was dating Emma's best friend, and Vee got a sinking feeling in his stomach. He didn't like Emma being objectified, and he flushed, probably visibly. "We've been best friends for a long time." It was said as a warning: *Don't talk about her that way*.

"Right." He drew it out. *Riiiight*. "Anyway, I thought you'd be interested in something I read recently." He produced an eight-by-ten envelope seemingly out of nowhere.

Vee shrugged. "Sure, I'll take a look."

He held out his hand and Trevor placed the envelope on his palm. When Vee's fingers closed around it, Trevor's tightened.

"You sure? This could change your life."

Curious, one side of Vee's mouth turned up as his eyes squinted onto the envelope. "I bet I can handle it."

Trevor threw up his hands in a mock *I tried to warn you!* way and swiveled his chair in the opposite direction from Vee, like a child on a ride in the park. Then he picked up his martini and slugged down the vodka as Vee pulled something out of the envelope. His eyes widened when he realized what he was looking at.

"What the—?" This time, Vee's dark complexion went alabaster. When the recognition made its appearance on Vee's face, Trevor knew he had him, and he laughed again. Vee immediately identified the headline in the newspaper from India. He didn't need to see the date; he already knew it: October 20, 2004. "Where did you get this?"

"I have sources." He moved his face a couple of inches closer to Vee's. "I know what you did," he said without blinking.

Vee pulled away and slugged down half of his Bud Light in one sip, then wiped his lips on the back of his trembling hand. The accident was so long ago that he thought maybe it didn't happen. Seventeen years. Almost eight thousand miles. Another Veejay. Another life.

Another life, so conspicuously tied to his current one.

When Vee didn't answer, Trevor shoved the article into his hands. "Read it."

Vee closed his eyes and dropped it on the bar. "I know what it says."

Vee heard slow, eerie music playing in his head, like a jack-in-the-box clown was about to pop out of Trevor's skull and drive Vee's fast-beating heart into cardiac arrest. His body shook, his whole reason for applying to Columbia about to be known.

"Please don't say anything," Vee said, knowing it was useless, and then asked the question that got him in trouble. "What do you want?"

9

ETHAN

Two days before the wedding, 2 p.m.

After having a cigarette on the balcony, Ethan watched through hazy eyes as his wife changed into a sundress and heels. He liked how the dress hugged her. She was still so, so tiny. It was hard to believe there was an actual baby in there. His child.

"Come here."

Emma smiled. "No. You've had too much to drink, you'll take forever, and we have to meet everyone downstairs. Plus, I just finished fixing my hair and makeup."

No.

He'd heard that a lot lately when it came to sex. She hadn't been the same for a couple of months. It was right about the time she became pregnant, and her hormones were likely out of whack. He twirled his wedding ring around on his finger, a habit when he was anxious. He was sympathetic to her moods, but he loved her and that came with wanting to be close to her physically.

"I want to see Fiona." She paused. "And, of course, Trevor."

Ethan hated the mention of his name and hated even more that his wife liked Trevor. It nagged at him, poked him in the ribs and then ran away like an annoying little sibling. Probably because Trevor was always all over Emma whenever they'd all been together. He mentioned it to Dutch once, that he didn't like the way Trevor looked at Emma, but Dutch had convinced him that he was being irrational.

Despite the fact that Trevor was a terrible human being, even Ethan couldn't deny that he was a good-looking dude. He was tall, around six-foot-one, and he had dark wavy hair and those mysterious dark eyes that melted all the girls. He could've been a Calvin Klein model. His build rivaled Dutch's although Trevor was somewhat leaner, less meaty. If he was honest with himself, he thought Trevor was out of Fiona's league. She was cute, of course, with brown hair and gray eyes, but she was average. A dime a dozen. Fiona didn't exactly turn heads as she walked down the street, whereas Trevor probably caused whiplash.

"We should get going," Emma said and layered a bunch of bracelets onto her wrist, which sounded like wind chimes when she moved. Exiting the bathroom, she moved to the bed and sat to lotion her legs. "Hurry up and change. It's so damn hot out." She waved her hand around her cleavage, like the mere motion of her tiny hand would have any effect on the heat they were experiencing.

"I know. I couldn't even finish my cigarette on the balcony. It's brutal out there."

Emma nodded, then switched legs and squirted a big goopy pile from the tube and rubbed it in, up and down, up and down. "You're quitting though, right?"

"Yes, Emma, I promised you I'd quit when you got back from the gynecologist. Right after the new year. Fresh start."

It would be hard; he'd tried before. But he'd do anything for Emma and the baby. It was time for him to quit being immature, in every aspect of life. Less Alcohol. Fewer nights out. No smoking. Work harder. Provide better. A beer after work with colleagues or hoops on weekends with the guys would be a thing of the past. He'd even skip some Rangers games at The Garden with his brother Timmy. He'd need to be home for feedings and diaper changes, and later, recitals and T-ball.

But it was okay. He'd be doing it with his Emma, and they were a unit. If Emma wanted to stay home with the baby in lieu of a full-time job, he wanted to be able to pay rent without her income. If she wanted to go back to work, he needed to be in the headspace to support whatever decisions she made. Doing it for her—for his *family*—was a no brainer.

Emma pursed her lips. "You know Cassandra, Eduardo, and Bianca are staying with us for a few days between Christmas and New Year's. I'd really like if you didn't smoke around them."

"I'll try, baby momma."

He called her that every once in a while, even though she made a face every time he did. On the bed next to her, he emptied some lotion into his hands and helped her with her routine. The lotion was greasy, and he pressed it into her skin at her ankle, then moved his hands north, kneading her shin and then her thigh. When his hand met her inner thigh, he didn't stop. He looked at her with intent and went in for a kiss. Her eyes closed and just when he was about to make contact, her head snapped back and her eyes went wide.

"We can't. We have to go." She jumped up off the bed and then pecked him on the head. "I love you."

"Hey," he grabbed her hand to stop her. "You hypnotize me." He meant it. No one, *no one* had captivated his heart the way she had since the first time their lips touched in college.

She smiled at him, but didn't give in, so he did as usual. With half a hard-on, Ethan changed to go downstairs, where he'd have to face that asshole for the first time since the summer.

Five months before the wedding, 12 p.m.

When Trevor texted Ethan and said he was in Midtown and asked to meet for a quick coffee, Ethan could've made an excuse. The truth was, he was just passed over for a promotion and he wanted to get out of the office and let off some steam. He'd held Trevor off until noon, when it didn't turn heads to add a little bit of Irish to his coffee. Trevor mentioned having a meeting in the neighborhood at one o'clock, so the timing was perfect. He'd be able to see him, get it over with, and Trevor would scatter off to his next meeting. Ethan wasn't exactly excited about seeing him.

Ethan's initial dislike toward Trevor started the first time they'd met over the winter, when he seemed to be more enamored with Emma than Fiona, and he thought Trevor to be quite smug. He snapped his fingers at waiters and whistled for cabs and always ordered for Fiona without asking what she wanted. Maybe *entitled* was more the word he was looking for. The guy fancied himself as some sort of Ray Donovan, but he'd mentioned several times that he had political aspirations as well.

When Ethan got outside of his building, he loosened his tie—God, the heat was like being stuffed under a damn polyester tent. It was only June thirtieth, but the temperatures had been in the nineties for well over a week. Trevor was already waiting against the huge call letters for the network that were displayed outside of the fifty-story building. He wore a black T-shirt and black pants, dark hair slicked back, and dark eyes hidden behind dark sunglasses. *Fucking vampire.*

"Hey, Ethan, good of you to meet me," Trevor said when he reached him.

Ethan shook his hand. "What brings you to our part of town?"

He said "our" because Emma worked only five blocks north of him on Sixth Avenue, and their condo was only a few blocks east. Dutch lived in a penthouse in the West Village, and Allie lived in a penthouse in SoHo while Vee lived in a new luxury building down in Battery Park. Fiona, before the move to Miami, was back in her hometown in Westchester County. Midtown was for people like Ethan and Emma Pierce, where you were able to walk to work from your eight-hundred-square-foot condo. Unless they all purposely got together for dinner or drinks, their paths never crossed in the local bodega or dry cleaner's. So yes, Ethan considered Midtown to belong to himself and his wife.

"Fiona and I are staying at the W this weekend. Not too far from here," Trevor said. "I thought you'd want to take a walk."

"Your timing is epic," he said. "I think I need something stronger than coffee."

"Right." He drew it out. *Riiiight.* "I heard that about you."

"There's a place just around the corner that I like," Ethan said.

They didn't talk, not even small talk, as they walked the block to Ernie's Pub. It was a dark, unassuming little hole-in-the-wall that he'd found by accident a couple years prior. He liked that he could pop in during lunch or after work and not have to run into coworkers. Trevor gave him a quizzical look when they stopped at the front, and Ethan shrugged and held the door open. He was sure Trevor was used to fancy places, but he didn't give a shit.

Just as he'd hoped, Old Man Ernie was behind the bar and nodded as Ethan and Trevor took their seats in the empty space. Being just shy of noon and not really the type of place for a power lunch, they were the first ones there. Ethan liked this place because he knew the staff—and they knew him. Within seconds, there was a hot coffee before him, and no one would know that there was a nice shot of whiskey in there. Ernie took good care of him.

Trevor rolled his eyes as Ethan took a sip. "A little hot out there for coffee?"

"We're inside," Ethan said with another slurp, the slow burn descending. "So, what's up?"

"Funny you should ask." He signaled for Ernie and ordered a shot of whiskey for himself. The heavy shot glass thumped immediately onto the thick wooden bar and the whiskey glub-glubbed to the top. Trevor slammed the shot and winced, clearly not used to brown liquid on an empty stomach this early in the day. "Guess what I know?" Trevor asked.

After the meeting Ethan had just had with his boss Patricia, he was in no mood for games. He even wore a tie in this heat, thinking he would be promoted today. He began to sip his drink again as he shrugged.

"I know about you and Fiona, how's that for starters?"

The hidden whiskey caught in Ethan's throat and he coughed, feeling the burn into his nose. He grabbed a paper cocktail napkin and wiped his face down. Trevor's voice didn't change with the proclamation, like the sentence he'd just stated was that that the sky is blue, and did Ethan know that? His expression remained flat.

He continued, "My guess is—actually, it's not a guess but I have *knowledge* that Emma doesn't know anything. About you fucking her best friend while you guys were broken up."

Ethan tried to play dumb, a quality that was not lost on Trevor. "What are you talking about?"

Trevor clasped his hand on Ethan's shoulder like they were old college buddies and gave him a good shake. "You know, she's my future wife. I'm proposing on Sunday in front of all of you when we go to brunch. She'll be so surprised." Trevor never took his gaze off Ethan, who still stared into his coffee, an abyss of alcohol and darkness, like his life had just become. "Look, I know Fiona wasn't Little Miss Innocent. The kindergarten teacher thing is a good facade, but she was obviously no virgin before me."

Ethan's hands were shaking, so he didn't pick up his coffee. He'd look like he had Parkinson's if he tried to lift the mug to his lips. He knew the mannerisms—the disease had taken his father.

The mistake—and it *was* a mistake—with Fiona was about five or six years ago, right toward the end of the yearlong breakup with Emma. Ethan and Fiona were from the same county in New York, they'd previously discovered in college, four towns away from each other. While the guys camped on Ethan's side during the breakup and the girls stayed by Emma's side, he'd texted with Fiona intermittently, mostly about Emma.

When Ethan was home for his brother's birthday, he went out with some friends from high school and saw Fiona at a bar, and tequila happened. One thing led to another when he was blackout drunk and just wanted the closeness of Emma. It had been almost a year, and Emma wouldn't see him, no matter how much he begged and professed his love. Hell, when he showed up to her place for his *Say Anything* moment, she wouldn't even remove the chain from the door. Her crystal green eyes welled with tears, even as she told him to go away and never come back. He thought he'd lost her for good. In his drunken state at the bar that night, Fiona was the next best thing.

A few months later, Emma was finally taking his calls—out of the blue. Truth was, he'd never stopped trying with Emma, no matter what else he'd had going on with Fiona. He and Emma had talked about reconciling, and that was the only relationship he'd planned on devoting any time to. He ended it with Fiona abruptly, stating that he was going back to Emma, and he hoped she understood. Fiona pretended she wasn't crushed—she'd already all but said *I love you* after barely two months. She had to know he'd never return those feelings, but she swore, in the name of friendship and the group, that she'd keep the fling to herself.

"I don't know what you think you know, but that's not true," Ethan stated to Trevor. He knew he was fucked. Trevor wouldn't have brought it up unless he knew the truth. Did Fiona *actually* tell him she'd been with Ethan? Why would she do that?

Trevor pulled out an envelope and opened it; inside was a picture of him and Fiona, against the back of a building at nighttime. He recognized it as the outside of Taggin' T's, the bar at home where he'd run into Fiona. After a fifth tequila shot, they started making out back by the bathrooms. Eventually, they'd stumbled out the back door. In the picture, his hand was under her skirt and thank God Trevor didn't have pictures of five minutes later. Fucking CCTV, drones, whatever captured the images.

"I'm no doctor but I'm pretty sure I know what came next," Trevor said. "Do you think I don't do my homework on the woman I'm going to marry?"

"Look, it was one time. We were drunk," Ethan said flatly, knowing it wouldn't land.

"Don't lie, Ethan. I found her diary in some of her stuff. It had details. About feelings. It caused me to do a little more digging. So, I have another gift for you." This time, he tugged a piece of paper out of his back pocket. He unfolded it and placed it on the bar. "One time? This seems rather... intimate. Christ, imagine if Emma saw this picture?"

Oh no. Jesus, he'd be sleeping on the couch for a year if Emma saw that picture. If he was lucky.

Trevor was so calm and sure in his demeanor, and Ethan tried to internalize the shaking. The front door of the bar opened, and a few people came in, laughing, but Ethan only heard Emma's inevitable crying. Emma could never, *ever* see that photo.

His legs trembled on the stool and he pressed down on one knee with his free hand. He didn't want Trevor to know he was losing his cool.

"Nuh uh uh, one more," Trevor said, shaking his index finger at Ethan, clearly enjoying Ethan's discomfort. "I found this one on her phone."

Before Ethan saw the picture, he knew what it was, but still looked at it like it was the first time he'd seen it when Trevor slapped it down on the bar. Ethan's vision swirled and he blinked rapidly to try to focus. Why was Trevor showing Ethan these pictures? Was he jealous because they'd briefly dated? It meant nothing—not to him, even if it meant something to Fiona. Emma was Ethan's whole world—everyone knew that.

Trevor continued, "Anyway, the past is the past, am I right? Hey, I didn't know her then. I don't care who she was with before me." His smirk was dangerous. "But man, if your gorgeous wife ever saw these pictures, I mean forget the first one, with her husband with his hand between her best friend's legs, but these other ones show much more of a—"

Ethan grabbed his arm. "Shut the fuck up, Trevor." He shot Trevor a stare that was deadly. If looks could kill, Trevor would have a fatal bullet wound.

But, of course, Trevor didn't rattle. He shifted his eyes downward until they rested on Ethan's hand clutched around his forearm, then lifted his eyes back to Ethan's. Smooth as silk. Ethan let go.

"Don't worry about it. She'll never have to see these. And I have the diary, detailing intimate things about you two, in a safe place. Just do me a favor," Trevor said as he stood. He wiped his arms and legs down like someone had spilled baby powder all over him. "When I propose in front of all of you, just remind Fiona how lucky she is and that I'm such a good guy. I don't want her to have any second thoughts about me, and she obviously trusts you, considering your cozy history. I mean, you can do that, right?"

Ethan stared straight ahead into the cracked mirror that decorated the wall behind the bar. How fitting that his reflection was fragmented.

"Oh. Also. You'll be a groomsman in the wedding. Say *yes* when I ask. Be enthusiastic. What a great way to show me that you have no lingering feelings toward my future wife." He threw a twenty on the bar. "Drinks are on me, bro. I'll see you at brunch on Sunday."

He walked out, and Ethan internally berated himself for ever hooking up with Fiona. What a stupid thing to do. Working in a newsroom, he knew there were cameras everywhere, and everyone took video of everything these days.

Nothing could be kept a secret.

Ethan had to find a way to make sure this one stayed dead and buried.

10

ALLIE

Two days before the wedding, 2 p.m.

One foot in front of the other, Allie thought to herself as she got off the elevator after unpacking. *You can do this. Don't let him get to you.*

The hotel lobby was expansive with two-story high ceilings and billowy white and gold chiffon curtains bookending the opening to the lobby bar. Visions of palm trees in the distance, through the glass wall that opened onto the terrace, was the cherry on top of the dessert. The sun drifted in at the perfect angle, enlightening the room as if they were in heaven itself.

And just when she thought she'd see an angel…

"There she is!" Trevor's deep voice boomed through the lobby to Allie when she walked into the bar. "Well, be still my heart, but your hair looks amazing that shade of blond!"

I miss my red hair, Allie thought. She didn't want to go platinum. For a reason unbeknownst to Allie, Trevor said he would keep her secret once and for all if she showed up to his wedding as a blond. He didn't give a shit what color Allie's hair was, he just wanted to prove that he could control her, which he did like a marionette. At that point, she almost didn't care if her friends knew—they'd protect her—but she couldn't do it to her father, and that's what kept her in line. She couldn't be in prison when he died. *I'm still your Good Girl, Daddy.*

"Yeah, well, we'll see if I keep it. I'm more of a redhead at heart," Allie said.

Trevor's eyes got darker, and he slipped his arm around Fiona's waist. Allie cringed at his fake display of affection. "Well, maybe you'll change your mind. It may grow on you," he said. "Although I prefer redheads myself."

Jerkoff.

Allie couldn't believe that Fiona didn't see the snarling wolf under the wool, the chunks of flesh between his teeth. She couldn't smell the copper on his breath from his latest kill. Seeing her old sorority sister under such a spell gutted her. She wondered if anyone else noticed.

No.

Everyone thought Trevor was such a great guy. Allie decided she would keep her thoughts to herself. After all, she was a bridesmaid, and speaking ill of your friend's fiancé, wretched as he was, two days before the wedding was a no-no. She turned her attention to Fiona.

"This place is gorgeous," Allie said, taking in the beautiful surroundings, but that was as much emotion that she could spew out next to the Devil. "You look great. Lost a few pounds."

Fiona slapped her ass. "I had to get rid of the dumper to fit into a wedding dress! Trevor needs a presentable wife." She said it and looked up at him again with such admiration that Allie knew Fiona was done for.

Like the predator that he was, he caressed her ass and then looked at Allie. "She's still got a few more pounds to go. Too many food samples the past few weeks."

How dare Trevor insult her like that—this guy was unbelievable. Allie thought about Vee and his alien books. At that moment she wondered if she could shoot a laser out of her eyes that would make Trevor's head explode. Is that what Vee read about? Allie hated herself for selling out her friend to this douche. But her father was *most* important. Fiona smiled at Trevor, the abuse not landing. Happy she was skinnier for *him*. Not for herself.

"Trevor, could I speak to you for a minute?" Senator Hawthorne appeared at Trevor's side. "It's important."

Trevor looked at him with raised eyebrows. "Are you okay, you look a little flushed." Then he waved his open hand out in front of them like a grand gesture. "Senator, have you met my friend Allie Whitton?"

Ugh, she was not *his* friend. Allie shook the senator's clammy hand. "Nice to meet you, Senator. I voted for you. I'm Fiona's friend from Columbia. Sorority sisters." *Not* Trevor's friend. She didn't want anyone mistaking it.

He nodded. "Thank you. Always nice to meet voters." He turned back to Trevor, a dented worry line visible between his eyebrows. "Trevor?" His head tipped to the right. He wanted privacy.

Trevor kissed Fiona on the head. "Well, if you'll excuse me ladies, it seems my work is never truly done." Allie was thankful Trevor had moved along, even though she felt his stare burning her bald in the back of her head.

Soon enough, Dutch showed up, then Veejay joined, and finally Emma and Ethan about twenty minutes later. Emma's eyes shifted nervously as they all made small talk about New York, jobs, and of course, vows.

"Hey, are you okay? You look white as a ghost," Allie whispered to Emma.

"*Estou bem*. I'm fine," Emma said, putting a hand on her forehead. "I'm just tired. And it's too hot. We were at the Rangers game last night, and then we got up so early to pack."

Allie whipped her head to Ethan, then back to her best friend. "Ethan and those damn Rangers! He forced you to go to a hockey game?"

"He didn't *force* me. Timmy got stuck at work, so he *asked* me. You know it's our thing."

Allie softened; she knew how proud Emma was to be part of that tradition. Ethan's father raised him and his brother Timmy on hockey, but their father died of complications from Parkinson's when they were all in college. Emma was the only one Ethan had ever taken to a game besides his brother, whom he now shared half a season of tickets with. Emma always said she felt special that she was the only one he shared his hockey love with— he'd never even taken Dutch, Veejay, or Roger to a game. It was for family only. She even had the Rangers app on her phone and tried to keep up with the news and the trades, the wins and the losses. It was all Greek to Allie. She didn't do sports, aside from her annual Yankees game with her father.

"Let's go to the bar," Allie said. Maybe a drink would give Emma a second wind.

Emma nodded, her eyes shifting to the other end of the room where Trevor talked with Uncle John, then immediately back to the group. She had not yet said a proper hello to him. In fact, she seemed to actively avoid him.

Allie couldn't blame her.

Allie had just returned from a massage and a Louboutin shopping spree on Fifth Avenue at Saks, and she was enjoying leisure time on her private roof deck, twenty-eight stories above the car horns and garbage stench. Armed with the latest contemporary romance novel and a cold bottle of prosecco, she lost herself in the heat of the sun, making sure she stayed tan, or as tan as her freckled Irish skin let her get, like a good little soon-to-be divorcée.

The papers were signed, but it wasn't final yet. None of her friends knew she and Wharton had separated, nor that he'd moved into the Plaza while he hunted for a new apartment. It wasn't like they had spent much time together in the last five years anyway. Her friends had all stayed supportive throughout the engagement and marriage even though he was old enough to be her father. A hedge fund partner, he didn't have much to do with Allie and her gaggling bunch of millennial friends. None of them would even realize they were divorced.

Fiona had moved to Miami the month before, but she was up North with her boyfriend for the weekend to gather the last of her things, and they were all supposed to have brunch together on Sunday. Maybe she'd bring up the divorce up then.

Maybe.

Her cell rang, interrupting her book's scandal—a typical enemies-to-lovers story—and she saw the number for her lobby on the caller ID. Her doorman Sal had called up and told her she had a visitor.

"Trevor Vaughn?" Her voice registered shock as she spoke. How did he even know where she lived? "Sure, send him up," she said warily.

Allie didn't know him too well, just that he was some big-time security guy, and he was tapped to head up his company's new south division in Miami. He and Fiona had barely dated—less than five months—when he got the job transfer and demanded that Fiona follow him down there. Not to be catty about one of her best friends, but Fiona wasn't a ten on her best day. Trevor, simply put, was gorgeous, and Fiona was spellbound and immersed herself into his life. Allie thought the phrase *tall, dark, and handsome* was invented for people like Trevor. He was chiseled and fit and confident, and she understood Fiona's infatuation.

That was something Allie wouldn't do—let a man dictate her comings and goings. Still, she was grateful for Trevor to come to the group. He'd given her some great advice without even knowing it.

Allie stood and tucked her wrap around her waist. As she descended the spiral staircase from the private roof deck to the main living area, she had second thoughts about her attire and went into her master bedroom, into her extra-large closet, and pulled down a full-length green maxi dress to wear over her bikini. She stopped in her bathroom and pulled her red hair off her face and into a slick topknot secured with two bobby pins.

When there was a playful knock on the door, she glided down her long hallway, past the round stone entryway table and reached for the doorknob. Before she opened it, she secured the chain lock. She wanted to make sure it was him first.

She had to be extra careful these days.

Opening the door to a sliver, she took a peek and sure enough, it was Trevor. His dark hair was loose around his face, and he was at least two days unshaven. Relief flooded her when she realized it wasn't the FBI.

"Trevor! What are you doing here?" She closed the door for a hot second and released the chain before welcoming him. "Couldn't wait until Sunday brunch to see me?" she asked with a smile. "Come on in."

His swagger propelled him inside. "Nice place," he said as his head swiveled around, taking in her floor to ceiling windows and state of the art chef's kitchen. The unfettered view to the Freedom Tower was her favorite part of her enormous, windowed living space.

Still not knowing what he was doing there, alone, she grew curious. She looked at her watch with purpose. "Can I help you with something? Wharton is going to be home any minute." It was a lie, of course, but she felt using urgency would help him get on with it. She was a happy little housewife as far as anyone was concerned.

Trevor found the living room and plunked himself down onto her custom-made velvet lavender couch, too familiar, and that's when his demeanor changed. "Oh, Allie, Allie, *Allie*. We both know Wharton isn't coming home. How long are you going to lie to everyone?"

He couldn't possibly know what was going on. No one did.

Used to being in control, she redirected the conversation to her favor. "I'm not sure I understand what you mean, Trevor?" Her voice went up an octave at the end. Quick blinks. Innocence. *Still married, see?* She said it even as sweat began to drip down her back. She hoped her voice didn't waver and give away her collapsing house of cards. "I'm not sure I understand?" That time her voice cracked audibly. *Shit. Get it together.* Her arms crossed, and she tapped her foot, the sound of the beat ricocheting in the room off the lofted ceiling.

"I think you do, Allie. I think you do," he said as he leaned back and put his arm on the back of her couch, spreading his legs, getting comfortable. "I know what's going on with your divorce. I know everything. Do you want your friends to find out *why*? Jesus, they think he still lives here. You really put on a great show on Instagram."

Her heartbeat raced, the tempo pounding as if it were a snare drum, her body melting. As though he just threw a bucket of water on her, and she was descending into a pile of green witch goo. *What a world, what a world!*

"Well, let's put it this way." This time he leaned forward with a direct stare, his elbows on his knees, the fingers on both hands interlocked with each other. "I'm the one who sent Wharton the letter about what you were doing behind his back."

What you were doing behind his back.

Oh, no. He hadn't said what he said in passing that time. He knew she would act on it. It was all a setup.

She flustered. "Trevor, I—"

"Shhh," he said, holding an index finger to his lips. Then he reached into his pocket and retrieved a small plastic electronic device and pressed a button, then held it to his lips before he spoke. "I know exactly what you did."

The distorted voice that came out of the contraption was unfortunately familiar.

It was him. *Trevor* was him.

And they all fall down.

So did Allie. The realization that her secret was not only discovered, but that Trevor set her up, dropped her right to her knees on her imported rug from Italy. Her trembling hands found her face to cover the inevitable tears.

"No, no, Allie. It's okay," Trevor said, one hundred percent unshaken, as he got off the couch and half crawled to where she'd collapsed, and he slung an arm around her shoulder as she cringed. "Shhh, it's okay. No one has to know."

He smoothed down some of her flyaway hair, but she wasn't about to let him touch her. She jammed an elbow into his arm. He laughed. But he moved away, now on the floor and leaning on the front of the couch, his legs crisscrossed and his hands behind his head.

"Your hair is really a beautiful shade of red, Allie. Just like your father's."

Her head whipped to face him with such fury that she thought she'd pulled a muscle. "Don't you ever mention my father. Ever!" He took the hint and stayed silent as the wheels in her brain turned despite the fact that he'd just killed the hamster. "Why?"

His face was incredulous, like how *dare* she have the balls to ask him that. "Come on, honey. You know what I do, right?" He was a condescending asshole now, but what could she really do? She didn't know his security arms reached into… lawlessness.

He continued. "I'm the best in the business." He looked around her living room and paused at the entertainment center, the right side of his upper lip curling as if someone were tugging it with a fishhook. "You'd probably shit a brick if you knew about half the things that I have on record and on video just from iPhones and computer cameras and smart TVs. Like that one right there." He pointed to the TV. "Tap tap, click

click—that's all it takes, Allie. That's all it takes for me to get into someone's life and stay there."

Had he been spying on her? Why would he target her? She tried not to let her voice warble, but it did anyway. "But I'm not in the business anymore." It came out in a whisper.

"Yeah, Allie. You are. Maybe not as much as before, but you are." He tapped the side of his head twice with his index finger, then pointed it at her with a relaxed smile. Always so slick. "Remember. I know things."

Yes, he knew things, *those* things, and her carefully cultivated world was up in flames. "What do you want from me, Trevor?"

"Oh. Right." He drew it out. *Riiiight.* "I'm proposing to Fiona at brunch on Sunday. In front of all of you. And you *will* tell her how great I am and egg her on to say yes." His face relaxed. "I know she's told you that she thinks she made a mistake by moving in with me so quickly. By giving up her job and her friends and her family. You're going to make sure she marries me."

"No." Her head shook furiously. "No way. You're sick."

"Allie." He said her name threateningly, then stopped. It was the whole paragraph, and he didn't need to say anything else.

"What do you want with Fiona? Why are you doing this? Why me?"

A chuckle escaped. "Why you? Because you were too damn innocent, but you're also judgmental about me— Fiona told me you said to dump me. Why, Allie? Just because I wanted her with me when I left for Miami?"

Allie had a sneaking suspicion that Fiona had told him everything—she didn't listen to a word of advice, even after asking for it. "You made her give up her life."

"Yeah, love is a powerful thing, am I right? Watch—everyone else will be happy about the proposal. If you want to alienate yourself, you'll be the one on the outside. But then," he paused as he spoke into the device again. "Then I can't make any promises about keeping what you've been doing a secret." The electronic voice no longer gave her the thrill it once did, but now filled her with panic over her illegal activities. He released the button to speak in his regular voice and shrugged, like a heartless sociopath. "I *know* you don't want your father to find out. Especially with him so close to the end. Tell me, do you think jailed criminals are allowed to go to funerals?"

The color so quickly drained from Allie's face at the thought of being in prison and not being there for her father that she was sure she'd need to have her makeup redone. There was no way her foundation was a match anymore. If Trevor exposed her, her father would know exactly what she'd done with her Ivy League degree.

"If you go near him, I swear to God Trevor, I'll—"

"You'll do nothing. Just do as I say, and it all stays hidden. How hard could it be to tell her how great I am? I mean…" He let his sentence sputter.

What an egomaniac. An egomaniac who *knew*. "You set me up."

He shrugged. Then he stood, his smile sadistic—too big and too menacing, like it was drawn onto a frightening Halloween mask. Cool as a cucumber, he swayed past her, leaving her in a crumpled heap on the floor. Allie's world as she knew it was about to disappear. Her life. Her friends.

Her freedom. Trevor was in charge now. The door opened and then slammed shut without another word from him.

She let out half a scream as she ran to the closed door and beat her fist on it, crying. The chain was secured, and the heavy bolt was turned with a weighty click. Her next frustrated slap onto the back of the door did nothing to calm the flames inside.

He knew.

11

EMMA

Two days before the wedding, 2:15 p.m.

Emma offered to grab the drinks for Allie at the bar for two reasons. One, she wanted to make sure she ordered herself something that looked like an alcoholic beverage so people wouldn't ask her why she wasn't drinking, and two, she wanted to get farther away from Trevor. Just seeing him again made her skin crawl.

Emma quietly ordered herself a club soda and lime (hold the vodka), and a prosecco for Allie. The bartender handed them over with a wink, and she turned to find Allie right behind her. She handed the drink to Allie, who then grabbed her by the wrist.

"Thanks. Hey, let's go get Fiona and take some pictures of the three of us for Instagram. I got a great new selfie filter."

Allie and her selfies. Emma was surprised Allie didn't pack her ring light in her clutch along with her lip gloss and granola packages. "Let's do it the right way. I'll find Dutch and have him get ready. You know he lives for this stuff."

Dutch loved capturing moments—pictures and videos were definitely his thing. *These are going to be some of the best times of our lives. You'll thank me one day*, he'd always said. He probably had an archive of videos that rivaled Warner Brothers.

While Allie wrangled Fiona away, Emma felt a tickle at her waist from behind and whipped around to see Trevor.

"Emma. Look at you." His dark, brooding eyes took her in from head to toe. "God, you look gorgeous. How long has it been since I've seen you?" he asked, gaslighting her.

He knew exactly how long it'd been. The heat outside was no match for the flames that tortured her from within at the memory. Her balance became unsteady as the room spun before her.

"Trevor." It was all she said. Beyond that, she didn't have a voice. She took a huge gulp of the club soda and finished it in one sip, wishing it were full of real alcohol.

"Whoa, slow down, Emma. We all know how you get after a few drinks."

I hope you die, she thought. Thankfully, Allie returned with Fiona, and it took Trevor's attention away from Emma.

"Hello my bride. I was just catching up with your best friend," he said knowingly.

Best friend. I know about you and Ethan, Emma thought. She shuddered when she remembered the circumstances of how she found out. It only made her task that day easier. Still—she couldn't say a word.

"Ladies, if you'll excuse me, I'm going to go hang out with my friends. The groomsmen," Trevor said.

As he walked toward Ethan and Dutch and Vee, they smiled at Trevor, and Emma thought how much she hated that Ethan thought highly of that wretched excuse for a human. Emma had such high hopes when Fiona told her

65

the story of how she and Trevor had met at the end of last year. Fiona was out at a coworker's bachelorette party in the city. Thirty-seven-year-old Trevor approached her in the hotel bar and said that he, too, had been at a bachelor party, but he ditched them for some quiet time—he wasn't into the whole scene of strip clubs and drinking until you threw up. Fiona immediately had a soft spot for him, one that got mushy as soon as he mentioned that he'd only been in love once and lost her, and now he was just waiting for the right one, so he could settle down himself. Have a wife. Two point five kids and a house in the suburbs. A dog.

"What exactly does he do again?" Emma asked Fiona.

Fiona shifted her drink from her left hand to her right. "He wants to get into politics. My Uncle John is trying to find a fit for him once he takes office. But right now, he does security stuff for big firms. Important people."

"Security like what? I don't understand." Emma persisted. "Is he a rent-a-cop? Or a high-end ADT?" she asked, fishing for information. She really wanted to know how he got what he had on her.

"No!" Fiona laughed. "I mean, that's part of it. Home and property cameras and stuff. But he also—" She looked from left to right and then lowered her voice. "These high-powered people that he deals with all have secrets. He makes sure to scrub it all from the internet. It's pretty extensive and involves payoffs." Fiona looked impressed, but Trevor could've shoveled dog shit for a living—she was just excited to get married to someone who looked like him. "He finds out stuff from facial recognition cameras. He can find people from years ago. People who are hiding. The technology is so good sometimes plastic surgery doesn't even fool them. And it got even crazier after quarantine and masks and stuff. They can even find you through that now."

Emma wondered how much Trevor had to pay, and where he even looked, to find what he found on her.

Five months before the wedding, 1 p.m.

"Mrs. Pierce, Paula just called me from downstairs. There's someone here to see you," the voice boomed from her desk phone. It was her assistant Tyler. Well, he was the *floor's* assistant, not just hers. Not yet. "His name is Trevor Vaughn. I don't see an appointment with him on your calendar. Can she send him up?"

Emma looked up from her manuscript to the picture of Bianca on her desk, then up to the ceiling in recollection. Trevor Vaughn? Oh! Trevor! Fiona's boyfriend! She looked at her watch; it was one p.m., a half an hour before her marketing meeting. Emma pressed the button on her phone to reply.

"Sure, Tyler. I'll be right out."

She waited a few minutes before she stood and exited her cubicle and strode down the beige hallway to reception, where she indeed found Trevor, dressed in all black, sitting on one of their plush couches, their newest best-selling thriller from the coffee table in front of him in his hand. He waved it in front of her upon her approach.

"You like these types of books? Where secrets and lies destroy families?" he asked slowly.

Emma chuckled. "I'm more of a romance girl myself."

"Ah." It was a statement. "Shall we take a walk?"

She looked at her watch again. "I have a meeting in a half hour. What are you doing here?"

He picked up a large manila envelope that was next to him. "I need to talk to you about something. I think we should grab a coffee. You don't want to do this here."

"Do what?"

"How's that place downstairs? Bean Addiction? Good espresso? I can use an espresso."

Emma's stomach warbled at his tone and his dismissal of her agenda for the day. However, he was already walking briskly ahead of her and placed his hand into the closing elevator door where some coworkers stood, so she went in, and he followed. The only noise came through the blaring headphones of a young bike messenger with a love of Eminem. There was no small talk, just people shifting around, getting on or off at designated floors, and getting more cramped and hotter than outside's ninety-plus temperature. Very hot, even for the end of June. Leaving the building was no relief as the air was thick and humid, constricting her chest even more.

Trevor opened the door to the coffee shop for her, his hand too familiar on her lower back. As they waited in line, she breathed in the coffee smell. It reminded her of her childhood in Portugal, when she and Cassandra would visit the coffee shops with their parents. They'd always gotten the whole beans, and then ground them in the kitchen themselves before brewing. French press was their favorite.

She lifted her thick hair off her neck in an attempt to cool down, and felt a soft breeze prickling her skin. Yet, it didn't have the arctic chill of the air conditioner, and when she turned, she was startled to discover Trevor blowing lightly on the back of her neck. Uncomfortable, she moved away and dropped her hair. He winked, then he ordered for both of them while she stayed silent.

Once settled with two espressos—a single for her, a double for him—she quizzed him.

"I thought we'd see you guys at brunch on Sunday. What's with the secret visit?" She sipped her espresso—too bitter. She would've preferred a cappuccino, but there was something in Trevor's insistence that made her just want to get this over with.

He swallowed his sip and cleared his throat. "Well, I'm proposing to Fiona on Sunday at brunch."

Emma let out a yelp so filled with volume and happiness that other patrons turned to look. "Oh my God! She's going to be thrilled!"

Trevor's head tilted ear to shoulder, ear to shoulder, like a boxer working out the kinks. When he stopped, they locked eyes. "Good Lord, Emma, you really are gorgeous."

Her stomach sank to the bottom of her abdomen. It wasn't a compliment; it was sleazy, especially after the inappropriate touching. How dare he mention proposing to Fiona and then stare her down like his prized pig? She lowered her eyes to her cup. "Thank you," she said and took a sip.

"Don't look down. Look at me. Those eyes are something. Mesmerizing."

Emma had been hearing about the beauty of her big green eyes her whole life. Her mother, sister, and a few of her cousins in Portugal had really light green eyes. So did Bianca. It must've been in the bloodline. It was always the first thing people noticed about her. But those big eyes only had room for Ethan. She thought she might tear up right in front of Trevor—she was beyond uncomfortable.

"So, you're proposing to Fiona! That's great news." She changed the subject.

"Oh. Yeah. Right, right," he said and snapped back into it. "Well, I think she's been having some second thoughts about our relationship lately."

Emma and Fiona had spoken on the phone a couple times since the sudden move to Miami. Yes, it was true—Fiona had expressed some concern, and thought she rushed into it too quickly and realized she gave up her friends and her job for a guy she barely knew. Emma thought that Fiona let herself get wrapped up in the fact that this gorgeous man paid attention to her at all; Fiona had been toying with moving back North after only a month.

"Oh no," Emma said. Fiona would be so upset if she didn't get her happy ending. But it was also Fiona's happiness that mattered to Emma, and she didn't know Trevor all that well. By the way he was acting, she thought he was a bit of a slime ball. Emma wondered if the proposal would make a difference to Fiona at all. "I'm sure it'll all work out."

"Yeah. *Oh no*," he mocked. "Anyway, you're going to convince her to say yes. You're going to be *so* excited and *so* shocked and *so* thrilled, that if she comes to you with any concerns, you're going to brush them under the rug and talk me up."

"Excuse me?" Who did this guy think he was? He couldn't threaten her.

He tapped on the envelope that he'd been carrying, which he now placed on the table in front of him. "Guess what I found out?"

She placed the small paper cup down and again looked at her watch. "I don't have time for this. Why are you playing games?"

"Games? *I'm* playing games. I see." He pushed the envelope toward her. "Go ahead. Look inside."

With a huff, Emma tore the envelope open and pulled out pictures. Five of them. Five different outfits. Five different places. All different, yet remarkably the same. The blood drained from her face before she spoke.

"He doesn't know," she whispered, her eyes closed. Her lips trembled, holding back her sob.

His was a smirk. "I know. I'm sure you want to keep it that way."

12

DUTCH

Two days before the wedding, 2:30 p.m.

"Pardon me guys, I think we have a damsel in distress," Dutch said with a laugh and pointed at a desperate Emma, whose eyes were squinting through the crowd, clearly looking for someone. He excused himself from Fiona's brother Jesse and his boyfriend Hector. He picked up his drink, a gin and tonic, and the ice rattled as he made his way across the room. He didn't expect so many people here this early—immediate family and close friends, sure, but there had to be at least fifty guests already enjoying drinks and passed appetizers.

The only one missing was Roger. And to hell with him anyway.

Still, it bothered him. Dutch had known the guy almost twenty years. He wondered how everyone else felt at his absence, but he wouldn't dare utter Roger's name. His friends banished Roger on their own—Dutch would never tell anyone who to be friends with, but he was glad they all stuck with him after that mess.

"What's up Em?" he asked after he pushed through the crowd to his friends.

"We need pictures and video. James Cameron is on location, so you're all we've got," Emma said, her brows raised with hope.

"Yeah, man! I'll direct," he said as he looked around for the nearest cocktail table to rest his drink on as the girls gathered around, waiting for their big moment. Dutch was a natural director, and always wanted everything documented when they were in party situations with their friends. It had proven to be hilarious watching old videos years later.

It was also the catalyst that could ruin his life. One of his videos was sitting in a police closet somewhere, now marked "evidence."

Fiona beamed at Dutch. "I still think it's so awesome that you guys are his groomsmen. It really means a lot to me, to have you *all* in my wedding. Well, I guess not all of you." Her eyes glazed over before she collected herself, clearly still sad about what Roger did, causing him to be removed from the wedding party and the wedding itself. They'd dated briefly freshman year of college and remained friendly ever since, until Roger made his feelings clear about the engagement. "Your support isn't going unnoticed."

Dutch was unsteady inside, his stomach grumbling and his head becoming light. His support came with strings. He hated it. He gave a crooked smile and a curt nod, and then he waved his phone around. Fiona stood in the middle of Allie and Emma, her white dress mimicking a wedding gown—she'd mentioned to them that everything she planned to wear all weekend would be white.

Dutch made the best of the situation and took pictures on the latest iPhone, the one with the amazing camera. All the girls knew they would be hashtagged with

#ThreeDaysOfFun, and Dutch documented everything. Then he switched to video and spoke with a heavy French accent making a mockery of their show while directing, "Vat eez dis? Give me sexy. Give me bored. Give me love!" Their expressions changed at his direction.

"Wow, you're good at that." Trevor's voice crawled up Dutch's spine from behind. "Maybe you should direct videos full time. With those all-American looks and those people you know in LA, you wouldn't have a problem."

Videos. LA. Dutch could never forget what Trevor said to him.

"I knew her."

His words still stung like battery acid every time he'd thought about it. Dutch's smile disappeared, and he stopped the video. "I think I have enough for now. We'll get more tonight at the welcome dinner," Dutch said dryly, picked up his now watered-down drink, and made his way over to the bar for a refill without turning to acknowledge Trevor.

As Dutch walked away, his legs were unsteady, and he felt his knees buckle. He'd had a couple drinks already, but he also knew he wasn't drunk. The rage started five months ago and had only increased as time went on. Tick tock, tick tock—he was almost off the hook. He hoped. He had to get through the wedding, even if he'd handed Fiona a life sentence with Trevor.

Five months before the wedding, 3 p.m.

It was the end of June, a hot as hell day in the city. After basketball practice with one of his little brothers that he mentored, Dutch looked at his cell phone and saw a missed call from a strange number. He yanked his shirt off the ground and wiped the sweat off his neck and had a sip of bottled water as he listened to his voicemail. The call came in at one-thirty. It was Trevor, Fiona's boyfriend. He explained that he got Dutch's number from Fiona's phone and needed to speak with him.

Even though they'd only moved away to Miami a month before, Fiona and Trevor flew into New York to visit her mother for the weekend and to grab some of her stuff that she'd left behind. They were all having brunch together on Sunday before the couple flew back to Florida Sunday night.

On his walk back to his penthouse, he dialed Trevor's number.

"Dutch. Glad you called back," Trevor answered. Curt. All business.

"Hey, Trevor. Is everything okay?"

"Well, that depends on your definition of okay."

Dutch's heart sank. "Oh God. Is it Fiona? Did something happen?"

Dutch stopped in his tracks, causing a lady walking a dog to bump into him and tell him to watch where he was going, as she walked around him with disdain. The little Yorkie on the leash turned around and yelped a high-pitched bark in agreement. Dutch was on a quiet stretch of Tribeca, away from the construction and the beeping horns, and he swore Trevor laughed.

"I think you should come to my hotel. I have something to show you. Trust me, you'll want to see it, and you'll want to keep it to yourself. The W in Midtown. The room is in my name. They'll call up to let you in. And don't say a word about this meeting to anyone. But you'd better come now."

The call disconnected, and Dutch stared, bewildered, at his phone. What the hell was that about? What could Trevor possibly have to show Dutch? And why was he so angry and insistent? Was it about his father? He stayed in his sweaty clothes and grabbed a cab.

Dutch looked out of place in the W in basketball shorts and a dark gray T-shirt that was stained with sweat down the middle, but still waited patiently to talk to the man in the suit behind the counter who called to let Trevor know he had a visitor. The man nodded as he hung up the phone and sent him up to the twelfth floor.

The door opened as soon as Dutch knocked, which made him think that Trevor was literally waiting behind it. Trevor offered no smile, no handshake—all he did was open it and walk away, leaving Dutch to follow him in. He got a bad feeling as he sat down on the couch in front of a pile of manila envelopes. His instinct usually didn't betray him.

"So," Trevor started, "I'm going to propose to Fiona on Sunday at brunch. I came up here to get her Uncle John's permission, since he's the man of the family now. He's practically raised her since her father passed. I had breakfast with him this morning and of course he said yes."

Dutch breathed a sigh of relief. His paranoia was unfounded.

"Wow, Trevor, that's great news. Congratulations!"

"But," Trevor said in a way that showed domination, "I've decided since all of you guys have been so close for so long—you, Ethan, Roger, and Veejay—that I'm going to ask you all to be my groomsmen at the wedding. You're going to stand up next to me and say nice things about me because I'm telling you to. I'm not asking you to. You'll make sure Fiona says yes, too. She's expressed some doubts about our relationship. I won't accept it."

Dutch blinked quickly and studied Trevor's face to see if it was a joke. He didn't know him all that well. Dutch could count on one hand the number of times they'd hung out in the five months since they'd met. If Trevor had wanted Dutch to be a groomsman, he'd do it for Fiona, anyway—but he didn't do well with threats.

"Excuse me?" Dutch stood up. He stood a good four inches over Trevor, and he was going to let him know that he wouldn't be intimidated. "I don't know where you get off—"

"Sit down."

Who does this guy think he is? "Screw you, Trevor."

"Don't you want to see what's on the flash drive?" Trevor never stood, and never raised his voice. He wore a smirk fit for a gangster, pushing it closer to the edge of the table. "Go ahead, Dietrich." Dutch flinched at the use of his first name. "Stick this in the laptop and press play."

Dutch was all thumbs as he fumbled with the flash drive, and his fingers trembled as he inserted it into the laptop. When what he was looking at became clear, he squinted, and then his mouth dropped open.

"Wait, wait. Keep watching. It's a greatest hits reel," Trevor said.

Dutch looked away. He remembered the party. He remembered what was about to happen.

"I said *watch*."

"Stop it." Dutch knew he was dead meat. Why make it worse? "Turn it off."

"Nah." Instead, Trevor tapped a few buttons and opened another file folder on the flash drive.

The one with the crime scene photos.

"Enough!" Dutch shut the laptop with a clap and sat back down, the sweat gathering on his back like he'd just run a half marathon. "What do you want, Trevor?"

"Now we're talking." He rubbed his hands together like a disgusting fly and Dutch wished he had a swatter. Despite the growing anxiety, Dutch was still floored at Trevor's next words. "You're going to pay for that, you motherfucker. I knew her. She was my girlfriend. And I've spent the past ten years watching you, making sure I get what I want."

What? Had Trevor been stalking Dutch this whole time? Ever since he…

Trevor cut into Dutch's worst memory. "Well, you've presented me with this terrific opportunity, finally. *Finally*, I find out that you have someone in your life who can be useful to me. So, this is what's going to happen, Dietrich. You're going to talk me up to Fiona no matter what you hear about me. If she has doubts, you'll settle her mind. When I present the ring, you'll smile. If not, this stuff is going to the press, like it should've when it happened. Daddy won't be able to buy back your reputation."

He couldn't wrap his head around what Trevor had said. *She was my girlfriend*. Trevor must've been the relationship Kelsey broke off to be with Dutch. That was before—

Shit.

Dutch had worked too hard to become a pillar of the community since that fateful day. He was a champion of the underprivileged. He assumed he could volunteer his way back into God's good graces. He'd been trying like hell. Forgiveness never came, but he kept trying. He'd *keep* trying.

"It was an accident," Dutch whispered, and the tears came.

"Sure didn't look like one, you asshole. Now, as I was saying…"

Dutch half tuned out as Trevor went on about how Dutch was to make sure that Fiona would accept his proposal—no matter what. That, or his days of freedom would come to an end. It dawned on him that Trevor wasn't randomly in his life, nor Fiona's. No, this was all Dutch's doing. And Fiona was about to be screwed forever because of his own shameful secrets.

His internal conflict raged until he resigned himself to the fact that he had to do what Trevor asked, to keep his reputation intact, to stay out of prison, simply so he could keep doing good in the world. It mattered to him. It was his penance for his past, or so he thought. When Trevor stopped speaking, Dutch nodded in lieu of saying anything that would send him further into the rabbit hole.

Just like that, he sold his soul. It turned out his father was right—anything could be bought for a price.

13

VEEJAY

Two days before the wedding, 6 p.m.

After a few hours in the lobby bar catching up, everyone retired to clean up and dress for the evening. Now, the entire gang was on the second-floor outdoor balcony of one of the hotel's restaurants, the one that was hosting the welcome dinner. It was an expansive space, but private to them for the evening and elegantly set up with tall cocktail tables and two makeshift bars, one on the north end and one on the south. The sunset had faded to darkness on a downward spiral to the west. The surrounding palm trees swayed in the breeze as if they were the rope in an invisible game of tug-of-war.

There, they all met Trevor's parents for the first time.

Vee couldn't believe that this spawn of the Devil came from two such lovely people. Margot Vaughn was a retired schoolteacher herself, which explained the bond Fiona always described them having. She stood around five-foot-seven, and her dark hair was dyed a harsh color that came off as unnatural, especially for a woman of her age, which Vee believed to be upper fifties, maybe even early sixties. She wore what old people would call "spectacles," with dark frames that appeared to be bifocal from the thin line cutting through the glass in the middle. Her outfit was a version of what someone wore on *Dynasty* in the eighties (he'd seen repeats in India), with sequins and shoulder pads; yet, on her, it draped elegantly down her thin frame. It looked heavy and he didn't understand how she wasn't passing out from the heat.

Harrison Vaughn was also retired—he used to write children's books. Trevor's looks were definitely inherited from his handsome father—it was clear that this man was a heartbreaker when he was younger. The dark hair, the cheekbones, and the charisma must've been in the Vaughn DNA. He wore a three-piece suit despite the grating heat, with a chain peeking from the lower vest pocket. *A pocket watch*, thought Vee. *How quaint*. Both of the Vaughns were accommodating and pleasant and showed no signs of the narcissism or sociopathy that fueled their son.

Vee and his travel buddies all stood at a cocktail table, taking in the moon hovering over the Atlantic, the water trickling onto the beach. The weather had cooled down a smidge, and he was dressed casually in chinos and a short-sleeved button-down shirt, as were Dutch and Ethan. Emma and Allie both wore sundresses. Vee breathed deeply to take in the smell of coconuts and pineapple, something that always fascinated him when he escaped to a tropical place like this, which he didn't do often. The first time he'd been around a palm tree as a child, he thought that pineapples, with their spiky skin and green top, grew up to be palm trees.

Trevor and Fiona interrupted his seagull-like serenity when they approached the table with a bottle of champagne and seven glasses. Trevor popped the top off the bottle the way they do in the movies (like a douchebag) with the cork darting across the room, and everyone turned their way and cheered at the loud noise. The champagne bubbles overflowed off the top of all the glasses and six of the friends picked them up.

Emma didn't.

Right. She mentioned something earlier about the bubbles bothering her stomach, Vee thought. That must've been why she'd been clutching it on and off all afternoon.

"Wait," Emma said, her fingers grazing the stem of the only glass still sitting on the table. "I'm glad it's just us right now. Look, I don't want to make a big deal, and I don't want to steal your thunder Fiona, but I won't be drinking this weekend. Or, for the next seven months."

It was a screech like a fire engine, the way Allie screamed. Immediately, she threw her arms around Emma. Dutch shook hands with Ethan, congratulating him. Emma glowed, while Vee flung his arms around her. He couldn't believe it, yet he could. Inside, he was bursting for one of his closest friends. The pride on Ethan's face was noticeable and Vee pulled him in for a big hug as well.

Vee figured it would be the happiest moment of the entire weekend.

Fiona stood with a closed-lipped smile, and Trevor didn't move a muscle. Did they think Emma was trying to one-up their wedding?

"Sorry about doing it now. Here," Emma said, reading Vee's mind. "We couldn't put it off until the twelve-week mark. We assumed you'd all wonder why I'm not drinking in Miami of all places. And it's your wedding. I mean, hello!"

"Why does everyone wait until twelve weeks, anyway?" Trevor asked.

Emma had to educate him. "Because there's blood tests and genetic tests and all sorts of things that can happen before that. I'm only about two months in. Technically, I'm not really in the clear yet." She paused and placed her open palm on her flat belly. Her light green eyes glassed over, obviously worried about what could still be. "We haven't told anyone in our families yet. We're only telling you guys for now."

"Well, we feel very special that you shared it this weekend," Trevor said with a sigh of resignation. He put his arm around Fiona and kissed her temple.

Vee didn't think he seemed sincere, but then again, he was a sociopath, and they weren't capable of empathy or true happiness for another. Still, Vee wondered why he looked like someone was about to push him off a ledge when he grabbed a cocktail napkin and wiped the sweat off his forehead.

14

ETHAN

Two days before the wedding, 6:15 p.m.

Fiona's eyes had long since glassed over. Ethan knew that she wasn't jealous. But it probably still hurt *just a little*. She grabbed a cocktail napkin and blew her nose, and then realized she couldn't control herself.

"I'm just so happy," she said, but she didn't look happy. Her smile betrayed her. "I have to use the ladies' room. Excuse me."

She turned on her four-inch heels and walked away, as everyone stood in silence.

"We should go check on her," Emma said to Allie. "Maybe I should've waited to say anything."

"No, I'll go," Ethan said. "Stay here. Enjoy your moment. I'll make sure she's okay."

Fiona had been stopped by a few people on her way to the bathroom, and she told everyone they were tears of joy and that she needed to get to a sink fast as not to ruin her makeup and she would be right back. Ethan trailed behind her at a safe distance, watching the pale white silk that draped over her thin frame as it bopped and weaved through the crowd of people. He shouted her name when her hands pushed on the tarnished brass handle of the bathroom door. She paused for an indiscernible second, then went in. He knew she heard him behind her, and he would wait for her to come outside.

He leaned against the wall with his hands in his pockets. He tried to quiet the buzz of regret in his head by concentrating on the space around him to pass the time. Actually, it wasn't regret. He didn't know what it was. Bittersweet memories? Ones Fiona clearly held on to, even if he didn't.

He looked up—it was still light out, the sky a shade of blue that looked as though it used to be royal blue but was faded by the constant presence of the southern sun. The air had become stagnant with the wearing on of the day, the humidity. He took out his iPhone to check the weather, finding that the heat would be worse tomorrow, hopefully capping off late tomorrow night with a thunderstorm to wash it all away.

He checked his watch, a secondhand Breitling with a blue face that Emma had gotten him for their one-year wedding anniversary, and only a minute or so had passed. He imagined that Fiona was figuring out what to say to him when she emerged—she had to know he'd be waiting by the door like a guard at Buckingham Palace.

Right then, he couldn't crack a smile either.

When he heard the whoosh of the door opening, he blocked her from going any further.

"Fiona, I—" He'd rehearsed it, and now it was gone, like a magician's parlor trick. *Poof.*

"It's fine Ethan. Really." Tears crept back to her eyelids, and she pushed them down. "You guys belong together. Congratulations on the baby. Really."

She smiled at him and went back to her fiancé's waiting arms.

Ethan didn't know what to do, or what to say. He was a stupid, irresponsible kid six years ago, and he didn't know how to handle her developing emotions, especially when he was still in love with Emma. Why twist the knife? She was already bleeding.

He wondered if she knew that Trevor knew about their past. God knows where he came up with the photos he had, but he said he found one of them in her phone. Why had she kept that photo? Fiona obviously loved Trevor, but Ethan couldn't waste any more time thinking about him. He had his own family that he was responsible for now. Emma. The baby.

He'd protect his family at any cost.

15

EMMA

Two days before the wedding, 6:30 p.m.

Emma was alone at the bar, grabbing herself a ginger ale so she could pretend she was drinking something bubbly and alcoholic with her friends. She didn't know how she'd be able to do it, just water and soda and mocktail fakes for the next three days while her friends imbibed in celebration. What she really needed was liquor—cold, hard, liquor. But she had no other options, so ginger ale it was. When the syrupy liquid slid its way down her throat, the hair on the back of her neck stood up. She could sense the presence of evil. When she turned around, her gut didn't betray her.

"What do you think you're doing?" Trevor said through clenched teeth. "What exactly *the fuck* do you think you're doing?"

Emma tried to remain calm; she had to keep her cool. This was her moment, the one she planned, the one she'd been waiting for. She knew he wouldn't take the news lightly and she'd rehearsed this little speech of hers, but in her version, Trevor was begging and submitting. She didn't expect the curse-filled confrontation.

"Careful, Trevor—you don't want to give away too much about your real self. You know it'll ruin your chance of getting into Fiona's family. I know that's your endgame. Her Uncle John. Politics."

He threw his head back in laughter. Then he leaned in too close to Emma and when his lips got near her ear to whisper, her skin crawled.

"Don't worry about me, my endgame, or my connections. You don't know anything about me, or my dealings with Senator Hawthorne. You just worry that you still have another month until you're 'in the clear' with this pregnancy, as you put it. Like you said, anything can happen. I mean, you haven't even told your family. Your whole, huge extended family in Portugal. Your sister, her husband. Your niece, Bianca. You know I know who they are."

The threat landed on Emma. She knew he was a sociopath, but was he capable of violence? How dare he mention her family.

"*Não me ameace*. Is that a threat? I'll expose you!"

"Oh yeah?" More laughter. The whole thing was a joke to him. "I'm going to make sure Ethan finds out what a manipulative, calculating little whore you are. Don't forget what I know. I should punish you for this little stunt."

Her plan wasn't working. In fact, she'd made the entire situation worse. She shoved her index finger in his face in a show of bravado. "You stay the hell away from me and stay the hell away from my husband. And if I find out you go near my family, I'll kill you myself."

Feeling eyes on them, Trevor laughed off her position like she had just told him a joke, and the finger pointing was the punchline. It had been all smiles and laughs and casual conversation on his side. Anyone watching them from a distance would see Fiona's fiancé and her college friend fawning all over each other.

When Fiona turned the corner, returning from the bathroom, her eyes were teary and Emma followed her trail—Ethan was a few steps behind her. It ate at her to see him follow her, knowing what she knew about them from the past. Keeping quiet was the second hardest thing she'd ever had to do.

The third hardest.

Okay, the fourth.

"They'll be calling people inside any minute." Trevor's demonic eyes bore a hole into Emma's skull. Another silent warning. *Keep your mouth shut.* "We'll see you later." He took Fiona's hand to lead her away.

Emma pursed her lips and raised her champagne flute, filled with ginger ale, in their direction. "Cheers."

They walked away, and Emma hoped she got her point across loud and clear.

16

ALLIE

Two days before the wedding, 10:00 p.m.

Once the pregnancy announcement died down, everyone remembered the real reason they were all there and celebrated Trevor and Fiona. He gave such a warm welcome speech that Allie was almost convinced that he did love Fiona, even though in her heart of hearts she knew he was as fake as a three-dollar bill. There were golf claps and clinked glasses as Allie slugged down prosecco after prosecco. After dinner, Uncle John gave a speech about his brother—Fiona's father—and how proud he would be of the woman she'd become. His oratory skills were only part of the reason he'd had Allie's vote.

Proud of her, thought Allie when he concluded his speech. *Not proud of her poor choice in men*. Then again, Uncle John seemed to love Trevor. Just like everyone else. Ugh.

Everyone was tired—it had been a long day. They were all up early and jammed into New York City traffic and then a metal tube and then alcohol on a steady stream, so everyone retreated to their rooms shortly after dinner. The next day would be another early one.

After visiting the ice machine for her end-of-day beverage, Allie changed into a long silk nightgown, dressed up for no one. She opened her minibar and was happy to see it was well stocked. The ice cubes plunked into the sturdy glass, making her favorite *dink-dank-ding* sound. In the mini fridge, she took out all the little Jack Daniels bottles—four of them—and poured two of them into the glass with just a splash of diet coke. Bypassing the minibar M&Ms and Pringles, she grabbed a homemade packet of trail mix from her bag to chomp on absent-mindedly while she drank. The balcony doors squeaked as they opened and the hot Miami air met the air-conditioned room. The humidity felt good on her face. Her skin had gotten drier since she'd hit thirty. She was starting over at thirty-two, even earlier than her planned thirty-five. She positioned herself in a chaise to face the moon and sipped her whiskey.

This fucking wedding, she thought. *That fucking guy*. She remembered the first time she'd met him, after he and Fiona started almost dating a year ago. Fiona was so excited to introduce everyone to her new boyfriend. She came into the city from Westchester and had planned for everyone to meet at a bar in Midtown on a Saturday night. Through Allie's perspective, Trevor seemed to pay a little too much attention to Emma and didn't like Dutch from the jump. It was just a feeling she got. She was a Pisces and had terrific intuition.

Allie's memory of that day was vivid, seared into her conscience like a raised scar. She'd asked Trevor about his work, while he was more interested in what she did. After telling him she was all but retired from finance, he made comment after comment about the dark web. Gave away a few secrets himself after too many drinks—mentioned how to get there, how to contact someone who called themselves "Blue" who bought information.

He constantly said that she was too sharp to accept a life of leisure, and after that night, she let his comments grate on her for a month. She *was* too damn sharp. Second in her class. She used to rule Wall Street. Order men around. Not match China patterns to wallpaper samples.

One day in another fit of boredom—how many damn pairs of shoes could one shop for?—she tried it. Getting to Blue was easier than she'd thought. He, or she, talked from a burner phone into hers with a voice distorter. Selling Wharton's financial secrets was either done with an untraceable web address or a burner—she had a closet full of them—and finished with a Bitcoin deposit into her account in the Caymans. It was not how she'd seen things playing out, but at least she got a thrill out of life again. She was using her brain for more than adding the cost of the Manolos to the cost of the Versace dress. Plus tax.

After college, she'd interviewed with Wharton's hedge fund. Being smart as a whip and somewhat of a math whiz, her Ivy League degree solidified her immediate hire and signing bonus. One of the only women traders, not only in his company but in the entire industry, she was described as a shark. She quickly became addicted to the lifestyle, commanding respect, ordering all the Masters of the Universe around. She'd take over everything and retire at thirty-five. Of course she was drawn to a man of such power like Wharton.

She had to quit her job after one of the partners found out about their involvement, and to avoid the scandal, they married—framing theirs as some super love story, not a man getting his rocks off with someone half his age, and she'd sooner die than be labeled a gold digger when she was just starting out. So, the choice was made. Well, actually, the situation was presented to her: she was to give up her career and be Wharton's wife, to attend functions and galas and to host dinner parties.

The life suited her, at first. She was a kept wife who'd upgraded from roommates and warehouse sales to a penthouse and an American Express Black card. But, like any good shark, once Trevor had teased that there was blood was in the water, it was hard to curb a taste for it. With her teeth sharpened, she began to look for something to bite. She *was* too smart to be the little woman, and that was how Wharton began to see her. The old coworkers she used to boss around knew her now as a lady who lunched.

She couldn't have that.

She pretended, of course, wearing short dresses and too much makeup and flitting from conversation to conversation at industry parties, stowing away all the financial tidbits that slipped out of old men's mouths after their third martini. They, too, had forgotten about her reputation as a shark. She used it to her advantage.

She'd pressed her own husband. *Pillow talk*, she'd called it with Wharton. He never imagined she'd be selling material nonpublic information. Ever since she became his wife, he acted like he'd picked her from a catalogue. *I'll take the redhead in her twenties.* His first mistake was treating her like an object. His second was forgetting her intelligence.

She'd waited, patiently, hunting her prey. The first time she'd gotten decent intel, she'd heard it from Wharton's study while he talked on the phone about Company A taking over Company B. She knew the value of the stock would jump by twenty percent, from twenty-five dollars a share to thirty, once the news hit the street.

She contacted Blue, who wanted the info for free, as a trial to see if she was full of shit or not. When the rumors proved to be true, Blue kept coming back for more information. Her Bitcoin increased, and she knew when to sell high. She was becoming a millionaire in her own right. It was a perfect situation, and she was back in control—she loved the power she had over men when they paid for her brain; it was like a drug, and she was always chasing that first high.

Then, six months ago, Wharton got an anonymous letter, detailing all of the information that Allie had been selling; her gig was up, and he divorced her, no questions asked. Allie only asked for the apartment, holding Wharton's company information by the balls—she could easily set him up to take the fall for selling the info. Insider trading came with a hefty sentence.

But Allie wasn't a blackmailer. She was a good girl trying to keep her rightful place in the world.

Wharton signed the apartment over and she didn't get another red cent. She was cut off from her former life, blacklisted in the industry, and she couldn't get information from him or his associates anymore. She'd been living off her Bitcoin earnings—she knew when to buy and sell other crypto currencies as well—and told her friends it was the divorce settlement. Not that she was a criminal.

Yet, here they were, at this hotel in Miami, less than six months after she was presented with the divorce papers. Less than six months after Trevor revealed himself to her as Blue. The asshole set her up from the get-go and he'd been holding it over her just to get Fiona to marry him. For politics, she was sure.

Didn't Trevor get lucky.

Going in for another sip of her old friend Jack Daniels, Allie didn't realize she'd already drained the entire cup. What was left of the ice cubes sounded pathetic at the bottom of the glass, no longer the sharp *dink-dank-ding*, but now a *thump-thump* sputter. She let them slide onto her tongue and chewed them up, and then decided to retire instead of drinking the other two bottles.

Sliding into the lush bed, she adjusted two down pillows under her knees and another under her head, grabbed her silk sleep mask, and opened the relaxation app on her phone to play as she fell asleep. This particular night, she chose an inner meditation monologue that was supposed to calm her center. Deep breath in, hold, deep breath out. *Breathe in positivity, breathe out negativity*. The woman's soothing voice could probably lull a snarling pit bull into submission, but as she tried to sleep, Allie had only one thought: how to save herself from Trevor Vaughn.

17

DUTCH

Two days before the wedding, 10:00 p.m.

Dutch settled into his room, ignoring the pings on his phone. He didn't want to deal with anyone back at home, especially if it related to his parents' divorce. He had enough to worry about where he was and who he was with. He was the one who led the wolf into the pen. And now Fiona was mixed up in it and about to be slaughtered too.

After he cracked a beer, he opened the door and settled into a chaise outside and took in the night air from his balcony, a nice deep breath that swelled his chest like he was a gorilla about to pound it. He remembered back to the time after he visited Trevor at the W in the summer. After he saw the video and pictures that Trevor presented to him, he knew his life was over. At least, his life as he knew it.

There it was: Dutch and his ex-girlfriend Kelsey. They'd met during spring break in Cancun. She was an aspiring model from LA, and a bit of a club rat, which was perfect for him—at the time, anyway. They were obsessed with each other—she'd even broken off a five-year long relationship to be with Dutch. He knew now that the relationship had been with Trevor.

They alternated weekends between New York and California. After graduation, Dutch was going to rent a yacht in LA for the summer, just him and her without the rest of the gang, and they were going to head back to New York together in the fall. He was going to work for his father developing real estate, and she was going to model.

Just hearing her voice, seeing her smile, seeing her move on the video—it brought tears to his eyes. The way she used to be. The way he wanted to remember her. Hundreds of other people were there too, on the video. Partying on the yacht in Los Angeles. When he was *that* guy.

He was high as a kite. So was Kelsey. He should've stopped pushing her to do more, but the table in front of them looked like it was the nineteen-seventies, covered in mountains of cocaine. That was what the little richie-riches he used to call friends did at the time—sleep all day, party all night, and sun themselves in between. It was all there on video—Kelsey refusing to do more coke, and Dutch acting like the entitled little prick he used to be until she did more. He insulted her in front of everyone. Badgered her to do more. Called her a lightweight. Said she couldn't hang with the big boys. He laughed at her.

Her overdose was caught on video too. She survived though. She was alive.

Not that it mattered. Alive, yes. Living? No.

Kelsey's life would never be the same. She'd lost too much oxygen during her overdose and that resulted in her losing more than half of her motor and speech functions. She had round-the-clock medical care. When Dutch's father paid everyone under the sun to make it go away and Dutch got off scot-free, his resentment grew. Toward his father, and toward his upbringing. Why should he be allowed to get away with what he did? Because of money? He swore he'd never be that guy again. He never went to work for his father, and instead volunteered with the schools and anything else he could get his hands in to help people.

It was about time he did something that wasn't one hundred percent selfish. It'd been his mantra ever since. He'd never paid for his mistake. Of course, he'd been paying for top-of-the-line everything for Kelsey since the day he came into part of his trust at twenty-five. Her family wouldn't let him see her—that hurt the most.

He'd never told his friends what happened. It never made the news or the papers. *Thanks, Dad*. When Dutch returned to New York early, he told everyone it was because they broke up. That's it. No drama. She was just gone. The gang felt bad for him. If they only knew what he'd done to her without penalty, and that he let it stay covered up, he'd lose them all. His good guy reputation, lost forever.

Just like Roger.

As much as Dutch hated Roger and what Roger did to his family, he had to admit he had an ounce of respect for the guy he'd known since freshman year of high school. It was a boarding school of sorts, less than an hour from the city, hidden behind ivy and wrought iron in suburban New York. Roger's family was from the Midwest, just outside Chicago, and they sent him to the school because he'd been getting into trouble. Half-Black and half-Irish, Roger didn't know where he fit in, and took it out on everyone and everything around him. Tall, fit, and light-skinned, he still didn't look like everyone else in his upper middle-class neighborhood. No one ever said anything to him or his parents, but he told Dutch he saw it. People crossing to the other side of the street when he walked their way. People locking their car doors when he was in the vicinity. His parents only wanted the best for him, so off he went, to a good school where he'd have more opportunity and diversity.

From Day One, Dutch and Roger became fast friends and did everything together. With Roger's family being so far away and Dutch's so close, he spent more and more time with them. Weeks at a time during summer breaks. Sometimes even holidays when Roger's parents were traveling. After making a pact and applying together, they both got into Columbia, and after college graduation, Roger started working for Dutch's father's company. They were like brothers.

At brunch, Roger's message to Trevor was clear from the beginning: *I won't play ball*. The happy engagement brunch ended with Roger leaving, his friends bewildered, and Fiona stuck with that asshole while Dutch didn't have the strength to stand up for what was right.

The next day, Trevor had no problem airing the dirty laundry to everyone: Roger had been having an affair with Dutch's mother. The information came anonymously, but Dutch knew that it had to come from Trevor—the timing was too coincidental, and it went to everyone *except* Fiona. It was the catalyst for Dutch's parents' divorce, for his family being torn apart, for his disgust whenever he thought of his mother and his former best friend.

Dutch knew he'd *have to* play ball with Trevor to keep his situation with Kelsey under wraps. Unless he could think of another way to get Trevor out of his life for good.

18

ROGER

Five Months before the wedding, Sunday brunch

It was hot, sure, but that wasn't why Roger was sweating on his way to brunch with his closest friends. Trevor Vaughn had visited him at his office that past Friday, holding a two-inch stack of pictures of him with Annette Von Ryan. Intimate dinners. Hand holding. Kissing. Inappropriate touching. And yes, pictures of sex and nakedness, of them, together. Sex with another man, with her son's best friend, while she still had her wedding ring on. How did Trevor get pictures of the insides of both of their bedrooms? He shuddered at the thought.

Roger's first instinct, of course, was to throw a punch, which he did. It landed on the exposed brick wall in his office as Trevor moved out of the way. Roger thought he'd broken his hand, but it was just a mess of bloody knuckles that he'd have to ice and wrap and make up an excuse for later.

Annette was a mistake—call it a boyhood crush at fourteen that never went away. The excuse for acting on it? Zero. Not only was it his best friend's mother, but it was his boss's wife. He'd been riddled with guilt and knew he had to stop, but he was out of time. Now he had to do what Trevor wanted: throw Fiona into the volcano as a human sacrifice. He didn't think he could do that to one of his best friends, but he'd lose the others if he didn't. He'd lose Dutch—his brother by all other accounts. The internal war was real.

Roger was the first to arrive for the eight-person brunch. Dutch had made the reservations because his name had the most pull, the prince of New York City. His best friend. He was able to secure them a table outside for their meal, and then a plush table in the back corner inside for the inevitable afterparty. Although Roger didn't feel much like partying.

Dutch showed up, then Emma and Ethan, followed five minutes later by Vee. They all looked tired. Dutch didn't speak much, just twiddled his thumbs and scanned the menu. Emma looked like she didn't even shower much less do her hair, and Ethan made no effort either, wearing a Rangers T-shirt and shorts. Vee had on golf shorts and a Polo and sandals—his typical outfit. However, his expression was anything but typical. Where Vee always wore a smile, he seemed distracted and forlorn. Allie arrived last, as usual.

Roger couldn't mention that he knew about the engagement—he didn't want to have to explain that he'd seen Trevor a few days earlier, and why. So, instead, he tried to act normal. He took his sunglasses off and slid them on top of his head. Their conversations seemed stunted to Roger. Whenever they all got together, it was endless jokes and catching up on the last few weeks. Work, relationships, the stock market, celebrities, the weather— you name it. Roger thought maybe he was overanalyzing because of the anxiety he carried with him into the restaurant. It was like he put it into a basket and passed it around as a party favor, because everyone just seemed so *off*. If only they knew what he was hiding.

The drinks arrived, the basket of bread and assorted pastries came, and the specials were read. Finally, Trevor and Fiona made their grand appearance while Roger squirmed. The look Trevor gave him said all he needed to know. *Comply*.

They all ordered food and made awkward small talk. That's when Roger realized they would later get dinner *and* a show.

Trevor had ordered a beet salad with goat cheese and apples, oil and vinegar on the side. On his third forkful, he clutched his throat and his face swelled, then turned the same color as the root vegetable on his plate.

"Is he okay?" Emma asked, motioning the fork from her egg white and spinach omelet in his direction.

Fiona took one look at him and sprang into action. "Trevor!" she screamed. He rolled off his chair onto the pavement, and Fiona skidded her chair across the concrete and turned her purse upside down. A small circle of patrons stared.

"Is he choking?" Emma asked, rather callously, Roger thought. She barely took her eyes off her plate.

"His allergies! I need his EpiPen!" wailed Fiona.

She dug through the contents of her bag, now splayed inside the roped-off outdoor seating area, until she saw what she needed. She pulled the cap off with her mouth and spit it out at the same time she plunged the needle into his left thigh. His head was in her lap, his half-opened eyes bloodshot.

"Call 911," she said to no one. "He has a deadly nut allergy."

No one immediately jumped to do the deed, so Dutch did, as Roger thought for a quick few seconds that maybe Trevor would die right there in front of him and then his nightmare would be over. It was nice to see him on the ground, seizing. He couldn't breathe, and his face paled where the hives didn't take over. He was vulnerable.

Fiona had her hands in his dish. "An almond! Jesus!" She held it in the air, waving it back and forth. "Where is that waiter? We told them no nuts!"

When the ambulance arrived, their brunch became like an accident on the side of the highway. People gathered on corners to stop and stare at them and point, like they were zoo animals. Foot traffic backed up as people took videos of the man breathing oxygen from the tank like it was a new reality show. Why? Was this going to be entertainment at home? *Let's watch the video of that guy breathing on the oxygen tank again!* Much too much attention was being paid, and that was when narcissistic Trevor saw his opportunity. He pulled the mask off his face and looked at Fiona and smiled. Then he got down on one knee and pulled a box out of his left pants pocket. He opened it and took her hand while Roger held his breath.

"Will you marry me?" Trevor asked Fiona.

He'd previously agreed to do whatever he had to do to keep the affair hidden, but watching Trevor drop down and open the little velvet box made something snap inside Roger. Before he was able to let his disgust register on his face, all his friends jumped up, cheering.

"Oh my God, Fiona, this is the best news!" Emma, doing a version of jazz hands.

"All right, man. What a perfect couple!" Vee, smiling.

"Look at that ring! Say yes!" Allie, clapping.

"It's about time!" Ethan, fist pumping.

"This might be the best day ever!" Dutch, patting Fiona on the back.

Ugh. All his friends really *did* love Trevor. He'd won; he was right. Roger would be the outsider if he didn't go along.

He didn't care. He couldn't do this to Fiona.

"Isn't this a little soon?" Roger asked in lieu of spitting out what he really wanted to say.

Seven pairs of eyes darted in his direction, Trevor's being the darkest and the most threatening. Fiona took her gaze from her huge ring to Roger, and she looked like she'd been slapped.

"What are you talking about? Aren't you happy for me?"

There were tears in her eyes as she spoke. Tears he knew would last a lifetime if he didn't intervene to rescue her from this jerk. So he doubled down. What was Trevor really going to do, blurt out Roger's affair, right after he'd proposed? Nah. He was bluffing. The whole thing was a big, bad bluff. Screw you, Trevor Vaughn.

Roger's upper lip curled. "Happy? You don't even know this guy. None of us do. Sorry, I can't stand around and pretend to be excited. To be honest, I'm surprised the rest of you are so gung ho about this. Why isn't anyone thinking about Fiona?"

It was the truth. No one—*no one* met his eyes. They all looked over his head, to the west, at the ground—anywhere but him. Fine, he'd had an outburst. He'd explain it to them tomorrow, after making up a reason for it. He'd smooth it over. They were his best friends. They'd understand.

He reached his hand into his pocket and tossed a fifty-dollar-bill on the table. "I'm out of here. Enjoy your celebration."

Even the medics looked at him with disdain as he turned his back on everyone. Sure, the gang would be mad at him for how he acted, but Trevor was full of shit, a wannabe powerful guy.

Trevor was no one. He wouldn't do a damn thing.

19

ETHAN

The day before the wedding, 8:00 a.m.

When the alarm blared into his ear, the last thing Ethan wanted to do was get up out of his comfortable bed and play golf with the wretched groom. After he lazily swatted at his phone to shut off that horrific siren, he rubbed his eyes and looked at the clock. It was just past eight a.m. There were light knocks in the hallway, with soft voices whispering *Housekeeping!* He hoped Emma remembered to hang the *Do Not Disturb* sign on the door last night, because he didn't do it. It would've been hell to jump up and stop someone from entering the room—he was practically naked. He turned over and spooned his wife.

"Mmm," Emma said and backed herself farther into him. He loved the little sounds she made when she was waking up. "Not yet. And I heard it too. I put up the *Do Not Disturb* on the door."

Of course she did. She was perfect. "I know it's early," he said, and kissed her shoulder. "Tee time isn't till ten-fifteen, although I want to hit the range for a bit first. I need to warm up my swing for about twenty minutes beforehand. What time is your first appointment?"

"Eleven," she said lazily, still dreaming. "Facial. Body scrub with fake tan. Manicure. Pedicure. All day long. I had to skip the massage because of Junior, but I'll still be stunning for tomorrow."

"Sounds like a dream," he deadpanned. Then his voice lit up. "And you're always stunning. At least you don't have to spend the day chasing a ball in this heat."

She turned to face him and pecked him on his cheek. "I get pampered, and you get to play golf. Don't make it sound like you're making a sacrifice!" she said with a laugh. "At least we're not at the office."

"I know. I love golf. It's just—" He stopped himself. He couldn't tell her that he didn't want to play with Trevor. "It's just that I think I injured my shoulder at the gym last week."

"Oh no!" Emma threw the covers off herself. "Which one?"

She was going to rub it and make it better for him. How did he get so lucky?

Emma kneaded his left shoulder for a good ten minutes before he began to stroke her arm in a way that meant business. Almost as soon as he was able to roll on top of her, morning sickness reared its ugly head and she got up and ran into the bathroom. The sound of the heaves certainly killed the mood.

When she crawled back to bed, eyes watery and clutching her abdomen, he tickled her hair for a few minutes in silence. He noticed the rhythmic tapping sound the clock made. It was digital, but the symbol between the numbers blinked for every second. Tap. Tap. Tap. A sound so faint he wasn't sure if it was real or if he was imagining it. That, and the sound of hungry seagulls on the balcony reminded him he needed to eat.

"I'm going to run downstairs and grab bagels for us in the café. You need to eat something. You're eating for two."

"Don't worry about me. I'll order room service." She glanced at the clock. "You should get ready to go. You can grab a bagel on the way."

He would've loved breakfast in bed with his wife, but instead, he dragged his ass in the shower, and Emma was on the phone ordering room service while he dressed. As he buckled his belt, Emma scrolled through her phone, her face lighting up, no doubt looking at her sister's Instagram—again.

"I have to go," he said, picking up his clubs and blowing her a kiss. "Enjoy your spa day."

"I love you," she said, without looking up. It was a reflex for her. She loved him, and that was that.

His heart swelled. He'd do anything to protect that woman. No matter what it took.

With his clubs hung over his shoulder, Ethan met up with Dutch and Veejay in the lobby at nine-fifteen. They both looked well rested and drank coffee from Styrofoam cups provided in the hotel lobby as part of the free continental breakfast. He said hello and set his clubs down near them and strode over to the coffee stand to fill his own cup. They were already out of bagels, so he scarfed down a blueberry muffin. The coffee was surprisingly fresh, not bitter and syrupy. Usually, the smell of coffee reminded him that he'd be up and alert for the next few hours, although at that moment all he thought about was the comfort of being snuggled up in the sheets with Emma.

"So, where's the groom?" Ethan asked upon his return. He tried to keep his tone light and cheery. *I love Trevor.*

Vee looked at his watch. "I don't know, but he said to meet down here at nine-thirty. Funny that we're all here early, ready to get going."

"I guess were all excited for golf. What a fun day this is going to be!" Dutch exclaimed.

Shit, they really do like him, Ethan thought. Then again, Dutch was acting like a child. A fun day? Was he hiding his misery as well by overcompensating? Nah. Dutch didn't have it in him to be fake, especially after the whole Roger debacle. Ethan was just eager to get it over with. The sooner they could begin this charade, the sooner it would be over.

"Right!" Ethan said. Ugh. Way too overenthusiastic. Smile, but don't clown smile. "So fun!" Jesus, he sounded like a first grader on their way to an ice cream shop. Just like Dutch. Maybe the boys' day had them both feeling nostalgic and young. They hadn't golfed together in a while. Adulthood got in the way.

The elevator doors dinged behind him, and Dutch and Vee's faces lit up. The sinking sensation in his stomach told Ethan it was his worst nightmare.

"Hello, groomsmen!" the slick voice behind him spit out, and the reaction to Trevor's voice felt like spiders were crawling up Ethan's spine. "I have an Expedition waiting outside. The course is only five minutes from here. Let's roll."

As soon as they exited the hotel, Ethan couldn't breathe. While yesterday provided a much-needed relief from the arctic temperatures up North, this was something else altogether. A heat wave in Miami was no joke. He set his golf bag down and took his clean towel from the hook that attached to the bag and wiped down the back of his neck, already shiny. He re-hooked it and a porter loaded the bag into the trunk with the others while Ethan clawed his way into the air-conditioned car. He'd been afraid of the leather burning the backs of his thighs. He went to the third-row seating to spread out while Dutch and Vee jumped into the second row.

"Warm out there," Ethan said, and uncapped a water bottle that was in one of the cup holders.

"Yeah, how do you do it in the summer?" Vee asked.

"Oh, come on. I'm sure Mumbai summer temperatures are no joke," Trevor said from the passenger-side front seat. "Actually, isn't it hot there all year round?"

"Pretty much. I guess I've acclimated to winters," Vee said with a shrug.

"Right." *Riiiight.* "You came here when you were a teenager, yeah? College lottery, you said?"

"Mmmm hmmm."

"Lucky you, Veejay Rahna. Lucky you."

Trevor's tone was so condescending that Ethan didn't understand why these other guys liked him so much. But he played along. Hell, if you can't beat 'em, join 'em. He slapped the back of Vee's head from the third-row seating.

"Fucking dork. Did you win because of those stupid science fiction books you read? Were you teleported here from your mother ship?" Camaraderie.

"Hey man, what gives?" Vee asked.

Dutch joined in on the mockery and put Vee in a headlock and rubbed the top of his head with a fist. "Are your leaders going to come down and punish us now, Rahna?" he said with a laugh.

With the roughhousing and teasing, Ethan almost felt like they were all there to have a good time.

Almost.

The heat outside proved to be too much during the last few holes, and they stopped after fourteen. The southern sun beat down on them like it wasn't ninety-three million miles away, but like someone was hanging it over their heads and shaking it, letting the fire droplets fall on them like lava. They were all soaked right through their clothes, and they needed to sit in air conditioning. Vee said he wanted to shower, Dutch wanted to take a nap, and Ethan just wanted to get the hell away. They got lucky, because Trevor said he had some things to take care of before the rehearsal dinner later that night. Ethan wondered if any of it had to do with him.

He'd planned and plotted all night on a way to make sure Trevor kept his word; as the old saying goes, two can keep a secret if one of them is…

But that was too extreme.

Even if he did wish for it. Even if he'd been wishing for it since July.

20

EMMA

The day before the wedding, 1:00 p.m.

Emma had just emerged from her body scrub and mud wrap, and she felt like a million bucks. Her facial was relaxing and much needed, and the technician would be attending to her nails momentarily. She went back to the spa's Serenity Waiting Lounge and Fiona and Allie were already there, clad in the same terrycloth-lined velvet robes and slippers that made her feel like a bunny.

"How do you feel?" Fiona asked. "That massage was heaven. Really worked out the pre-wedding tension!"

"No massage for me." Emma rubbed her abdomen. "But so far, I'm never going home," she said with a smile. "Where's the rest of your family?"

"They all had their nails and toes done already. It's just us for manis and pedis. We're all going in at the same time."

"Oh, fun."

The truth was, she didn't want to spend any more time with Fiona than necessary. She hated what she knew about her. She didn't want to feel that way about one of her oldest friends, but sometimes when she closed her eyes, she saw it, in glorious detail. That picture of her husband making out with Fiona against the back of a bar. Gross.

How she'd gotten a hold of the picture was yet another memory she wanted to forget. Fine—she and Ethan were broken up when it happened. It was still a breach of the worst kind. But what could she do? She had her own secrets to deal with, ones that were much, much worse. Because of her hidden past, she didn't even feel the need to forgive Ethan, but she was struggling to forgive Fiona.

Though she had no right to feel that way either.

It'll all be over in one more day, she thought.

"So, Fiona, tomorrow you're a wife. You'll be married to that Trevor Vaughn," Allie said.

She said *that* Trevor Vaughn, and Emma stifled laughter.

"Yeah," Fiona said faintly.

"That was a quick turnaround though, no? I mean, last spring when the three of us went out you said you felt like he was suffocating you and isolating you, and then all of a sudden *BAM* you move to Miami and then *BAM* you're engaged a month later and now *BAM* you're getting married less than six months after that." Allie pulled no punches and didn't mess around.

"I know it's fast. He's got his quirks, but I'm not perfect either."

Quirks? Emma not-so-accidentally made a *pfft* sound and then covered it by pretending to sneeze.

"Bless you," said Allie, then turned back on Fiona. "I'm just saying." Her lips were pursed.

"You guys like him, right?" Fiona asked.

"What does that matter? Who cares what I think of Trevor? Or even her for that matter." Allie snapped, and pointed to Emma before turning her attention back to Fiona. "You love him, right?"

Fiona's eyes welled up and she tilted her head toward the ceiling. Allie was never a warm person to anyone but her father, which is why her weird marriage, while it lasted, made sense. Emma never saw either of them overly affectionate to each other, or even affectionate at all. Wharton was twice Allie's age when they married, and Emma had only met him a handful of times. Christ, his three children from his first marriage were all older than Allie. She'd only met them at their wedding. They weren't fans of Allie's.

She'd never fawned over anyone, so it was no different that she didn't get gaga over Trevor.

Three technicians called their names, and they went into the nail salon section of the spa, where the three of them sat in a row with Emma in the middle. She chose that seat on purpose because she didn't want to listen to the sniping anymore. Allie seemed to be well on her way to giving an opinion no one asked for when she was saved by the bell. Did Allie hate Trevor, just like Emma did? She couldn't even risk asking. She couldn't explain to Allie *why* she hated Trevor.

Emma sat in the plush pedicure cubicle and sank her toes into the warm, frothy water that glowed green in the tub lights. She had chosen a green tea pedicure, which included a clay mask, paraffin oil, and a ten-minute foot massage—she'd read it was good for circulation during pregnancy, though she made them go light with the pressure. She leaned back into the leather chair and turned on the back massager—just because she wasn't allowed a Swedish rubdown didn't mean she couldn't work out the kinks in her back. Her eyelids were heavy, and she decided not to fight it—she hadn't taken much time for herself in the last couple months, when everything went to shit, and telling Ethan about the pregnancy a couple of weeks before the Miami trip was half a relief and half a mountain of pressure.

The girls stayed quiet. Emma, enjoying her closed-eye silent time, Allie, playing with her phone and probably uploading pictures of the spa to Instagram with the hashtag *#HateMeCauseYouAintMe* and Fiona—well, she was reading a bridal magazine, probably making comparisons and picking on everything that she did wrong.

Like her mind was being read, Fiona turned to Emma and pushed an open page in her direction.

"Do you think I should've chosen dresses like this for you guys instead?" she asked.

"No!" they both shouted at once, even though Allie didn't see the picture. She barely lifted her head when she was lost on her phone in the Instagram world.

Emma and Allie both liked the bridesmaid dresses, which was a first. They were pale pink chiffon, perfect for a wedding at the beach. They were flattering and flowy and didn't have anything remotely bridal about them— no puffy sleeves, no boning in the chest, and no taffeta. Emma's olive skin stood out against the light color, and she planned on wearing her dark hair in a soft side bun, held together with bobby pins containing small pink and white crystals.

Allie had said she particularly liked the dress against her copper hair—the pink against the red was stunning, with her pale complexion and smattering of freckles across her nose. Now, at platinum blond, Emma wondered if the pale color would wash her out.

"Hey, so what's with the blond?" Emma asked. They'd never properly talked about it.

Allie dismissed her with a wave of her hand, still not looking up from her phone. "I told you, it's fabulous."

Emma wasn't convinced. "You send us snapshots of yourself from dressing rooms asking for opinions on T-shirts—I can't believe you didn't tell us about such a huge change."

"Well, I just didn't, all right?" she snapped. She typed furiously for a few more seconds and then put her phone on the armrest beside her. "It was a spur of the moment decision. I just wanted to be different for a change. Whatever, it's just fucking bleach. It'll grow out."

Yikes. "I didn't mean anything by it," Emma said. "I'm sorry, I didn't mean to upset you. It really does look great."

Her sigh was heavy and said more than she'd intended. "Thanks. Sorry. I was up too early today for all this stuff. I hit the Jack pretty hard when I got back to my room last night. Yesterday was a long day with the travel, and then the drinking all day, and everyone together and the pregnancy announcement and dinner and more drinks—it caught up to me. I'm just being a bitch." She maneuvered her body forward to look past Emma and to Fiona. "And I'm sorry about before. As long as you're happy, I'm happy."

Fiona smiled weakly. Why didn't she look like a glowing bride-to-be?

21

DUTCH

The day before the wedding, 6:00 p.m.

After the wedding rehearsal on the beach, everyone stood around the outdoor bar, waiting to be called in for dinner. This time *everyone* was drinking water—not just Emma. The heat was too much. Dutch pulled at the buttons on his linen shirt, trying to pump some air between the material and his chest.

"Holy shit. Remind me of this moment if I start bitching about the cold when we get home," he said. "This is *fucking* ridiculous." He looked at Vee. "Sorry."

"Can't wait for the tuxes tomorrow," Ethan said with an eye roll.

"Ugh," Vee said. "It's going to be brutal. You girls are lucky. Short dresses!"

"Yeah, that and ten pounds of makeup. We'll be melting," Emma said with a chuckle. "And I'm not slicking my hair in a bun like I originally wanted to do. I don't have the cheekbones for it. I'll have to think of something that won't make me look dreadful. Maybe a side braid, so my hair is off my neck."

Ethan pulled her close and kissed her temple. "The face that launched a thousand ships."

She blushed and gave him a coy smile, then jumped up to meet his lips. "*Eu te amo.* I love you."

"I think it's time for a drink." Allie fanned herself with her left hand, but it wasn't doing the trick for her shiny chest.

"I'll grab them," Dutch said. "Why don't you guys see if there's a spot inside, in the air conditioning. There's that landing right up the stairs with those big windows overlooking the water. I'll grab some beers and a bottle of prosecco. And some water," he added, looking at Emma. "I'll have them send a bucket of ice."

When Ethan opened the door, the cold air immediately formed dew marks on everyone's damp skin. They all looked like a cold bottle of beer, left out in the sun. Dripping wet. Emma held her thick hair off the back of her neck while Ethan fanned her from behind and Vee cursed the humidity with his PG-words. Allie pursed her lips as if she'd be able to stare down the heat—and win.

Dutch found them on the landing in the wicker chairs and couches with plush white cushions. They were able to get comfortable without sticking to the bottom of their seats like they would have on the leather couches on the other side of the room. Dutch carried one bucket full of beer bottles in his left hand, a bucket full of plastic water bottles in his right hand, and a bottle of prosecco tucked under his arm.

"They're bringing an ice bucket and some glasses," Dutch said to Allie. He handed Emma a water, and she looked deprived as her friends pulled at the various libations. Dutch, too, started with a water to cool his core temperature, and unscrewed the cap as he talked. "By this time tomorrow, they'll be married," he said to his friends. "Awesome."

I'm sorry, Fiona.

He wondered if the angst would ever subside.

"Yeah," Vee said. "Another member of our little family."

Emma and Ethan both gave a thumbs up, silently, while sipping their respective drinks.

"It's not like we're going to see them all that much," Allie said after popping the top of the prosecco and placing the cork on the table. "They live here. We all live there." She pointed up to signal north, then drank right from the bottle since no one had brought over glasses yet.

Dutch figured he had an ally in Allie, but never mentioned his distaste for Trevor to her. He was waiting for Allie to snap, to come out with it, to say something, anything that would make him feel comfortable with echoing her sentiment. But he knew Allie was practical—never emotional.

She didn't date much in college—everyone was either "too this" or "too that." Too sappy, too fratty, too nerdy, too psycho. She was smart—second in their class—and didn't want to settle. It didn't exactly shock him when she married someone powerful like Wharton.

Dutch was at the wedding. He'd noticed she didn't beam as she walked down the aisle, her smile stiff and forced, like an untalented artist drew it on her face. Her impatient stance proved she'd rather be scrolling through Instagram when Wharton said his vows—Dutch even thought he saw her tapping her foot, signaling *"Let's get on with this already!"* Their kiss was a mechanical pact—her lip gloss didn't even smudge. In fact, the only time she showed any proof of life was when the minister mentioned her mother's memory. It was a quick flinch, but it gave everything away.

She spent the reception dancing with Emma and Fiona and her family members, while Wharton pressed palms and smoked cigars with his older friends and associates. They seemed like acquaintances at the morning after brunch, and all the pictures she posted on Instagram from almost three weeks in the Seychelles for their honeymoon were selfies. No kisses under the sunset or them lazily lounging by the pool, his hand on her knee while they read books and took in the rays. She never did seem interested in anything long-term or till death do they part. Dutch happily thought she'd do better single anyway. The divorce would be good for her.

Vee popped the top off one of the beers and took a long swig, then held the dripping bottle to his sweaty forehead.

"Trevor's not that bad. I just don't know him that well," Vee said.

"Then why are you a fucking groomsman? Sorry, Vee, but I've had enough of policing my language today." Allie rolled her eyes again, and Dutch thought she'd pull a muscle—they certainly were getting a workout.

Vee shrugged. "He asked us. Why not? It's for Fiona." He drank half of his beer. "Plus, Trevor's an okay guy."

Dutch began to wonder if his friends were telling the truth.

22

EMMA

The day before the wedding, 8:00 p.m.

Emma held Ethan's hand as they walked into the rehearsal dinner. It was the same restaurant in the hotel as the welcome dinner, half inside and half outside. And just like the night before, the humidity had dropped from ninety-five percent to about eighty percent. It wasn't exactly comfortable, but they'd make do.

This time, they'd been seated with the usual suspects—Dutch, Allie, Vee—and Fiona's brother Jesse and his boyfriend Hector. Emma had met Jesse during his random visits to Columbia and the odd birthday celebration in the city over the years. He resembled Fiona—you could definitely tell they were related, with dark wavy hair and gray eyes. He stood about Ethan's height, but he wasn't as nice to look at, in Emma's opinion. He was twenty-seven and weighed about a buck-forty soaking wet. He tried to make his Coke bottle glasses look hipster but miserably failed. He usually wore mismatched outfits and red sneakers, but today looked dapper in his button-down and slim-fit pants. Unfortunately, he had used too much gel in his hair to try to tame it in the humidity and now looked like an extra from *Grease*. If Pee-wee Herman and the cast of *The Big Bang Theory* had a wonder child, this was it.

"How's the firm?" Vee asked him, always accommodating. "And how's the world of finance, Hector?"

"Great," Jesse said, adjusting his glasses. "I still can't believe I passed the bar. They have me running ragged over there, but it's my first year. I'm learning so much more there than I ever did at Villanova." He paused to hold Hector's hand. "Hector moved from Merrill to Goldman a few months ago."

Vee nodded. "You're making your father proud."

Fiona's father, before he died—as well as her Uncle John, before he ran for senator—were both lawyers, and Jesse wanted to follow in their footsteps, which Emma thought to be admirable. "I think my uncle might run for higher office. I want to be an asset. My father would've wanted it that way," Jesse said.

They all pressed their lips together and nodded, and Allie, who sat next to Jesse, even patted his forearm in an unusual show of emotion. She knew what it was like to lose a parent. Fiona and Jesse's father had been killed in a car accident when Fiona was in grade school. He should've listened to the television when they said not to drive in the snow and ice storm, but he was determined to get to his office. A tractor trailer with bad brakes had other plans.

By the time the servers cleared plates later in the evening, the tablecloths were dotted with red wine stains and cloth napkins were caked with grease. Emma placed her hand on Ethan's stomach and chuckled. He'd eaten every last morsel of the filet mignon and vegetables and advised Emma to do the same—eating for two and all.

She hadn't finished her food.

Just before dessert was served, a sharp, high pitched clink-clank boomed throughout the room and everyone's head swiveled to the front where Trevor stood with his arm around Fiona.

"I'd like everyone's attention," he said, the left side of his mouth jerking into a half smile while everyone in the room beamed at him. "I just want to thank all our friends and family for coming from near and far to celebrate our wedding. It really means a lot to me, and to us." He made a gesture with his champagne glass toward the table of their friends. Fiona's friends. "Special thanks to everyone sitting at table three—that's our bridal party. I've grown close to Fiona's best friends from college, and they are doing me the honor of becoming my best friends, too. Thank you."

Everyone *oooh*'d and *aaah*'d and did a soft golf clap while looking at them as if a spotlight were shining on top of the table. Then their attention turned back to Trevor, who dipped Fiona like you'd see in the fifties movies and kissed her lips, then stood her upright and twirled her around, gesturing his open palm out toward her like *Look at my wonderful bride-to-be*. Then came the *awwwww*s while servers came around with dessert and coffee.

Emma didn't understand how no one saw through him. She wondered if Fiona's family was thinking *Finally, Fiona's getting married!* And in three days, they'd all start badgering her about having kids. Why did people do that? Why was everything such a rush? Emma thought of the celebrity gossip rags she loved to read. Two actors would be photographed standing near each other, and a week later there were reports of canoodling and then another week later, engagement rumors. Then, obviously, the woman half of the equation was pregnant— WITH TWINS!—less than a week later. People seemed too conditioned to move to the next step too quickly. According to said magazines, poor Jennifer Aniston had been pregnant with twins at least once a month for two decades. Most of the time, they were Brad's. For the love of God, leave the woman alone.

Emma and Ethan were obviously not like that. They met at eighteen—young. They were both doing their college thing, as they should've been, but there was always a spark, and neither of them wanted to take it a step further and ruin the friendship. Until one day, after a writing class that was a requirement for Emma's English degree but an elective for Ethan, he asked her to "hang out" after class. Later, after a few beers, they had their first kiss. He looked deep into her green eyes, and then he stroked her cheek with the back of his fingers. He lifted her chin and kissed her with a soft peck on her lips which lasted for about seven seconds, and then both of their mouths opened.

She was done from that point. In love. So was Ethan. They both knew there was no one else for them. They didn't rush anything.

Ethan—the things she'd done for him, to keep distance between her love and her secrets.

As Emma bit into her rehearsal dinner cake, Dutch's phone pinged. It was sitting right on top of the table. He looked at it and his brow immediately furrowed.

"Unknown number," he said, then tapped the screen. To say he looked uncomfortable was an understatement— it was like he'd eaten a bad clam and it was about to regurgitate. His eyes flew to Ethan. "Hey, buddy, can I talk to you for a second?" he asked.

Ping. Allie's phone.

Ping. Ethan's phone.

Ping. Emma's phone, from her purse on the table.

"Don't!" Dutch screamed across the table and stood up. "Don't open it."

"What is it?" Vee asked. "I left my phone charging in my room."

Too late. It was like when someone said, "Don't look now but..." Curiosity *did* kill that damn cat. Everyone opened it. Vee leaned over and looked at Dutch's phone.

Everyone's eyes flew to Ethan.

Emma took her phone out of her little black clutch and opened the message. It was a picture. It was her husband, her Ethan, her world. Not only that, but he was kissing Fiona. In his Rangers jersey. She recognized the background—they were in the arena at Madison Square Garden. He had one arm around her shoulders, the other hand on her chin, positioning her face toward his as they kissed through smiles. It was on the goddamn *Kiss Cam* for all eighteen thousand patrons to see. To *oooh* and *ahhh* at Ethan and Fiona, in love.

He took Fiona to the Rangers game? And ended up on the *Kiss Cam*?

Sure. A couple of months ago, she'd already seen the picture of them half-fucking against a building. She'd silently come to terms with it—they weren't together when it happened. And she'd done far worse.

But the Rangers? She barely had time to process what she stared at before...

Ping. Dutch's phone.

Ping. Allie's phone.

Ping. Ethan's phone.

Ping. Emma's phone.

Emma's phone was already about to be crushed in the grip of her hand and she opened the message immediately. This time, she transported out of her body as she cried, right there at the table, in front of everyone. It was a picture of Fiona with Ethan, Timmy, and their mother. The banner in the background said, "Happy Fiftieth Birthday." His mother was wearing a paper crown and holding a cupcake with two lit candles, a five and a zero.

Ethan had lied to her when they got back together, when she said how sad she was for missing his mother's big birthday. He told her all everyone did that day was ask where Emma was. The betrayal stabbed her in the heart and for a second, she was happy about what she was hiding from Ethan, no matter how terrible it was.

Ethan and Fiona didn't have a quick hookup, like she'd thought. They seemed to have had a relationship.

Even worse, now everyone knew. Her dirty laundry was aired. *Dutch* knew that Ethan slept with Fiona. *Vee* knew. *Allie* knew. Of course this was Trevor's doing. He said he would punish her for the stunt yesterday afternoon, for threatening him. He wanted to embarrass her. Job well done, you asshole. If he was able to get *those* pictures of her from so long ago, there was no doubt in her mind that he'd been the one able to track down these little gems.

Stunned faces stared at Emma from around the table as her heartbeat swelled to a dangerous rate. Dutch and Vee looked dumbfounded, yet sympathetic. Allie looked disgusted. Ethan looked caught.

Emma slammed her phone on the table and stood. She'd forever associate her text message alert with Ethan's betrayal.

"Emma, wait. I can explain," Ethan's mouth said, but his eyes betrayed him.

"Explain what?" she asked in a tone that was way too loud for the company around them. "*Eu sabia que você*

126

não era perfeito. I'm not perfect either. But this?" Tears ran down her face, taking her mascara with them. "All you've done is lie to me."

She'd secretly dealt with her feelings on the matter, but they all came racing to her heated head once everyone else knew. Allie tried to grab Emma's arm, but she was no match for the rage as Emma pushed back from the table, grabbed her phone, and headed in Fiona's direction, near the bar, talking to people Emma had never seen before. Emma stormed up and yanked Fiona's arm so hard that she'd thought it came out of the socket.

"What the hell, Emma?" Fiona said, her round eyes completely devoid of the knowledge of what Emma had just seen.

On second thought, she didn't want to make a scene in front of the family. "We need to talk." Emma dragged Fiona to the side of the room like she was dirty laundry. "*O que é isso?* What the hell is this?" Emma turned her phone's screen and held it an inch from Fiona's face.

Fiona squinted and pulled back, aware that half the room was staring at them.

Fiona took the phone from an angry Emma and her eyes widened when they recognized the images on the screen. She lifted her head and Emma's eyes were damn near red, matching her overheated face. Behind her, Ethan skipped toward them with Dutch holding him back by his arm. Vee sat at the table, immobile, his head in his hands. Allie had her hand over her open mouth.

Trevor appeared by Fiona's side. "What's going on?" he asked.

Like you don't know. Emma thrust her index finger in his face. "*Va se foder!*"

His face showed disregard, like she was speaking Klingon, not Portuguese. "What the hell does that mean?"

"Don't ask, but it's well deserved," Ethan said with his palm toward Trevor as he got to them, having heard to fuck off a time or two in the past. "Can we talk, Emma?"

Allie rushed over and jumped between them. "Come on girls, let's take this to the ladies' room."

Once, in college, there was a cricket in their dorm room. When Allie saw it stretching its body and its gangly legs across the floor, she chased it with a shoe while screaming. Emma calmly trapped it underneath a Tupperware that usually housed leftovers and took the disgusting thing outside, even though she wanted to kill it. That was Emma's normal demeanor—saving things—but seeing this, she was capable of body slamming Fiona. She really, *really* wanted to.

Allie turned and addressed the few people that looked in their direction, their stares hot on the back of her head. "Overdramatic girls." She rolled her eyes. "This'll be over in a minute. It's a misunderstanding."

Allie led the two girls out with Emma shouting a string of obscenities in Portuguese. Ethan tried to follow them, and Allie stopped him. Ethan looked defeated as Allie stayed between Emma and Fiona on their way to the bathroom. Emma was five steps ahead when she barreled through the ladies' room door.

"*Saia!* Get out!" she screamed to the two girls who were touching up their faces.

They got a glimpse at Emma's tears and her flaming eyes, then glanced at Allie who gave them a sympathetic look and nodded her head back toward the door. "Go," she mouthed, not uttering a sound. Emma needed a win.

Allie locked the door behind them and then stood between her two friends, Emma at arm's length away on one side and Fiona at arm's length on the other. She looked like the rope in a game of tug-of-war, which Emma knew she'd easily win. She'd be able to pull a Mack truck right now without breaking a nail.

"Emma, I'm sorry. Let me explain," Fiona started. She stared at the floor, probably willing the tile to swallow her into the depths of hell rather than explain that she had what looked like a meaningful relationship with her best friend's boyfriend-slash-husband. "It was a long time ago when you were broken up." Fiona was crying, destroying the professional makeup job carefully applied a few hours earlier. "As soon as you came back, he dropped me like yesterday's news. He never wanted me, he always wanted you."

Emma scoffed, then realized what Fiona said. The timing. "You were *dating* him when he and I got back together?"

Fiona clasped her hands in front of her like she was praying to God, which Emma thought was in her best interest at the moment. Emma wanted to kill her. "It was only a couple months, I swear. I know, I screwed up. He always loved you. We were both lonely, it wasn't done on purpose or to hurt you."

Emma sniffled, sucking back the buildup. "You went to his mother's fiftieth birthday? Don't you dare say you weren't trying to hurt me. We're friends. How could you?"

Fiona's face opened up like a busted damn. "I hadn't seen you in so long, Emma. It's not an excuse, but you barely even texted me back. You were like that with everyone for a while. I'm so sorry. I know you've never been with anyone but Ethan. I'm sorry." This time, Fiona fell to the floor, her face in her hands. "I'm sorry. I'm sorry. I'm sorry!"

The statement gutted Emma. How could she carry on like she was, knowing what she'd done?

Allie stayed silent. Emma spun around and looked in the mirror, then wet a paper towel and cleaned the raccoon makeup out from under her eyes. With a splash of water on her face, she took another towel and patted herself dry. Running her hands over the front of her dress, with a sniffle said, "I have to go." She unlocked the door and closed it behind her.

"I'm sorry!" Fiona shouted after her.

What a mess Trevor created. That asshole was going to pay for this.

23

ETHAN

The day before the wedding, 9:30 p.m.

When Ethan saw his wife exit the ladies' room, he pounced.

"Emma, wait."

She strode right past him like he didn't exist. Like she didn't even know who he was.

He caught up to her. "Emma, I'm sorry. I'd never want to hurt you."

She headed to the restaurant entrance and walked to the landing that overlooked the bay, where they all celebrated with drinks before dinner started. When they were all still friends, with no betrayals between them.

Ethan kept in hot pursuit. "I'm not leaving you alone. I'll follow you all night, Emma."

Ethan felt the presence of Dutch behind him by about fifty feet, which he was grateful for. Far enough away that he couldn't hear every word uttered in the fight he was having with his wife, but close enough to catch him when he would inevitably fall.

Emma hauled down the stairs with Ethan trailing and calling her name. It was quite the scene, apparently, as other bar patrons stopped and stared at the man chasing the teary-eyed woman through the lobby. The doors squeaked when they opened, and then she was back outside in the thick heat, heading toward the pool. The smell of chlorine enveloped the soupy air and Ethan thought about how nice the area looked at night with the multicolored lights changing in the pool like a drunk rainbow. Something he wanted to share with Emma—she loved rainbows. Red, orange, yellow, green, blue, indigo, violet. They changed the color of Emma's dress hue by hue as she trailed along the concrete.

The doors squeaked again, and Ethan knew that Dutch was still behind him. *Thank you.*

"Emma, please stop. Think about the baby."

She stopped dead in her tracks, and so did Ethan. She didn't face him, but was he supposed to approach her? Was he supposed to wait for her to make the first move? He couldn't bear the thought of her being upset, of her knowing what she knew, and he didn't care if it was the right move or the wrong one—he wanted to hold her. He approached with caution, and she stared at the dark sky over the beach beyond the pool.

"Em," he said softly, his hand on her shoulder, and she flinched at his touch. That hurt the most—that the thought of him touching her gave her such disgust. She said nothing. "Em, I'm sorry. I have no excuse. I don't know what to say. Just that I love you and I've always loved only you."

She turned to face him, still the most beautiful woman he'd ever seen, even with her makeup- and tear-stained face. There was a reggae band in the distance playing Bob Marley, and with the heat and the palm trees and the song, it reminded him of their honeymoon. The contrast in his mood then and now was unbearable and he'd never felt like more of a shit in his entire life. How could he have done what he did? If he lost Emma, he'd never recover.

"I've always loved only you, too, Ethan. Just remember that." She looked up, at the moon, a witness to their declarations. Having a witness made it real—notarized, signed, sealed, and delivered. They loved only each other. Always had. "I want to go lie down. Can you not follow me anymore? I want to be alone. Go out with Dutch and Vee and have a few drinks."

She nodded over Ethan's shoulder, and he turned to see Dutch still lagging about fifty feet behind him, his hands in his pockets, pretending to look around at the nighttime scenery.

He clutched Emma's hands in his and kissed them, one after the other, again and again. "I don't want to go out with Dutch and Vee. I want you. You're the only one in the world who ever meant anything to me, Emma. The *only* one. I love you more than you'll ever know. I'd do anything for you. I never want to hurt you."

But he did hurt her. It was unimaginable, the pain she must be going through. If he ever saw her intimate with someone like that—much less one of his friends—he'd die inside. Maybe even on the outside.

She pushed her tears back down—at that point they were like lemmings, following each other one by one over her lower eyelid. "I know."

She sounded like she meant it, but she let go of his hand and walked away.

Ethan was gutted, as she took a piece of him with her. He bent forward, his hands on his knees. Silence. Silence, and the reggae band. *One love, one life, let's get together and feel all right*. He'd never feel all right again. Dutch approached and patted him on the back.

"Hey, man. You okay?"

Ethan stood and interlocked his fingers behind his neck. "Nah, man. What do you think?"

The unspoken words between them were indicative of their friendship—nothing needed to be said. But Ethan felt like he had to clear it up.

"Look, Dutch, I know it's a shock. It was a weird time, and it was when Emma and I were broken up. I don't know how—" he stopped. He'd seen one of the pictures before. He knew *exactly* how.

Dutch waved his hand in nonchalance. "You don't have to explain anything to me. I just want you guys to be okay." His head trailed to the direction where Emma had disappeared. "Poor girl."

It was a gut punch. What else was Trevor planning on doing to him? Trevor still had Fiona's diary. Ethan had to end this. Quickly.

"What do I do?" Ethan asked. "Everything is so fucked."

"I gotta get out of here!" Dutch screamed at the top of his lungs to no one, frustrated as well. "Let's get out of this hotel for a night. I've gotta get away from these people."

Ethan gave him a half smile. "Nah, you go with Vee. I just gotta—well I don't even know," he said with a laugh. "Thanks, man. I love ya." With that, he embraced Dutch for a bro hug, and walked away.

Alone in the dark, he thought about the last time he and Emma got back together. They'd broken up because Ethan was still immature. He'd blown off work due to hangovers, he still wanted to frequent the college bars they went to while at Columbia, and he just didn't treat her right in general. She was worth more—she knew it and left.

He'd thought about her every damn second of every damn day and was worried about her. No one had seen her. Dutch and Vee and Roger had said they'd only spoken to her intermittently for almost a year. He didn't bother contacting Allie—he wasn't close with her, and she was married to that old dude, doing her *now-I'm-a-rich-girl* thing. That first time Ethan was with Fiona, he remembered talking about Emma, but didn't *really* remember anything thanks to the tequila.

Despite Fiona occupying the absent Emma-shaped space next to him, Emma was never far from his thoughts. He wasn't sure if she had changed her number, so he called her at work one day. She was flabbergasted with his casual, "Hey, it's me," like no time had passed between them. She agreed to meet him for a drink that night, where he proceeded to beg for her forgiveness, again, and promised that he had changed, which was true—he'd made himself a better man for her. And he'd been wasting it on Fiona.

After being back together for less than a year, he proposed on top of the Empire State Building, underneath a pink sky and in front of a hundred Japanese tourists. They were only twenty-nine. He didn't want to wait any longer, and he didn't want to lose her again.

He'd do anything to keep her. So much so that he tried to push away the evil thoughts that enveloped him about how to keep Trevor's mouth shut.

Surely it wouldn't come to that.

24

DUTCH

The day before the wedding, 10:00 p.m.

As soon as Ethan walked away, Dutch texted Vee and asked him to go get a drink somewhere else. He'd hoped that Vee had gone to retrieve his phone, but there was no answer after fifteen minutes. Dutch had been waiting at the outside pool bar, nursing a beer, waiting for a response. A couple of wedding-goers asked him what had happened, and he blew it off as nonsense and gave them his million-dollar smile to prove that everything was okay. That smile could melt polar ice caps.

Dutch's vision had slowly started going double. He grabbed an Uber and told the guy to take him wherever there was a happening scene.

From the back seat, Dutch looked out the window as people partied without a care in the world. Groups of girls in sashes celebrating bachelorette parties lined the strip as muscled guidos stopped to talk to them. He remembered being young and wished he was able to be as carefree, but he had responsibilities now—most notably, the kids he mentored, and also stopping his father from jacking up everyone's rent in East Harlem.

Where did those pictures of Ethan and Fiona come from? His first thought was Trevor, with his digging into the past, but he wouldn't embarrass his future wife like that—not the night before the wedding. Was someone trying to break up Ethan and Emma? Or Trevor and Fiona? Did other people have secrets as well? Dutch would kill Trevor if he found out he'd been messing with his friends. They were the people closest to him. Especially true after being betrayed by Roger.

A couple days after Fiona and Trevor got engaged at brunch, Dutch—along with all their friends—was emailed a file from an untraceable web address that disappeared as soon as Dutch opened it. It didn't matter; he didn't need to look at what was sent a second time. They were pictures that he could never unsee, of Roger with his mother. Along with receipts, proof that she showered him with expensive watches and dinners and even bought him that car he said he'd been saving for.

When Dutch confronted Roger, he admitted the affair, and begged for forgiveness that never came. His parents split because of it, and his friends were disgusted and cut Roger off as well. Fiona told Trevor to kick him out of the wedding, even though Roger hadn't committed to it in the first place.

Every time Dutch thought about giving up the ghost and telling everyone he was being blackmailed, he thought about Trevor releasing the information about Kelsey to the press. And Dutch knew he'd do it—he had no problem destroying Roger. Since Roger was involved in the high-profile divorce, Dutch's father, with his developer background, made sure Roger lost his real estate job and any additional opportunities for gainful employment that were available to him in New York City. Last Dutch had heard, Roger had moved back to the Midwest to start over.

Banished. All the good times they all had together—gone. Because of Trevor. Dutch couldn't be next.

Dutch's Uber driver dropped him off at a bar on the strip, not far from the hotel. Micah in the Kia Sorento assured him it was the place to be that night because of college football, and the local team was playing a rival. Dutch took a few pictures of the chaotic scene in the bar and sent them to Vee, hoping to lure him out, but Vee never wrote him back.

After a couple hours, after the local team won the game and everyone celebrated, the alcohol settled in his brain, and he wanted to go back to his room. Alone. He felt out of place, with people with painted faces and college flags and team chants. It just wasn't for him anymore. He was a grown man. And he still wanted to work on his speech. The mayor's event was only four days away.

The Uber ride there was only five minutes, so he assumed it would be an easy walk back to the hotel. He set out on foot after checking the route on his phone. The night air felt good on his hazy eyes, as the surrounding lights slightly blinded him as he made his way up the coast, one tall, rowdy, hotel after the next. Dressed in summer clothes, it was surreal to see all the palm trees decorated with wreaths and Christmas lights, Bing Crosby playing in the background when Drake and Beyonce weren't. Living in this atmosphere year-round had to make every day feel like Christmas vacation—he almost forgot the holidays were coming up, however fractured they'd be this year. He hadn't liked spending time with his father, but he always had dinner with his parents on holidays for his mother's sake. That was taken away from him too. Right now, he couldn't stand the sight of her either. Her little midlife crisis came with a price: divorcée with a kid who couldn't stand to look at her.

When he stumbled back into the hotel, it was eerily quiet—not like the ruckus of wedding mania he'd dealt with the past two days. Checking his watch, he realized the lobby bar would be open just late enough for a nightcap before he had to go to the wedding tomorrow. As much as he despised Trevor and the thought of Trevor together with Kelsey, it was still better than Fiona and Ethan together. Dutch walked into the lobby bar and squinted his eyes.

On a stool, with the near end of a Jack and Coke, was Allie. He made his way over and surprised her with a tickle from behind.

"Ass!" she said with a laugh as she turned and saw who it was. "You're lucky I didn't crack you in the face with my elbow!"

Dutch took a karate stance. "I can take you, woman! Don't forget I'm a black belt!"

It was true. Dutch had the best of everything growing up, and that included the top schools for anything he wanted to practice, which was mainly golf, karate, and swimming. If he'd tried, he probably could've been the next Tiger Woods or Michael Phelps.

"Fancy another?" Dutch said as he nodded to her drink.

She took her final gulp and pushed the drink away from her to the edge of the bar, the glass sliding on the wood with a whoosh. "I shouldn't. I've had enough." For seemingly no reason, she reapplied her lip gloss. "But why not?"

Dutch got the bartender's attention with a wad of one-hundred-dollar bills. "One Tito's martini and another Jack and Coke, and I'll settle up the bill, including whatever she had before."

Allie gave him a tense smile. "Thanks Dutch. You don't have to do that."

Dutch didn't mind and waved her off and took a seat beside her. They didn't say anything until Allie's drink was refreshed and Dutch's was placed in front of him. The bartender took his bank roll from the edge of the bar.

"Keep the change," Dutch said, ever generous, then turned to Allie. "So, blondie. Let's talk. What the hell was that about tonight?"

She started to laugh. "Good God. Ethan and Fiona? Did you know?"

He put both hands up defensively as his head shook wildly. "No way, man. I found out just like the rest of you."

"Who sent that text?" Allie asked quietly. "And why?"

"I don't know, man." Dutch decided it was best to ignore the question. "What happened to Fiona?" he asked.

"Hmph," Allie scoffed as she took a sip of her drink. She shook her head back and forth and pursed her lips. "I'm not getting involved. Not my circus, not my monkey."

"I hear you," Dutch said with a sigh. "Ethan was in pretty bad shape. I followed him when he was talking with Emma. You know. Just in case. But then she took off, and he said he wanted to be alone."

Allie took a small sip of her drink. "Look, I always thought Emma could do better, but the fact is they clearly love each other. I hope it works out. I really do."

"So, you still believe in love, then?" he asked, his head cocked to the side like a puppy in a cage just hoping to be adopted.

There was a hush that fell over the entire area, and she stared at him so hard, with such determination, that her next words didn't shock him after she finished her drink in one gulp and slammed the heavy glass onto the wooden bar.

"Want to get out of here?"

25

VEEJAY

The day before the wedding, 10:00 p.m.

Once the chaos died down, everyone was gone, and Vee was left alone in stunned silence. It wasn't like Emma and Ethan to fight in front of everyone—they'd had their little spats, sure, who didn't? But they'd made a scene.

Nothing was left on the dinner table except for half-empty champagne glasses, one smeared with lip gloss that he knew was Allie's. A couple of plastic water bottles had to be Emma's. One—make that two—completely empty scotch glasses. Ethan's, naturally.

Vee noticed one of his friends left a purse behind. He didn't know whose it was—everyone had small black clutches that evening. Not wanting to be intrusive, he opened it just to find the owner. Inside, it was a typical female purse. Lipstick, check. Powder compact, check. Tampons, check. Wallet, check. Well, what could pass for a wallet in a bag so small, anyway. It was more of a card-and-cash carrier. He tugged the small leather pouch out and unclipped the contents. There was sixty dollars in cash, and the license and ATM card inside belonged to Emma. He remembered she had her phone in her hand when she tore off with Ethan following close behind.

Vee didn't know where she'd stormed off to, and if she was back in her room fighting with Ethan, he didn't want to interrupt them. They'd clearly had something to work out. It was bonkers to even think about—Ethan had slept with Fiona. Even more than that—they seemed close. Vee couldn't wrap his head around it. All those times they were all together, no one had a clue.

Vee walked on the beach, clutch in hand, and listened to the roar of the night ocean. When he sat on a piece of driftwood on the sand to reflect on the events of the evening, the moon lit such a clear path into oblivion that he almost took off his shoes and followed it into the water, letting the ocean punish him for his own sin. One more day and it would all be over. If Trevor kept his word.

The minutes wore on. Vee looked at his watch and it was almost midnight—time for bed. Tomorrow was already going to be a long day *before* all tonight's nonsense. He wondered if the wedding would go smoothly at this point, considering what was going on between Emma and Fiona, and Emma and Ethan.

When Vee got back to his room, he saw his phone resting on the dresser, plugged into the charger. There were a million texts. (Okay, a slight exaggeration, but only slight.) Dutch had wondered where he went. He wanted to meet up and "get the fuck away from this hotel" at a bar in town. He ended up going alone, evidenced by the last text message from him, a picture of him smiling from ear to ear with each arm around a girl. He wrote "are you sure you don't want to come?" along with it.

There was one text from Emma.

I need to talk to you.

He sighed and texted her back.

> I have your purse, you left it on the table.
> I'll bring it by your room tomorrow morning.

There was no answer after a few minutes, so he assumed she was in the middle of a fight with Ethan or passed out already. He crawled into bed himself and hoped Emma really was asleep, resting. Stress like tonight wasn't good for the baby.

His eyes opened, and he shot up out of bed so fast he swore he tore a hole in the sheets.

The baby.

Why did a pregnant woman have tampons in her purse?

Part Two

26

EMMA AND VEEJAY

The Wedding Day, 9:30 a.m.

Emma woke to the click of the door of their hotel room closing. The clock read nine-thirty, and she heard Ethan re-entering the room. She focused on his side of the bed. It hadn't been slept in. She got up and went into the living area and sat on the couch. Ethan had coffee and bagels in his arms. He wore his New York Rangers hat and his eyes were rimmed red. One of the pillows and a blanket were crumpled on the couch in the corner of their room.

"I brought you some decaf," he said. "And some bagels."

She wanted to say *thanks* but when she opened her mouth, disgust threatened to pour out, so she shut it. As much as she wanted to blame him, she had no right. Her secrets were far worse. Being female was complicated.

But, if she decided to go through with what she planned a couple months ago, she'd have to pretend everything was okay. She needed him on her side, just in case. It wasn't manipulation, it was marriage.

"Thanks," she said quietly.

He brought everything over to Emma while she sat on the couch. She was furious because he should've told her as soon as they got back together. He'd started off their marriage with a mistruth and stayed silent as she chose Fiona to be a bridesmaid. But she wasn't any better in that department.

She was worse.

"Emma, I'm sorry," he said. "For keeping it from you."

"I know," she said, surprisingly upbeat, a major departure from the night before. "I knew you were with other people when we weren't together. I just—" She stopped. "Did you love her?"

He sat on the bed next to her and took her face in his hands and kissed her forehead. "I've never loved anyone but you Emma." It was the whole, entire truth. "I understand you may want some space, but please don't leave me."

"I'm not going to *leave* you Ethan. I love you. Really, I love you more than anything."

With that, there was a knock on the door. Ethan kissed Emma's head again and slowly rose to answer the door. Vee stood under the door frame with a black purse and coffee of his own.

"Hey, Vee, how are you doing?" Ethan asked him, one arm holding the door open, yet blocking an entry.

"I wanted to check on you guys. On Emma." His head turned and looked past Ethan and to Emma sitting on the couch. She waved, and he waved her clutch. "I have your purse."

"Thanks. Come on in, Vee," she said.

Ethan stepped aside, and Vee entered the hotel room. He awkwardly stood next to Ethan as they both stared at her.

"Ethan, can I have some time alone with Vee?" she asked. "I just need a different perspective on this whole thing."

"Whatever you want, babe." He shifted his way toward her, and she slightly turned her head away and winced and he gave her an awkward kiss on her cheek. "Take your time." As he moved to the exit, he clasped a hand on Vee's shoulder and whispered, "Please make it okay between us."

Vee nodded as Ethan picked up his coffee, opened the door, and walked out. The door clicked closed behind him, signifying that Emma and Vee were alone. She smiled at him, and he lifted her purse in the air, waving it to and fro.

"Do you want to explain this to me?" he asked, his voice accusatory.

Her expression was puzzled. "Sorry. You know I rushed out. I didn't realize I'd left it." Her gaze never left the bag, her eyes trained on the prize. "Thank you for returning it. I don't know how I'd be able to get on the plane without my ID and—"

He showed her a palm and placed his coffee on the table, which caused her to stop speaking, then opened her bag and retrieved a tampon. He held it in the air as the image floated in front of her like it was a magic wand. "I may not have seen my sister in years, but I know what this is, and what it's for."

Emma's face went blank, and then she finally put her head in her hands and wept. Vee was beside himself; he didn't want to make her cry, but he needed to know what was going on. When she picked up her tear-streaked face, she looked directly at him. "I have to tell you something."

"I bet you do."

"No, Vee, sit down." She motioned toward the leather chair near the desk and swung her legs over the side of the couch, so she faced him. She took a deep breath and spoke in a whisper. "You're right. I'm not pregnant."

Not pregnant.

The whole thing was a farce. The announcement, the belly clutching, the no-drinking—she made it all up. Vee's gaze drifted to the balcony door and beyond, where the palm trees swung, the sun shone, and the Atlantic trickled, all like they didn't hear a thing. *Move on, buddy,* they mocked him. *So, she's not pregnant. Nothing to see here.* Nature didn't feel the betrayal of the one closest to them.

"Oh my god, Em, why would you lie to all of us? Does Ethan even know? Or is this just some sick role-play you guys have?"

Her voice was barely audible. "Ethan doesn't know the truth. He thinks I'm pregnant."

Vee rubbed his face with his hands like he was scrubbing it with a washcloth. "Why are you doing this? Is it because you want attention?"

"No! When have you ever known me to be like that?"

"I don't get it. Why lie about—"

"I'm not pregnant *now*," she interrupted. "But I was. Six years ago."

"Six years ago? Did Ethan—"

Six years ago. Vee heard a train whistle in his head, like it was moving toward him at a thousand miles an hour, and he was tied to the tracks. *Move, idiot.* The whistle screaming, *move! Moooove!! Moooooooooooooove!!!* Then boom. Lights out. "Oh God. It was mine, wasn't it?"

Emma had met Vee out one night, right when she and Ethan broke up for the final time. They were around the corner from his place, so they decided to go back there and sleep it off—it wouldn't have been the first time Emma stumbled into his apartment. He caught her before she fell. There was too much alcohol between them, and he thought of Emma like a sister, so he didn't understand why the blood rushed from his head to his pants so quickly. The first kiss was fast, a mistake, until she approached him again, and their clothes ended up in a heap on the floor.

The next morning, she was gone. Veejay realized he had messed up in more ways than one. He'd had sex with his best friend, who was his other best's friend's ex. It was a no-no on all fronts. He was tortured about it, and afraid of losing them both over something that really was a mistake. He'd never wanted to screw up his friendship with Emma, even though that's exactly what happened. For a while, anyway.

He thought the guilt must've caught up with her a few months later, and she stopped returning his phone calls. They didn't see each other for a long time. He'd always tried to reconnect with texts and emails, but she was distant. He internally berated himself for letting it happen; he knew that she had only ever been with one person, Ethan, and he felt like a schmuck for letting it get as far as it did that night. Eventually, she came around and let it go, and their friendship resumed normally right after she had gotten back together with Ethan for the last time. Vee also knew that her heart belonged to only Ethan, and he loved that about her. Vee and Emma were never meant to be romantic, but they *were* meant to be best friends. He was happy the whole thing was behind them.

Now he knew the truth about why she was distant.

The revelation was shocking to say the least, and Vee wasn't prepared for how to react. They don't exactly teach a class on what to say to the girl you accidentally knocked up, especially when you didn't know a darn thing about it. His initial instinct was compassion, so he went with that.

"Emma, why didn't you tell me?"

For the first time since it happened, she let her grief overtake her, and she sobbed louder than she ever had before. Vee leaned forward, and his arms clutched her, so frail, so broken in that moment that he didn't know if he, or anyone else, would ever be able to put her back together. He didn't pressure her to talk; he just held her.

Eventually, she crawled out from underneath him and rose to go to the bathroom to blow her nose. When she reentered the room, she sipped some coffee and made a face, then put it back on the table.

"I'm so fucking sick of this decaf." She retrieved a bottle of water from the minibar and then apologized for her language. "Sorry. Anyway, I had to fake morning sickness yesterday to avoid sex. I wouldn't exactly be able to explain having my period."

Vee chuckled, still unable to process what she had told him.

"Look, Vee." She sat down and took his hand. "There's more."

He interlocked his fingers with hers. "I would've been there for you, Emma. I would've gone with you." His hazel eyes filled with tears. "I'd never leave you to do that alone. I'm so sorry."

She was going to have to tell him everything. *Everything*. Even the *really* bad stuff. Now was the time to spill it.

"I—it wasn't—no, Vee. It wasn't like that." She shook her head softly. "I found out, and you know how I feel about that stuff. I couldn't do it."

Vee looked at her like he'd never seen her before. "Couldn't do it? I don't get it."

"Don't hate me," she whispered. "It was a girl. A beautiful, healthy girl."

He jumped up from the bed and whipped around to face her when his voice hit a fever pitch. "What? *What?* We have a *daughter*?" Breathing at that rate couldn't be healthy. "How could you never tell me this?"

His heart raced, but she couldn't see that. The sweat on his head and the betrayal in his eyes told her everything she needed to know.

She began to cry again. "Please, Vee, don't be angry with me. I was so confused. I knew I couldn't get rid of it. I also knew that it would ruin both of our lives. What happened between us was a mistake. We were young. And to be honest—" she stopped talking and put her palm in the air for a moment of silence, then closed her eyes and pinched the top of her nose.

"What?" Vee's face had turned red. "What, Em?"

She lifted her face to his. "I still loved Ethan. I didn't want him to know. I still don't want him to know."

The silence between them was the loudest sound Emma had ever heard. It spoke volumes. And he didn't even know the half of it. She had to find the courage to tell him the rest. Somewhere, deep down in the underbelly of her conscience was the good Catholic girl she was raised to be.

Even though she'd already destroyed her pact with God. She'd broken one commandment to save her marriage, and she was well on her way to breaking another. It was all for her marriage. And until Vee knew all the details about both, she needed to finish her story.

"She's... she's been adopted. She's fine."

"What's her name?" Vee asked, and when Emma took a breath to answer, he held up his hand. "No. Don't tell me. It makes her real." The frustration, guilt, and anger on his face was palpable. "But she *is* real, isn't she? I have a daughter out in the world." He looked out the window as if he could actually see her, walking along the beach, holding hands with her mother and fath—"How could you do this to me? How did you even hide this? How does no one know?"

She took a deep breath. "My really pregnant months were in the winter. I'm tiny, so it was easy to hide under big clothes. I went to Portugal that year to visit my parents when I had off around Thanksgiving. I was barely showing. They wanted to come for Christmas but—I told them I was spending it with Ethan's family. They thought we were back together. I just didn't want to see them. I was definitely showing by then."

The tears dripped down her face like a leak as the memories flooded back. She'd spent Christmas alone that year. There was no champagne toast at a bar on New Year's Eve. No hot date on Valentine's Day. She'd taken a cab to the hospital late on that March morning, and Baby Girl Santos was born naturally six hours later.

"What's her name?" Vee asked again. "I want to know."

Emma put her face in her hands, attempting to hide her shame. Her name. Her daughter's name. *Their* daughter's name.

"Her name is... Bianca."

He nodded. "Bianca. Just like your—" He stopped. His face went blank, and Emma was terrified at what he would do at the realization that her niece was really his daughter. "Bianca. She's our daughter." His head shook, unrelenting, unbelieving. "She was your flower

154

girl—with Ethan. I met her. How could you do this to him? To me?"

"I needed her close. I couldn't keep her, but I couldn't give her away. Right before I had her, I called Cassandra. You know how close we are. I made her swear not to tell my parents. She flew in, we talked to a lawyer, and we signed some papers. After I had her, Cassandra came back and got her, and she went to Portugal. My parents think Cassandra and Eduardo had a surprise pregnancy they were keeping quiet, and that she delivered early. I needed my parents to love Bianca like she's their own grandchild. She is. They just don't know I'm her mother. She needed to be raised by my family. And this way I've been able to watch her grow up. I've seen it all."

Bianca's eyes were sometimes hazel, sometimes green—a perfect combination of her birth parents. Often Emma wondered if she would be inclined to do well in math, like her father, or English, like her mother. Were those traits inborn or learned? Would she take piano lessons like both of them did as children? Would she go through a tomboy phase like Emma did?

Just like the Christmas pictures that were sent to her phone two days ago, Emma always got the professional pictures. In the ones taken for Easter, which was shortly after Bianca's birthday last year, she was dressed in a pink dress with ruffles, holding yellow sunflowers in one perfect hand and a basket of colorful eggs in the other, surrounded by white stuffed rabbits. Her smile was contagious. It was like looking at the best parts of both of them. She was thriving. Bianca always smiled in her birthday pictures, leaning against blocks with numbers that dictated her age, sometimes holding balloons, sometimes with a birthday hat on her perfect little head. Her summers were spent at the beach and her winters by the mountains. She was happy. She was safe.

One thing Emma knew, is that she hoped Bianca turned out more like Vee than like her. Vee was the greatest person she'd ever met, and that included Ethan—but you can't help who you love. And she loved Ethan with her whole self. She'd sooner die than let him find out about her lies.

Lies. She still had so, so many lies in her. Having Vee's baby and passing her off as her niece only scratched the surface. She could barely stand to look at Vee; she'd gutted him like a fish with her declaration. And she had to finish. She *had to.* As soon as she found the strength.

"Look, there's more. It's why everything happened with the fake pregnancy this weekend."

"Oh God, I can't even imagine what the rest of this story is. Was it twins? Do we have a son too?" His voice dripped with disdain, and it saddened Emma.

"You're going to hate me. You're going to think less of me. *I* think less of me. It's lower than lying to you about carrying your child and giving her up."

His daughter. He'd never kissed her head or told her that she was Daddy's little princess. He'd never changed a diaper or woken up for a feeding or bought a onesie. He'd met her and didn't even know. When he made googly faces at her at Emma and Ethan's wedding, did she know he was her father? Did she feel a bond? Fine, she was only two or three back then. She had beautiful dark skin, a great combination of his Indian heritage and Emma's Portuguese one. Emma's green eyes—she'd always said it was in her bloodline.

"Good grief Emma, what else have you gotten yourself into?"

It was all he could say—he had to push the rest of it down, sweep it under the bed where it belonged. Part of him wanted to run to his best friend and hold her, pat her head, and tell her everything was going to be all right. The other half wanted to throw his coffee in her face and walk out of her life forever. But he couldn't—their tie, their miracle, their *secret* would bind him to Emma for life. They'd put something out into the world that was *only* theirs. His head spun like a merry-go-round.

"So, what's the other big secret? Just come out with it," he said.

Her green eyes were wet when she looked at him. "Trevor knows. He's been blackmailing me."

And the train whistle came again, because it didn't kill him the first time. *Move, idiot. Moooove!! Mooooooooooooove!!!* Then boom. Lights out again.

"Trevor? *Trevor?* That a-hole, I'm going to flippin' kill him!" This time Vee did throw his coffee, but at the wall—not at Emma.

She shrank back and covered her face, never having seen an angry side of Vee before.

"How does he know? What's he been blackmailing you for?" Vee's eyes had turned crimson, like he was a vampire that had just fed.

Her hands were around her bent knees as she rocked back and forth. "You're going to hate me, Vee, and I'm not sure that's something I can live with."

"Emma, please. I think we're past hate. We've created—I want to—but—" He paced a bit, then sat back down on the leather chair and hung his head between his legs. *Look at me, reacting this way*, he thought. *Like you're so perfect.*

No, Vee wasn't perfect either. He'd kept secrets. He'd lied to those closest to him. He had to tell her—now was the time. "He's been blackmailing me, too."

Emma's head whipped up. "What? Trevor's been—you too?" Her eyebrows pushed together. "Impossible. What did you do? You're the nicest person I've ever met!"

"Right. Because you met me *after* I moved to the States." He literally twiddled his thumbs from the chair. "Tell me first. What else is there? I promise I'll tell you everything."

Well, here goes nothing, she thought. He deserved the truth. She took a deep breath.

"He came to my office a couple of days before we all had brunch five months ago. Right before he proposed to Fiona." She took a sip of water. "He had pictures, Vee. Of me, in various stages of my pregnancy—when I withdrew from everyone, and no one saw me. It was easy not to see Ethan since we were broken up, and Dutch and Roger mostly hung out with him. Allie was wrapped up in her marriage. Fiona was in Westchester. And you—it was easy to make an excuse to be weird with you and avoid you. Now you know why I did it. I'm sorry," she said, as if that could make anything better.

Vee just stared at her, as his silence urged her to continue.

"I don't know where he got the pictures," she continued. "Some of them looked like they came from traffic cameras, or CCTV in a supermarket. I didn't even know him then. I don't know how he found out anything. Probably that high-tech facial recognition software that Fiona said he works with." She gulped the water until it ran down her chin, and she wiped it with the back of her hand. "He threatened to tell Ethan. He told me he'd been having some problems with Fiona but planned to propose. I knew a bit about the problems from Fiona, but he told me to talk him up and make her see how great he is, and he'd let it go. I don't even think he loves her. I think this all has something to do with getting into her family and getting involved with politics and Uncle John. Who knows, he's probably blackmailing him too." The tears flowed, and her fists clenched. "But I did it. I sold Fiona out to save myself. I fucking hate him, but I told her he was awesome. Looking at it now, I'm so mad at her after last night, finding out she was in a relationship with Ethan, and I think she and Trevor deserve each other. But I didn't know that then, and I did it anyway. I'm a horrible person."

"Jesus." He never looked up. "But why did you fake a pregnancy? To everyone? Even your husband?"

"Because I needed something on Trevor, too." Her lower lip trembled, and her voice vibrated as she choked out the next sentence. "So, I slept with him."

27

ALLIE

The Wedding Day, 9:30 a.m.

Allie woke up early, which was a miracle considering the energy she'd expended the night before. Sex with Dutch was everything she'd always thought it would be. Rough, in that they tore at each other's clothes and pushed each other against walls, but gentle in the way they stroked each other. Experimental in the sense that one time was on the bathroom sink, but traditional in that once was romantic and in bed. Either way—hot.

The alarm clock said it was nine-thirty a.m. *Shit.* She had to be in hair and makeup by eleven, which meant they probably didn't have time to order room service. If he even wanted to stay. Without turning over, she knew Dutch was still beside her—she'd forgotten how the heaviness of a man in your bed tilted the mattress, and how her sheets wouldn't kick up easily because they were wrapped around someone else's legs.

Despite her drunkenness, she remembered everything. He didn't pause before he took her hand and led her out of the lobby bar right after she'd propositioned him. In the elevator, he smiled at her and then pulled her toward him and kissed her. His lips were soft and hungry, and his tongue's presence in her mouth reminded her how badly she'd wanted him. Her legs were wrapped around him before the door opened. She fumbled for her keycard as he unzipped her dress in the hallway in front of her door. They'd barely made it inside fully clothed.

He lazily flung his arm around her and made a sleeping noise. A purr. She smiled to herself and then slithered out from underneath him and snuck out of bed to check herself in the mirror before he woke up. Her hair was still in one piece, but her face had a flush—either from the kissing or the orgasms. After swirling mouthwash, she grabbed her toothbrush and went to town, then splashed warm water on her face to wash away any sleep grease that had accumulated. She'd considered applying her lip gloss, but that was too much. Even for her.

Dutch was awake and staring at her as she exited the bathroom.

"Good morning," he said, then smirked sexily.

"Hi," she said, and sat on the bed next to him.

He looked at the alarm clock. "I'm going to go—"

Her heart sank, but she didn't want to give away her disappointment. "I know, it's okay," she interrupted in lieu of having him finish the sentence. "Look, we were drunk and—"

She was stopped by Dutch's finger on her lips. "Shhhh. *I'm going to go* and get us some coffee from downstairs. Maybe stop and brush my teeth in my room. I'll be back in ten minutes." He pecked her on the head, found his clothes from three different piles on the floor, then dressed and left.

Allie plopped herself down on the bed on her back and stretched out her arms, staring at the ceiling. Was this going to change everything? Their dynamic had always been on the flirty side, but he was *Dutch*, and she was *Allie*. They were friends, and friends couldn't be... could they?

When he returned, he was holding two coffees and a plate of pastries. Allie wanted to say something to him, something to blanket the sea of questions she was sure they both had. But look at him, so adorable—his wavy hair was tucked behind his ears, and he'd changed into a T-shirt and gym shorts. She eyed the pastries, but they were immediately placed on the table as he lifted her up and brought her back to the bed. Questions answered.

A half hour later, Allie complained from beside him on the mattress. "Shit. I have to go soon. Hair and makeup." She shook her head back and forth and raised her eyebrows. "I wonder if Emma is going to show up. I wonder what happened with her and Ethan last night."

"Oh, before I forget to tell you, I ran into Ethan downstairs. He saw me with two coffees."

"Oh, shit."

"I didn't really say anything, just that I went out last night and—and I let him think what he wanted. We don't have to tell anyone. Or we can tell everyone. Whatever you're comfortable with."

What a doll. "Honestly, I'd rather just keep this a secret if that's okay?" Because more secrets. Why not?

"Sure." He pecked her on the head again. "So, is this you throwing me out?"

She nodded her head. "Raincheck."

He smiled. "I'll see you tonight."

After Dutch left, Allie turned on her meditation app. First, she put on "Soothing Rainforest," and did a few yoga poses and stretches. She didn't realize how long it'd been since she'd enjoyed sex. Sure, there were one or two here and there after Wharton, but nothing like Dutch. After she spent twenty minutes in downward dog and warrior's pose and child's pose, she turned on her positivity meditation. *Think of what you're grateful for*, the woman's buttery voice said. *Expel negativity at every turn.*

Easier said than done, lady.

She showered, and as she dressed in clean yoga pants and a tank, she felt apprehensive about what was to come. The wedding, sure, but more important, the getting ready part. Her friends facing each other.

When Allie got to the salon, Fiona was there already with some family members. The flower girls (her cousin's five-year-old twins) were having the finishing touches put on their updos, with fresh flowers tucked behind their ears. Aunts and grandmothers and cousins were there. That was it.

Allie sat and waited, wondering what Emma was doing, and if she would even show.

28

VEEJAY AND EMMA

The Wedding Day, 10:00 a.m.

"You *what?*" Vee's face was contorted like he'd just sucked on a lemon.

Emma thought she'd finally broken Vee. This was too much information for anyone to absorb in twenty minutes, much less him of all people. The quintessential nice guy, and she was dumping all over him, telling him everything that would ruin his life. And hers in the process.

"I did it for a reason," she said, rather unconvincingly. She took the scrunchie out of her hair and ruffled up her long, dark waves with her fingers. "Listen to me, Vee. I need you to understand everything."

He sighed and crossed his arms. "Go ahead."

"Trevor texted me a couple months ago. He was in the city and said he wanted to talk to me because he had something he wanted me to see. Of course, I freaked out because of what he already had on me, so I went without question. I met him in his hotel room."

"Bad idea, Emma."

"I know," she said and put her hand up in defiance. "Anyway, Trevor had a picture with him. Ethan and Fiona in—let's just say—a compromising position. I had no idea about them when he showed it to me, and I snapped, then I raided the minibar. When I was good and sauced, he started to comfort me, which I'm sure is what he planned all along."

Vee jumped up and took both Emma's hands in his. "That's rape, Emma. I'll flippin' murder him."

"No, wait. Listen. I knew what I was doing. I made up a plan right then and there."

"Please don't tell me you had sex with flippin' *Trevor* for revenge."

"Only one percent. A half percent really. I know it's impossible to believe after everything I've just told you, but I truly did it to save my marriage. To save my friendship with you." She took a deep breath. "I planned on faking the pregnancy, and I was going to blackmail him. Tell him the baby was his, and I'd 'take care of it' once he swore that our secret was dead and buried. The only way to do that was to *actually* sleep with him. I had to. The timing was perfect for me to scare the shit out of him this weekend. I had to commit to it one hundred percent. I stopped drinking. I downloaded a sonogram off the internet. You know Ethan, he's a typical guy and doesn't know to look in the top corner for my name. I was going to tell him I had a miscarriage next week."

"You're lying to your husband? That's sick, Emma. You're sick. How could you do that to Ethan?"

"I did it *for* Ethan." She swallowed hard, only half believing her own lies as she heard them out loud, even if it was the truth. "And for you. But it's all out the window now anyway. When I threatened Trevor on Thursday night, he alluded that he was going to tell Ethan everything after the wedding. So, I did it all for nothing." The couch pillows were crumpled in her fists, her knuckles white with rage. "I think that's why he sent out those extra pictures to everyone last night. To punish me for threatening him. It's one thing for me to see a picture of them halfway to sex two months ago, which was bad enough. I could forgive that as a one-time mistake. But it was another to see—to see *them*—like *that*. At the Rangers game. And with his family." She shook her head, trying to rid it of the memory, and pointed to her head. "It's burned there, you know. I can never unsee that. It's all I see whether my eyes are opened or closed."

"But why would he do that to Ethan? Or even Fiona?"

"Casualties of war. He wanted everyone to know, to embarrass me." Her expression clouded over as the memory returned. "I knew he was the type to cheat—girls just know. He practically hit on me every time we've been together since day one."

"Ick." Veejay clamped his hands over his ears.

"I know. At least it was fast. Then I left and went home to Ethan. When I cried the second I stepped through the door, I told him it was because I lost an author that I was coveting to another publisher, and that I was PMSing so I was overreacting."

"Oh God." Vee's hand was on his head. "Poor Ethan."

"I did it for Ethan first, but for you too, Vee. I didn't want to have to explain this if it came out. You'd figure it out. You'd figure out she was yours—that was the one thing Trevor didn't know. He didn't know you were the father. If it came out, and you figured it out, would you lie to Ethan? Would you have lied to him then if you knew? Think about it."

Vee couldn't sit still so he stood and went from one side of the room to the other, back and forth, back and forth.

Finally, he opened the balcony door and let the Southern winter air flow into the room. The sound of the light wind entering the room and the smell of the salt seemed to take him down a notch and he took deep breaths with his eyes closed.

"My life with you will never be the same," Emma said from behind him. "I know this, and it kills me. But everything is going to be over. Ethan is going to know about the real pregnancy *and* the fact that I slept with Trevor. He's going to know you and I slept together." She shook her head softly. "There's only one way out of this whole situation."

Vee thought his Fitbit might blow out firecrackers before noon from all the pacing he'd been doing. But still, it was Trevor versus Emma, and that was a competition easily won. Whatever she had to do to get out of this nightmare, he would support her.

"No matter what it is, I'll help you, Emma."

"First, do you think there's any other way to blackmail him?" she asked.

"Please, I barely know the guy. None of us really do, I guess. I'm sure he's got his own secrets. But we have to face it Emma—we'll never get one over on him in the next few hours. I'm a science fiction nerd and you're an editor. We don't have the connections he does."

She paused, because she knew what she was about to say. She wanted Vee to understand the impact of her statement, because why stop now?

"Then I have to kill him."

He finally stopped moving. "What are you talking about, kill him? Are you *fucking* crazy?"

It was the first time since they'd met that he'd broken the swear word rule. The bad f-word, too. She started to think that yes, maybe she *was* crazy.

"I know a way," she said with conviction.

No way. Vee had had lived through enough death to last a lifetime. "Are you listening to yourself?"

She lifted her eyes to his and changed the subject. "Hey, what did you do? You said you were going to tell me. Why was he blackmailing you?"

And the pacing was reignited along with the train whistle in his head.

Emma had started the conversation by telling him that he was going to hate her. He felt the same at that moment. While her secret involved him and Ethan, Vee's secret involved another as well.

"I—I—I don't even know what to say. I did something bad in India."

Her face scrunched. "India? When you were a teen-ager?"

"Yes. Look, first it's necessary to tell you that I lied to you about my past." This was going to be harder than he thought. He'd never prepared a speech to divulge the information because he never thought he'd have to. "I didn't grow up how I said I did, in a poor village. We had money. A lot of it. My dad is an engineer. My mother is a doctor. I went to prep school."

Emma's face was blank as she shrugged. "Why is that such a big deal? Dutch is a damn federal reserve and we all still like him. Allie has her huge settlement and she's still our best friend. So, why did you lie?"

Her words stung.

"Because of why I got sent here. I didn't win a school lottery. I attended a boarding school in Vermont for two years before Columbia. I was shipped here because I shamed my family." He sat back down and covered his face with his hands, like what came out of his mouth would cease to be true if he didn't look at her as he said it. "I got drunk. A friend and I took his brother's car out joyriding. We—I—killed someone."

"Oh my God." Emma's hand was over her open mouth.

"That wasn't even the worst part." He paused, the pain on his face apparent. "The Rahna family influence ran deep where I was from. So, basically, it was swept under the rug—my name was never even involved, and it was pinned on someone else, a poor chap who decided to take the heat and the jail time to set up his wife and four kids for the rest of his life. I was a kid myself—I didn't know what was going on, what they were doing behind the scenes. My family knew a few Dons, which was the equivalent of the mafia, and paid off the officials, the judge, everyone involved. Then they put me in a box and slapped on an address label to the USA and shipped me off like a FedEx package. The poor victim's family never got real justice." His head shook in disgust. "My parents paid off everyone but the family."

"Oh no. What happened to them?"

"That's the worst part. The woman I killed—" He couldn't believe he was about to say it out loud. It would be the first time and saying it out loud made it real. "She was an American, there on business. Her name was Whitney Tanner."

Emma searched her brain for the name recognition, and when it came to her, she placed her hand over her open mouth. "It was Allie's mother."

She said it as a statement, a truth, a fact. Whitney Tanner was Allie's mother who died in a car accident while on business overseas. Of all the people in all the world—literally—Emma couldn't believe what she was hearing, and her tears returned. It wasn't just her that would break up the group. It was him too. He must've been tortured. If any of this came out—any part of it—no one would ever talk to anyone again. Poor Dutch would lose all his friends, and he didn't even do anything wrong. He was the only one not involved.

Vee finally let go and the pressure of the last half hour finally became a powder keg and exploded. He sobbed with such a gut-wrenching noise that even Emma didn't know what to do. He collapsed on her lap and cried, and she stroked his head.

"I found out everything about her, Em," he said. "I made trips down to Connecticut from Vermont on weekends just to follow Allie around. I made a fake Instagram account and followed her and all her friends. I visited the ice cream shop where she worked. I needed to make sure she was okay. When I found out she was going to Columbia through her social media, I called in a favor back home."

"A favor?"

He nodded. "They might as well use their money for good some of the time."

It came to Emma at once. "The Rahna-Patel Court Project." Emma recognized it immediately and wondered why she'd never made the connection to the garden and statues on campus. "Same Rahna?"

He nodded again. "Patel is my mother's maiden name. I didn't want it to be too obvious. They pay for the upkeep to this day." He sniffled. "I got in, and I just wanted to know her. To protect her. Now she's one of my closest friends. I love her like a sister, and I can't have her know about this," he heaved through gasps. "Trevor's never going to let this go. I know he's going to tell her. He's going to want everyone to hate me. He wants Fiona to hate her friends and dedicate her whole life to him and help him rise to power with her uncle. Allie is never going to talk to me again. No one will."

"It's okay, Vee." She was crying too. "You'll always have me."

Trevor. That sadistic son of a bitch. Emma wouldn't let him put Vee through this anymore. Not on her watch.

"Will you help me, Vee? I know a way to get rid of him. I even did a trial run when I originally thought about it two months ago."

Vee didn't say anything for a minute or so, then finally "Wait. You were serious about that? About killing him?"

She nodded, and possibly smiled. "We know he has a deadly nut allergy. We saw what happened at brunch that time."

Despite the aches he had all over his body from the last half hour, Vee stood and challenged his Fitbit yet again. He plugged each ear with an index finger.

"La la la la la la—"

"Vee!" Emma jumped off the couch and turned him to face her. "Vee, listen to me. You know as well as I do that he's never going to stop. We can jump through hoops. The fact of the matter is, by tomorrow, or Monday the latest, Ethan is going to know what I did. And what *we* did. And what happened because of it. All our friendships are going to be over. The whole group is going to disperse. My marriage is going to be over."

He wouldn't face her as she confessed her plans and kept turning his head to the side.

"Allie's going to know by tomorrow," she said to convince him.

He snapped his head toward her that time. "That's fucking low, Emma."

The f-word again. She was getting through to him.

"Just listen to me. We know he has a deadly nut allergy."

"You're not going to do this."

"I am. With or without you. But it'll be easier with you."

Vee looked at Emma, the mother of his child. He couldn't believe the amount of betrayal she'd put him through. She was right. Part of him did hate her. But the other part loved her in a way that no one would be able to understand. She was his Emma. His best friend. His touchstone. What would he do without her?

And Allie. Poor Allie, with her dying father and the recent divorce—he had no idea how messed up her life had been lately. If she found out, now, that it was Vee who killed her mother, she may never recover. Vee was the good guy—and no one would look at him the same again. Not her, Fiona, Dutch, or Ethan. Ethan, one of his best friends, would hate him anyway, but this would be more of a reason.

Almost fifteen years of friendships and memories, and they'd all be ruined. All because Vee couldn't man up at this very moment, when Emma asked him to help make it all go away.

He would help her.

"So, what did you have planned?" he asked.

Emma's eyes glowed and she finally exhaled. "You know peanuts are vaguely the same consistency as coffee beans, right?"

"No but go on."

"I went to Whole Foods and grabbed a handful of the loose peanuts they have in the back. The ones they sell by the pound. I brought it to the coffee grinder. You know how the machine has like six levels of coarseness?"

"Yes."

"You can grind them really fine if you get the dry roasted ones. They come out like coffee grounds. I even put it in the little brown coffee bag."

He threw his hands in the air. "Terrific. Now someone else with a nut allergy is going to bring home tainted coffee."

"Do you think I'm a moron, Vee? I ran coffee through after and complained to the coffee manager that it came out fine when I switched it to coarse. I mean, it didn't, I switched it back before I got him, but he got the brush and said it needed to be cleaned out and he was going to bring it to the back. He was taking care of it. Anyway, I brought it home and did some tests."

"Tests?"

"Yeah. Like, I know it doesn't dissolve in coffee, it's just floats noticeably on the top. And you can't really see it in champagne because of the bubbles. I can put it everywhere. On my clothes, in my hair. I can wipe the residual dust on Fiona's dress. I'll dump it in the glitter bin. It'll be everywhere."

"She'll have an EpiPen."

"I know. I'll be with her all day. I can make it go missing."

"The venue will have one for sure." He was going to try to poke a hole in every theory she had until she submitted and realized it was a bad idea, and they'd think of another way so save their fates.

"Well, by the time everyone realizes she can't find hers, it'll be too late. He'll be breathing it in everywhere." She looked down, then back up. "It'll kill him. Either he'll choke, or his heart—if he has one—will stop. Hopefully it'll fucking explode. It'll be too much. I can put it every-where. On everyone. Anyone who tries to help him will be making it worse."

"Jesus, Emma. Are you sure? Because a lot of people can get in trouble."

"I'm sure. Remember how Fiona said they're dropping all those balloons and they're going to have that glitter barrel come out during 'Celebration' for the Instagram video? I can mix it with the glitter. That's the best way. It'll fall all over the dance floor."

"You really thought this through."

"I did. Right before…" Right before she'd slept with that slimy son of a bitch to save her marriage and her friendship with Vee. "… before. I almost went through with killing him two months ago instead of sleeping with him, but I knew I'd be caught immediately, being the only one with him. I went with the lesser of two evils. But now it's a good backup plan because over two hundred people will be around when it happens. It'll be damn near impossible to pin it on me."

"What do you need me to do?" he asked.

She glanced at her wrist, but her watch was in the bathroom, so she went into the bedroom and looked over at the alarm clock on the nightstand on Ethan's side of the bed, where the digital display mocked her. "Crap. I have to leave for hair and makeup soon. My appointment is at eleven and I have to shower first. It would really help me out if you went to Whole Foods to get the peanuts and grind them. Make sure you get the dry roasted ones— the other ones come out creamy. We need them to be powdery. Just text me so you can give me the coffee bag when you get back. I'll take care of the rest."

He looked uncomfortable at the thought of being caught. "Everyone has iPhones. Everyone will be taking video. Someone will see something."

"No one is going to focus on me."

"You're a bridesmaid."

"But I'm not the bride."

Vee stayed silent for a moment. He looked again toward the balcony and let the bright sun shrink his pupils while he squinted. His life was going to change, right at this moment: Do or die, literally. If he went through with it, he'd be an accessory to murder. First degree murder, too, because there he was, planning out the whole thing with Emma, step by step. But on the other hand, wouldn't being an accessory still be a step up from what happened seventeen years ago? Manslaughter, they called it. They got the slaughter part right. However, the alternative of not doing it would most likely end up ruining his life. Emma's life.

His brow furrowed, and his hands shook in his pockets, where he'd placed them to wipe his clammy palms. He had no choice. He shifted his gaze to Emma and nodded. It was an unspoken agreement. He was all in.

29

ETHAN

The Wedding Day, 10:00 a.m.

It was the wedding day. You could feel it in the air with every breath. The flowers were being delivered, all white lilies and hydrangeas and tulips. The cake was already there, and the trellis was being set up outside on the beach behind the hotel. It was a typical upside-down "U" shape, decorated with an array of small flowers from white to baby blue, which blended in perfectly with the ocean behind it. The white silk aisle runner was being rolled out and the chairs were being set up. The hustle and bustle of porters running around taking orders from the wedding coordinator surrounded him.

Ethan saw all of this as he ate breakfast, in paradise, alone. Table for one.

The buffet was included in their room rate, and he and Emma had skipped it the previous morning for their respective golf and spa days. He'd decided to indulge by himself—he knew Emma had to be out and about pretty soon for the bridesmaid stuff, but he didn't have to be in the suite with Trevor and the guys until almost three. And he wanted to give Emma as much time as she needed with Vee.

Although he did plan on getting to the groom's suite just a tad bit early. He certainly had something to say to Trevor about releasing those pictures. To *everyone*.

It was a shame Emma missed breakfast. It had all her favorites: fruit, yogurt, and an omelet station. The first time she'd encountered an omelet station was on their honeymoon. They'd gone to an all-inclusive resort in Aruba; they weren't exactly flush with cash, and he still remembered the look on her face as her custom omelet was cracked and stuffed and flipped right before her eyes. He'd promised to always take her places with omelet stations, but since their honeymoon, they hadn't been anywhere of significance. A quick weekend to Vermont for fall foliage didn't count. A night to Atlantic City for her thirtieth birthday ended in her drinking too much and vomiting until two p.m. They had to skip breakfast entirely that time.

They'd always lived by the "We're young, we'll do it later. We have nothing but time" mantra. And now she was about to have a baby. There was never going to be time for anything again. But currently faced with the very real prospect of losing her, he decided he would've quit drinking, married her younger and had five kids immediately if he could do it over. Anything to keep her and erase the entire Fiona mistake.

After he finished, he went down to the bar near the pool to have a cigarette. Yes, another one—he'd already decided to quit as soon as they were back from Miami. He promised her he wouldn't let her sister see it when they came in a couple of weeks. He wasn't outside for two minutes when sweat marks poked through his clothes. Another day of record-breaking heat and humidity. He'd checked the forecast and of course this was the last day. A horrendous thunderstorm was supposed to pass through later in the night and take the remaining hell heat with it out to sea, just in time for them to be flying home to twenty-five degrees. He could barely suck in the cancerous toxins due to the thickness of the air, so he mashed his cigarette out after three puffs and went back inside.

Tugging at his T-shirt, slicked to his torso, he ran into Dutch, carrying two take-out coffees and some pastries on a plate. He looked worse for wear when he spotted Ethan heading his way.

"Hey, man, what's up?" Dutch asked, crookedly lifting his right elbow as a substitute for a high five. His hands were full.

"Ah. You know. Just had breakfast alone." Ethan eyed Dutch's bounty. "What's all this?"

"Oh. Well. Yeah, I—" He looked down at the coffees. Then he smiled at Ethan. "You know. I went out last night, and…"

Ethan put his hands up. "Say no more, man. Good for you."

"Hey, so what happened with you guys? Everything work out?"

Ethan sighed. "I hope so. She's talking with Vee right now. I just want her to—you know what? Just go," he said with a smile. "Your coffee is getting cold. We can talk later."

Dutch gave him a sympathetic, crooked smile. "Thanks man."

"Hey, thanks for being there last night."

"Anytime," he said, then looked at the plate in his hand again and winked. "I'll catch ya later."

Ethan checked his phone, and there was no text from Emma or Vee. He decided to go back to the room. They'd been talking for about an hour, and he wanted to speak with Emma before she left. It would break his heart if the next time he saw her was when she walked down the aisle.

At his door, he held out the key card and then decided on a soft knock first. There was no answer, and he didn't hear voices inside, so he opened the door. The shower was running.

"Em?" he shouted as he poked his head in the bathroom.

"Yeah, it's me. I'll be done in a minute," she said.

"Take your time."

He ambled around the bathroom for a few seconds, then went and sat on the bed and nervously laced his fingers in and out of one another. When the shower stopped, he waited patiently until Emma emerged, one towel around her head and one around her body.

"Hey," he said softly and waited for her to say something.

"Hey." She went back into the bathroom and took the towel off her head and ran a comb through her long, dark hair. Then she applied a moisturizing oil to her face and grabbed the hair dryer.

"Can we talk?" he asked.

"Yes." She turned the machine on and blasted it over her hair. Passive-aggressive behavior was not new to him. "I just have to get it dry really quick," she said loudly, over the whizzing of the dryer. "The lady is doing my hair, so I don't have to make it look nice now. I can leave it frizzy, I just have to dry it. I wanted it clean."

"Okay."

He wondered if this was some sort of punishment, making him wait. Fine. He deserved it.

Five minutes later, the hair dryer turned off. She threw on a robe and then took her towel off from underneath, hiding her nakedness and any trace of a pregnant belly. She came back into the room and stared at him.

He twisted in his own shame and disgust. "Did you have a good talk with Vee?"

"Yep."

Her answer was curt, but she didn't look mad. She still had her eyes trained on him.

"Emma, I'm sorry." He didn't care how many times he'd have to say it. "I love you. Please tell me we're okay."

She sat down next to him and put her hand on his thigh. "We're okay, Ethan."

He looked at her through teary eyes. "Swear?"

"I swear. I mean, I'm still not happy, but big picture." Distracted, she looked at her phone on the nightstand. "I have to go soon, I'm already a few minutes behind. I think I'm going to do a side pony like this." She gathered her hair over her right shoulder. "But, like, puffier and stuff. With crystals so it looks dressy. What do you think?"

And just like that, she'd moved on to something else. They really were going to make it.

Allie texted that she was already at the salon, so Emma threw on workout clothes for comfort for the next three hours, grabbed her dress and heels, and left. Ethan had a cigarette on the balcony, almost in a good mood. He had her back. The heat took him again, as it had all weekend, and he went back into the air-conditioned room, and then closed the blackout drapes behind him. He needed a nap before the real fun began.

30

Allie

The Wedding Day, 11:10 a.m.

When Emma arrived in workout clothes at the salon to get ready, Allie held her breath—it was the exact moment that Fiona stepped out of the bathroom, her hair already done, wearing a white silk bathrobe with the word "Bride" emblazoned on the back in silver crystals. Their eyes met, and for a hot second, Allie thought Emma was going to pounce and then scream and the wedding would be ruined. Which didn't bother Allie in the least. In fact, she crossed her fingers, still not breathing. It was either that, or Emma was announcing that she and Ethan were booked on a flight home in the next hour to visit a divorce lawyer.

"Hey," Emma said to Fiona. "I'm sorry about how I acted last night. I just—it's fine. It was a long time ago." She smiled. "It's your wedding day. It's a happy day."

Her smile was fake as shit, Allie knew, but Fiona bought it. She took one step forward, cautiously, and so did Emma. Before Allie knew it, they were hugging, and she exhaled. There would be no pile of hair extensions on the floor. No makeup covering bruises.

"I'm sorry," Fiona said. "I don't know what I was thinking. I'd never want to hurt you. It was me being lonely, and him missing you. He's always loved you more than anyone or anything in the world."

Another fake smile. The speech didn't land with Emma. Truth be told, with Fiona in Miami, married to the douchebag she was about to marry, she'd eventually fall off the face of the earth. Allie and Emma had always been the closest anyway—really, who's closer than college roommates?—and Allie thought Emma was taking the news quite well that Fiona had secretly slept with Ethan back in the day. Maybe a little *too* well. She deserved a Nobel Peace Prize as far as Allie was concerned. Maybe Emma would only forgive Fiona for the day, and starting tomorrow, they'd never speak again. For now, it was business as usual with the three of them, and someone named Alexa started to work on Emma's hair.

Allie's hair went quick. She had it parted in the middle, with soft pieces on each side of her temple curled back and secured with a crystal, making her look like a hippie. She cringed when she held up the pale pink dress—she much preferred it when she tried it on originally, when the hues of the rose in her cheeks played off her red hair. At the time, she looked like one of those cards you grab at the paint store, where all the pinks complement each other in one fashion. Now, her hair was the color of the inside of a ripe banana—almost a baby white, and she felt she needed to overcompensate with makeup.

She'd asked her artist, a tattooed girl named "C" with dark spiky hair with blue tips to give her a smoky eye, but not to make her look like Pam Anderson in her Kid Rock days.

"Hey, Blondie, I don't do your lids and brows with a sharpie," C said to her. "I know what a smoky eye is."

Allie assumed she knew what the letter stood for.

After her hair, Emma was being worked on by a man who looked so much like Kevyn Aucoin that Allie thought he'd been resurrected. She, too, went with a soft smoky eye, which always made her huge green eyes look model worthy. Her hair was gathered loosely into a side pony, showing off her tan shoulders. Fiona, however, went with a totally neutral palette. It made her look much younger than her thirty-two years. Her eyes were a very light gray, so her shadow matched her irises while her cheeks were blushed peach, her lips displaying a matching peachy gloss. The part in her hair was severe where it was pulled back tightly into a bun, but the bun itself hung low on her neck in big, bouncy, messy curls.

They sipped champagne and prosecco—Emma drank water—as the photographer invaded their personal space wanting detailed pictures of them before and after their transformation from hardened city girls to bridal magazine covers. The camera made that drowned out clicking sound, which reverberated in her head over and over, and she wanted to tell him to take his shot and get the hell away from her. The dude could seriously get a job as a TMZ paparazzi.

When Fiona's mother and aunt came into the room, the photographer followed them outside, where Fiona posed in a private outdoor area that ran the full length of the salon. They were away from earshot, so Allie decided to bring up last night.

"Sooooooo," she said to Emma, extending the word as she finalized her approach. "How'd you sleep?"

Emma laughed out loud, and that made Allie giggle.

"It was an interesting night. Ethan is tortured."

"Good. Make sure you torture him some more. I mean, Fiona, really. What was he thinking?"

Emma took a deep breath. "Look, when I wasn't with him, he was free to do what he wanted. I broke up with him both times, he never broke up with me. You know all he ever did was try to get me back. Subconsciously, maybe he did it to get back at me. I'm no peach." She clearly wanted the conversation over with.

"Well, I'm sure he'd feel differently if you slept with *his* friend. But we all know that would never happen." She glanced toward the open bedroom door to make sure they were all still outside. "Plus, you won at life anyway. Ethan, with all his faults, loves you. Even I know that. She gets *Trevor.*" Allie thrusted her thumb toward the outdoor area.

If only Emma knew what that asshole was really about. *One more day*, she reminded herself for the millionth time. *One more day.*

A million and one.

31

VEEJAY

The Wedding Day, 11:15 a.m.

Vee exited the hotel, a different man altogether. He got Emma pregnant. She had his baby girl. His daughter was being raised in Portugal. He *met* her.

What would he have really done if he knew? Emma didn't want an abortion, and that was fine. Really. But what would've happened with them if she kept the baby? What would've happened with Ethan? With the rest of their friends? Maybe it was better this way. At least she didn't dump the baby off with strangers, never to be seen again. She got to be Aunt Emma, always in Bianca's life, and he had to admit—Cassandra and Eduardo were terrific parents to their first child, Emma's nephew Ricard. When Vee saw Bianca—the baby that looked exactly like she belonged in the family—it all made sense.

He should be happy. Still, it was hard to wrap his head around it. He'd never had a say. Emma never gave him the benefit of the doubt, and as close as they were, that bothered him.

Back to his mission to keep it all a secret. He'd searched on his phone—there was a Whole Foods five point eight miles away. He didn't want to Uber there. He wanted no record of ever being there, so he walked down Collins Avenue, two hotels over, and waited outside for a bellman to hail him a cab. He paid cash at his destination.

Inside, everyone around him was *shopping*. Shopping, like nothing was wrong. Like there wasn't a potential murderer among them. *They know what you're doing.*

Anxiety wasn't new to him, and he wished he'd popped a Valium before he left, but he didn't. His heart rate stepped up just enough to alter his breathing, and his head felt hot—this time, it wasn't the humidity. *You're just grocery shopping.* He picked up a basket and headed to the produce aisle and perused the apples. Macintosh. Delicious. Granny Smith. Gala. Honeycrisp. Fuji. Organic or regular. He plunked two of them, the Gala ones, into the basket. *Plastic bag, stupid!* Shit. He was forgetting the most basic stuff. Behind him, he saw a roll of produce bags, so he tore one off and placed the apples inside, then back in the basket. He slowly walked toward the prepared salads and took an arugula mix with him after pretending to read the back.

Ahead of him, he saw the loose nuts. A whole wall of them. Sweat ran down his back as he approached, but like a good little worker bee, he grabbed a plastic bag. His hand shook like a leftover winter leaf as he opened the plastic top. He thought the scoop would slip from his clammy palms as he poured them into the bag. *Veejay. They're just flippin' peanuts.* He smacked the heavy bottom of the bag, so it spun around and made a little twist at the top to stay closed.

He turned into the condiments aisle and pretended to look at the shelves. He saw a small bottle of peanut oil and tossed that into the basket as well. Then, the score of a lifetime sat on the shelf before him. There was a large jar of organic peanut powder on the shelf second to the bottom. Powder! Even better than tiny, chopped peanuts which were sure to be discovered. He swiped it into the basket.

Then he took two jars of capers—he didn't want the checkout person to think he only wanted things that were associated with peanuts. Not that the checkout person gave a damn what he was buying. Did he still have to go to the coffee barrels?

Like Emma was pushing on the small of his back, he followed the aroma to the coffee beans. The grinder was there. No one was getting coffee. The bread department behind it had a line, but Vee didn't see anyone looking his way. He took a paper coffee bag out of the holster and placed his murder basket at his feet, staring at the clear plastic bag full of peanuts.

Thump. Thump. He had read "The Tell-Tale Heart" by Poe.

Everyone around him heard his heart. They had to. It was pounding in his ears like a drum.

He stood and looked from left to right. Look at these people, going about their day. They weren't even concerned with him, with what he was doing. With the crime he was committing.

He'd decided the powder was enough, but wanted to get fresh ground coffee anyway, just to hide the poison in the bag. Before he changed his mind, he filled a coffee bag to the top with Organic French Roast beans, then opened the lid of the grinder and poured them inside. They dinged as they collected in the machine. He slipped the bag under the receptacle and turned it all the way to the right to *fine*. His arm rose as he stared at the menacing "on" button. *Go ahead, you murderer,* it beckoned to him. *Do it. Get coffee just to hide the real murder weapon.*

He pushed it.

The machine buzzed as the beans swirled inside, and then they piled back into the opaque brown bag as coffee grounds. The whole thing lasted ten seconds, and then the bag was folded over, and the clasps were clasped. He wrote the SKU number for the Organic French Roast on the front and plunked it into his basket.

When he looked up, the same woman was still being served in the bread department. Everyone else was still waiting impatiently behind her. To his left, a woman was placing cookies from the bakery into a white cardboard box. To his right, a different woman with a baby strapped to her was deciding which organic chocolate bar to select.

No one cared about him, or what he was doing. No one noticed all the peanut stuff in his basket.

As he made his way to the register, he grabbed a hunk of cheddar cheese, a bag of frozen peas, and a big bottle of Smartwater. He placed everything on the conveyor belt one by one, waiting for someone in a green smock to point and scream from behind him, *That's him! That's the guy who's going to kill Trevor with the peanut powder!* But nothing happened.

The pretty checkout girl's name was Kellye with an *e* on the end, and normally he'd make conversation with her and asked why it was spelled that way, or if it was pronounced Kell-yay like Kanye, but he didn't want to draw attention. He didn't want to be memorable.

She asked him if he had the app to get discounts. Of course he did, but he didn't use it. She scanned the items, one by one as he bagged for her. When her hands touched the peanut powder, he froze and held his breath. She scanned it, then slid it over to him where he quickly hid it in the paper bag. She picked up the plastic bag full of whole peanuts, tapped a few numbers into the register, and slid that over to him too.

Then, like he was just an ordinary shopper on an ordinary day, she gave him the total, he paid cash, she told him to have a nice day, and he smiled and said, "you too."

Then he walked out the door.

It was over.

Beep beep. His watch told him it was noon. He'd seen a fast-food restaurant not too far from where he was while in the cab over. He walked there, in the stinking heat and ordered a burger and fries, and had them put the regular brown paper bag inside of a plastic carry bag. Outside, he retrieved the Smartwater and drank what he could, which was a lot considering he needed to replace all the sweat from the last half mile. He reached for the coffee bag and dumped out the contents and unscrewed the jar of peanut powder. He poured as much as he could fit into the coffee bag and resealed it—that should be plenty. He grabbed the mini peanut oil bottle, and put both of them in with the burger and fries he was dying to eat, and tossed everything else he bought into the nearby garbage receptacle, including the whole peanuts and the rest of the powder.

Then he got an Uber to pick him up and bring him back to the hotel.

Once there, he texted Emma.

32

EMMA

The Wedding Day, 12:30 p.m.

Emma's phone vibrated in her hand as the finishing touches were put on her eyelashes. She couldn't move, much less look at the text. It could be Ethan with another "I'm sorry and I love you," but she knew it wasn't. She knew it was Vee, and there were only minutes until she'd be up, out of the chair, and then have to get dressed and do all the things she'd committed to when she agreed to be in this damn wedding. Fiona had called for a limo to take them to certain areas of South Beach for pictures. It was going to take hours. She had to see Vee before she left. She had peanut dust to spread around.

When she was finally able to look at her phone, it was, in fact, Vee. The text said: *the eagle has landed.*

Wow. Really? She laughed inside at what a cheeseball he was.

"Hey, Fiona. I forgot my earrings." On purpose. "I just have to run to my room really quick before I get dressed. I'll be right back."

"Okay. The limo won't be here until one, so you have time anyway," Fiona said.

"Got it. Be right back."

It was time. Time to go and get the proverbial bullets that would shoot Trevor in the head. When she exited the salon and the smell of shampoo and hair products faded, she was on her way, and there was no going back. She walked faster and faster to mask the shaking.

Knocking on Vee's door, she was happy when he answered—she'd felt as if a spotlight had been shining on her for the whole walk.

"Hey. Get in here," he said, peeking his head out the door to see if anyone else saw her there.

"Stop being such a nervous Nellie, Vee," she said. "You're only making us look guilty of something."

"Well, aren't we?"

He was freshly showered, his hair wet, and the smell of soap lingered around him. He wore gym shorts and a T-shirt. His tux was hanging on the frame of the bathroom door.

"So, you have something for me?"

Vee stepped back and stared at her. "Wow. You look beautiful."

In all the action from the morning and the anticipation of what was to come, Emma had forgotten about her morning makeover, even though she'd literally just left the chair. She blushed—she knew she was doing it—and pressed her lips together in a smile.

"Thank you."

He took her hand to hold it. Not in a romantic way, but in a Vee way. She hoped his feelings toward her wouldn't change once they were all back in New York, and the reality of that morning's discussion set in. As it was, he'd still only had two hours to absorb the news, and she was sure he took it the way water absorbs oil.

"I still have to run to my room for my earrings, Vee. Let's get on with this."

Vee pointed to the greasy paper bag on the desk. "It's in there."

"You got fast food?"

"No Emma, I didn't. I took a cab to Whole Foods from two hotels away and paid cash. Then I had to shop for a whole bunch of unnecessary shit, so it didn't look like I was buying deadly peanuts only—by the way, I was able to avoid killing innocent people. I found organic peanut powder, so we can use that instead. I put it in the coffee bag to hide it. Then I walked almost a mile to get the burger and fries so I could hide the peanuts and the peanut oil in the fast food bag. I Ubered back from there. Any tracking of me shows I was hungry and got a burger. Not that I went to Whole Foods to help murder someone."

There was a tinge of anger in his tone during his explanation.

"Peanut oil?" was all she could come up with.

"Yeah. Peanut oil. I saw a small bottle and grabbed it just in case you needed... extra."

She nodded. "Good thinking."

At the desk, she opened the bag and looked at the pound of peanut dust. She couldn't hide her smile.

"Good thinking. This is perfect." She replaced the bag and then picked up the peanut oil. "Shit. This is too big." It was only about the size of her hand, but she wouldn't be able to carry it in her clutch. What if it fell out? "Don't worry about it," she said with a wave. "I'll take care of it. I'll find a way."

"How are you getting that in?" he pointed at the bag.

"The less you know the better. Plausible deniability."

He didn't seem convinced as he stood with his arms crossed. "Right. I don't know anything." The he plunked himself down on the chair in his room. "There's so much I wish I didn't know."

Tears rose again. She waved her hand in front of her face to stave them off.

"I've got to go, Vee. I just got my makeup done. I can't ruin it right now. Tonight and tomorrow are going to be chaos if this works, especially since we're going to have to leave for the airport around one. Can we have dinner Monday, back in the city? Just the two of us?"

"Of course."

"Okay. Good. I have to go." She picked up the bag and headed out. At the door, she stopped and turned around. "Thank you, Vee. You know I love you right?"

"Yes. I love you too."

It wasn't the first time they'd exchanged the sentiments, but it meant the same thing to both of them. Not romantic love, just love.

She left and rushed to the staircase—her room was one floor above his and she didn't want to be seen on the elevator with the contraband. She climbed the flight, trying not to sweat too much and ruin her hair or makeup as she barreled down the hall. In front of her room, she said a silent prayer and waved her key card on the lock and the door clicked open.

Inside, the blackout shades were drawn, and Ethan was in bed, out like a light. She removed her flip-flops at the door—she didn't want the clop-clop sound to disturb him—and tiptoed toward the bathroom. Using her cell phone's flashlight, she located her earrings in her jewelry roll and grabbed the medium sized silk sachet that housed her bracelets. She reached in and tried to stop the jangle as she removed the bracelets and placed them on the counter. Then, she filled the sachet with as much peanut dust as it could hold—it really was a better option, thank God for Vee—and pulled the drawstrings closed very tightly. She tied an extra knot around the top, and tucked the sachet inside her clutch.

She tried to fit the peanut oil in, to no avail, so she googled uses for it and found it was an excellent source of moisture for hair, and also prevented breakage. Double score. She removed the top and poured some into her palm, and then massaged it into the ends of her hair and rubbed her hands together and smoothed back any flyaways on the sides and the top of her head with her palms. She repeated the pouring and the hand rubbing until she'd smoothed it over her entire ponytail, then rubbed some on her elbows and legs. It really did feel good, and it absorbed easily without a greasy residue or strong scent, just like the organic coconut oil she'd left at home. She screwed on the cap and buried it under the rest of her junk on the counter. There was no lingering smell, but she spritzed some extra perfume on her hair and her skin just in case.

She tiptoed back to the door and picked up her flip-flops. One last look over her shoulder confirmed that Ethan hadn't moved, so she snuck out. In the hallway, she looked for the vending machine and ice machine area, and when she found it, she disposed of the paper coffee bag in the public receptacle.

With her earrings on, she headed back to the salon to get dressed.

33

ETHAN

The Wedding Day, 1:45 p.m.

On the bed, Ethan could barely lift his head from the pillow when he woke. He'd been out like a light. Sure, Emma said she forgave him, but if there was one thing he'd learned in his thirty-three years, it was that he didn't understand a damn thing about women. Maybe her talk with Vee was helpful. It was good to know he could count on Vee when it mattered.

Groggy from the nap, a final look at the clock, which told him he had just over an hour to get ready and then take pictures with that jerkoff before he married Fiona. He'd get it over with, hopefully Trevor would burn the diary, and Emma wouldn't be in danger of being hurt anymore. Ethan didn't know what he would do if that asshole made digital copies.

One thing at a time.

He lazily got up and ran the shower to boiling, just the way he liked it, hoping that scalding his skin red would disguise the redness around his eyes. Trevor thought he was breaking them apart, but what he didn't know was that nothing would come between him and Emma. Ethan would see to that.

After toweling off, he grabbed a dry washcloth from the counter and ran it over the mirror—something Emma hated at home because it streaked, but hey, they had housekeeping for one more day so why not? Emma used a blow dryer to fight the steam, and there were a hundred different tools near her sink as it was. He was afraid of electrocuting himself if he touched the wrong one.

Ethan turned to her side of the bathroom to look for extra toothpaste. The utter amount of shit she took with her when they traveled bewildered him. He didn't understand why all the compacts and jars and droppers were needed. He rummaged through her vanity bag and picked up objects like he was inspecting them. What the hell was a highlighter used for? The only highlighter he ever knew was neon yellow. And why was there a bottle of peanut oil? That woman had a mini kitchen in their bathroom at home, with coconut oil and vitamin E tablets and apple cider vinegar, all used on her face. Some nights he didn't know if he was going to bed with her or a salad. Then he spotted three mascaras—black, almost black, and brown-black. Huh? Did women really notice the difference? Ethan certainly didn't.

He decided not to question anything. He still felt like a fool from that one time, when yet another rectangular box delivered from Bloomingdale's, and she explained to him that they were black heels. He told her she already had black heels. She laughed for days. He still didn't know why that was funny.

In robotic movements, he put his tux on, the first time he'd worn one since his own wedding. Fastening his cuff links, he thought of the humidity outside before pulling on his tuxedo jacket. They'd been to beach weddings before, and the men were usually allowed to get away with linen and untucked shirts. Leave it to that asshole to make sure they were as uncomfortable as possible.

He checked his watch and he'd be early to take pictures. Good.

Once he got off the elevator, he charged toward the groom suite. The door was open, with the security latch stuck between so it couldn't fully close, and he pushed his way in.

"Trevor?" he called.

The suite was massive—the biggest hotel room Ethan had ever been in. It had an entertainment area, a small kitchen, and a dining area. He poked his head around the corner and into the open door of the private bedroom with a balcony overlooking the water. The bathroom was luxurious, with gold accents and black and red towels, so thick Ethan thought he'd be able to sleep on them. Down the hall there was another half bath. Back in the entertainment area, the sixty-inch TV was on but muted, and there were a few empty bottles on top of the bar. When he heard muffled voices, Ethan swiveled his head from side to side and realized they were coming from the terrace behind the dining area. Through the glass, he was able to see Trevor smoking with Fiona's Uncle John. He had on gym shorts and no shirt. Ethan didn't care who else was out there. He needed to do what he had to do and yanked the door open.

"Trevor. Can we speak?"

"Hey! Ethan!" Trevor said with a smile, holding a lit cigarette. "You're early! Come on out. I'm just having a little discussion with—well, I guess you're sort of going to be my father-in-law, huh?" Trevor asked Uncle John.

Uncle John nodded. His eyes betrayed the smile that followed, and he looked at his watch. "Actually, I should get going."

"No," Trevor said and shot him a look that meant business. Strangely, Uncle John acquiesced and took another drag of the cigarette, his gaze far into the ocean that faced them.

Ethan gave Trevor, who was exhaling himself, a questionable look. "You smoke? Since when?"

Trevor laughed. "I kind of don't. Cigars, mostly, on special occasions. Our friend Dutch even said he was able to get a box of Cubans for us to have at the reception tonight. But who am I not to be social on my wedding day? Uncle John wanted a cigarette, and we all know how accommodating I like to be. I know you're a smoker. Come out."

"I'd really rather talk inside first," Ethan said, disobeying Trevor, and the defiance was noted all over Trevor's rigid face. "I'll wait in here," he said and closed the door without an answer.

Ethan sat on the couch and turned on the Rangers game—he'd forgotten they had an afternoon game against the Devils today. At least for now, he could concentrate on something that wasn't Trevor related for the first time all weekend.

Trevor took his sweet ass time, but when the door squeaked Ethan knew he'd entered the room. Trevor's build was threatening, much leaner and more muscular than Ethan's, and he began to have second thoughts about the confrontation.

"Okay, Ethan, what's this—"

Nope. The sound of Trevor's voice ticked him off. Ethan jumped up from his seated position and got so close to Trevor's face that he could smell the cigarette. He wanted to grab him by his throat but didn't. "What the fuck was that last night? How could you send out those pictures to everyone?"

Trevor didn't rattle. He just smiled.

"That picture wasn't just me," Ethan said in an enraged whisper. "Why would you do that to Fiona?"

Trevor exhaled and took one small step backward, submissive. "Okay. Okay, I admit, I didn't think Emma would say anything to Fiona and make a scene. That was my bad. I didn't know Emma had that much fire in her." He stopped and smirked and raised an eyebrow. "Hey, maybe I did. You've got one more day to pretend, Ethan. Remember, everyone likes me, and no one knows it was me who sent the pictures. If you tell Emma, or anyone else, that diary will be in her inbox before we cut the cake. This is almost over. She forgave you, right? Don't make it any worse for yourself."

Ethan never wanted to take a swing at anyone more in his entire life. "I swear to God, Trevor, if you—"

"Nuh uh uh," Trevor interrupted with a shake of his finger. "None of that. Come on, pour yourself a drink, we have a full bar over there in the corner. Dutch and Veejay should be here any minute now. And remember—all good things. Only good things. Right, groomsman?" He slapped Ethan on his shoulder. "Take off the jacket. Loosen the tie. Relax, Pierce. It's a wedding."

34

ALLIE

The Wedding Day, 1:30 p.m.

The limo careened along the main strip of South Beach, air conditioned almost too much, and Allie had a shiver. It still beat the alternative—everywhere she looked, it was bikini-clad women and men in swim trunks. The occasional half-suicidal jogger—really, who could run in that heat? The limo wasn't a relaxing ride; it was packed. Allie was next to Emma, of course, and Fiona also had her mother, grandmother, and cousin there, along with the two flower girls, the twins Stacey and Tracey. The photo shoot itself this afternoon was meant to be a girl-power thing. The men were having their own fun with a different photographer in and around the hotel. Allie's eyes watched the destinations of South Beach pass them by from the tinted window seat.

"You okay, Allie? You've been pretty quiet," Emma said.

Allie smiled a bright, closed-lipped grin. "Yes, just tired. I was up most of the night." *Shit.* "Minibar reared its ugly head."

Truth was, she was upset but didn't want to talk about it for fear of crying and ruining C's makeup job. C was a bitch for sure, but that weirdo knew her way around a palette and Allie thought she looked amazing. After being happy with her makeup *and* reliving the night with Dutch, Allie had gotten a text from Val, her father's nurse, about an hour ago. A text saying that he was complaining of pain and wanted to up his meds; they were waiting for the doctor to call them back, but it was tough because it was Saturday. She immediately called when she saw it, but it was too late. Val said her father was sleeping.

Allie pictured her frail little father in his worn burgundy leather chair, the one with the torn piece at the bottom that always tickled her ankle when she leaned in to give him a hug. He was probably covered with that blue and beige patchwork crochet blanket that was her mother's favorite. Allie had originally made plans to go out to Connecticut on Monday morning, but she'd decided she was going to have Ahmed drive her there right from the airport. They landed around six tomorrow night. She probably wouldn't get there until well after dinner, but that was okay. She'd just sleep in her childhood twin bed and wait for him to wake up.

And pray for him to wake up.

The limo pulled over in the art deco district to use the funky buildings as their newest backdrop. They'd already posed their way through Ocean Drive and smiled their way through a rooftop pool. The heat was so thick that Allie wondered how Fiona didn't just jump in the water, with ten pounds of hair extensions and more makeup than she'd ever worn. That, coupled with a relatively heavy, beaded dress, had to be absolutely stifling. She didn't think Fiona had expected this brutal heatwave when she booked the wedding for December. Who would? Warm, sure.

Record breaking heat and humidity was quite something else.

She opened her clutch and took a handful of trail mix into her mouth—she hadn't eaten yet. She'd skipped the Danish that Dutch brought back with the coffee. Then she reapplied her lip gloss.

Emma laughed. "You know those stupid quizzes on Facebook and Instagram about what you'd take with you on a deserted island? I don't think anyone in the world would have the same answer as you. Lip gloss and trail mix. All the time."

She smiled. "The gloss has been around since middle school. We all have our thing. You're obsessed with your barre classes; I'm obsessed with lip gloss." Her mother bought her first one and taught her how to apply it. Being in front of the mirror and watching her lips go from dry to shiny was a memory she held close.

"Don't make fun of my barre!"

"Is it okay to do that stuff while you're pregnant?" Allie asked.

"Yes. There are tons of pregnant women in my classes. It's going to be great!" Emma said.

There was something in her enthusiasm that Allie didn't believe. She was still a bit miffed that she wasn't told privately, as soon as Emma peed on the stick. She supposed she was being selfish, demanding information about a private couple's future, but still—they were best friends.

Then again, Allie had kept her night of passion to herself.

35

DUTCH

The Wedding Day, 2:30 p.m.

Dutch yanked on the tight collar around his neck, the tuxedo being the albatross that was sure to drown him, and then ran his hand through his wavy hair. He was used to getting dressed up, having been to galas since he was a small child. He was probably the only child in kindergarten who had custom-made suits.

He looked good, and he didn't know why today was different than any other day. It couldn't have been that particular tux—a rental, because Trevor had insisted that they all have the exact same lines—so what was it? The rosy glow peeked through the smile on his cheeks. *Wow. Allie.*

He never saw that coming. Even as she asked him upstairs, all he thought about was getting laid, certain that was all that was on her mind as well. It was late, they'd had many drinks, and there was too much drama between the group—they'd both needed to be close again. But it ended up being more than that. It was comfortable. Not *we've-been-together-for-twenty-years* comfortable, but Allie comfortable. She was one of his closest friends. He'd known her since he was eighteen and knew everything about her. Right? It suddenly dawned on him that he knew nothing about her, yet he wanted to know everything. Where did that feeling even come from?

A quick glance at the clock told him it was time to go to Trevor's suite on the other side of the hotel. They had to go through the lobby and take a special elevator for the north suite. He texted Vee and Ethan that he'd pick them up in five minutes so they could go together. Ethan had texted back that he was already there, watching the hockey game. *Terrific.* Ethan was palling around with that schmuck. Sometimes he forgot that everyone else loved Trevor. He tucked his phone into his jacket pocket and left.

When he knocked on Vee's door, the apprehension set in. How was he going to go through with this? The door clicked and Vee stood before him, shirt half buttoned, holding a bottle of beer.

"My man!" Dutch said and gave him a high five. "Looking good!"

He had only seen Vee dressed up at Ethan's wedding, where they'd both served as groomsmen. Dutch actually *wanted* to do it that time.

"Yeah. We're obviously twins," Vee said with a laugh. Vee's dark skin and hair against Dutch's blond curls and piercing blue eyes were going to look amazing in the pictures. "Come on in. Grab a beer. I'm almost done."

Dutch entered Vee's dark suite and closed the door behind him. "Vampire much?"

Vee looked toward the closed drapes. "Oh. Yeah. I hit the blackout shades before. I ran out for a burger, and then it upset my stomach, so I took a quick nap." He walked over to the remote on his nightstand and pushed a few buttons until the whirring sound started, and the shades went up.

"Ah, there it is," Dutch said as the ocean came into view. "It's gorgeous here."

Dutch loved the water. He grew up in the concrete jungle, from one penthouse to another, until his parents finally settled on a brownstone in the eighties just off Fifth Avenue, near the park. A house. But it wasn't a *house*—it was in New York City. And as nice as that part of town was, there was still the constant presence of car horns and ambulances. A *house* was surrounded by other *houses*, with big patches of grass in between. They weren't connected to your next-door neighbor. They stood majestic on their own—maybe there was a swing set or a vegetable garden in the yard, and the only sound heard during the day were kids playing kickball at the end of the cul-de-sac, and at night all you heard were crickets.

Sure, he spent summers at their estate in the Hamptons, but that wasn't a house either—it was a mansion. There wasn't a big patch of grass between them and their neighbor, there were acres. When he wasn't in the Hamptons, he was in Santorini. He was in Cannes. In Melbourne and Maui and South Africa.

He often wondered what it was like to have the same friends in the same places his whole life. He'd been too compartmentalized growing up. His summer friends in the Hamptons were just that—summer friends. He'd never call them to get together for hot toddies at Christmastime. His friends around the globe were people he'd party with when he needed to escape. He'd never have a serious talk with any of them about his life's dreams.

Now, he had one family left. His best friends. He'd already lost Roger.

And Kelsey.

But so had Trevor. Sometimes, he had to remind himself.

"Gorgeous view, yes. But it's too hot." Vee said while fiddling around in the bathroom.

Dutch put on his sunglasses and grabbed a light beer from the minibar and cracked it open, then lounged on the couch in the corner. "Yeah, the weather this weekend has been awful."

"Hey, so how'd it go last night? With those girls?"

Right. He'd sent Vee a picture. Thank God Vee was still dressing in the bathroom and couldn't see his face while he lied. "Nothing happened, man. Struck out every-where." *Crap.* Ethan saw him with two coffees and made assumptions, which Dutch didn't correct. "I mean, I met someone in the lobby bar once I got back here, but you know. No big deal."

"Of course you did. Only you, man."

He heard Vee laughing, then the faucet turned on and off. He came out fully dressed, drying his hands with a towel and then put on his own sunglasses. Dutch took a gulp of beer and stood up next to him, where he caught their reflection in the full-length mirror on the back of the door.

"We look like a Tarantino movie," Dutch said. "Hey. I saw Ethan this morning. He said you were with Emma. Is everything okay with them?"

Vee flinched noticeably, enough to make Dutch panic. *I can't have my friends break apart.*

"Yeah, everything is going to be fine with them," Vee said. "Don't worry about it."

Dutch took another sip of his beer and sighed. "Where'd that picture come from? I mean, did you know?"

"About Ethan and Fiona? Hell no! I would've flippin' killed him," Vee said. "Did you know?"

Dutch held up his hands defensively. "No way, man." He knew how close Vee and Emma were. He couldn't blame Vee for the way he felt. He swallowed a last gulp of his beer and set it down on the table and picked up the box of cigars he'd brought for the boys. "Come on. Let's get this show on the road."

36

TREVOR

The Wedding Day, 3:00 p.m.

Trevor Vaughn stood outside on the terrace with Fiona's uncle, another puppet, while he waited for the rest of his groomsmen to arrive. It was brutally hot, again, because of course that's what would happen to *him* on *his* wedding day. Ethan, a heavy smoker, wouldn't even come outside for a cigarette. Trevor wondered if that had more to do with the company or the weather. Or the Rangers-Devils game that Ethan was parked in front of on the television.

He internally thanked Dutch. He may have turned the love of his life into a vegetable but having Fiona Hawthorne as a close friend proved beneficial.

Shortly, he'd marry Fiona, that boring, unattractive former schoolteacher. He'd targeted her once he found out who her uncle was, and he needed a way into her family—he wouldn't stop until he was an advisor to the President of the United States, and this was the way. This chubby, frizzy, gummy-smiled *thing* was the way. He'd surveilled her and found out where she would be one Saturday night and went in with his made-up story about escaping a bachelor party. She bought every goddamn word he'd said.

Trevor wouldn't be at a bachelor party. He didn't have, or need, friends. He used to be a pretty social guy, but fuck that. He was vulnerable once when he fell in love with Kelsey and look what happened. She cheated on him, then left him—after five fucking years. She took his youth. And for *Dutch*.

He'd had no use for people since. They were objects to him. Rungs in his ladder to the top. Ten years of finding out everything about those closest to Dutch, just to take them all down. That was the plan. Isolate Fiona. Make her work for him. What an insecure little twit. Easy pickings. Low hanging fruit. So *not* up to his level. But hey, he'd had her wrapped around his smooth finger like a telephone cord.

"Hey Pierce!" he screamed toward the half-open door. "How's your shitty team doing?" *God, even your hockey is subpar.*

"They both suck," Ethan said, trying to keep it low, but Trevor heard.

Used to hearing Ethan curse at the television, the stir of voices inside made him curious. He looked through the glass to see Dutch and Veejay had arrived. *Puppets*, he thought with a snicker. Trevor excused himself from Uncle John to greet his guests. First, he glanced at the television as he passed Ethan.

"Why the Rangers, Ethan?" Trevor said, motioning toward the television.

"My father," Ethan said. "He was a fan."

"*Was*, huh? I bet he gave up on them when they started to suck. Typical fair-weather fans."

For the first time, Ethan removed his stare from the game and turned toward Trevor, his face a mixture of ice and hatred. "My father's dead, you asshole."

Oh. Well. Even Trevor knew when he crossed a line. He shrugged. "I'm a Devils fan. Nineteen ninety-five, baby! Our first Stanley Cup. Best year ever!"

"Fake season," Ethan said under his breath.

"What was that?"

He stood up and got in Trevor's personal space, something that Trevor hadn't expected. Ethan sure was being aggressive that afternoon. "Rangers won The Cup in ninety-four, and then the strike happened. They only played half the games in ninety-five. You can hardly count that as a legitimate win."

Trevor was undeterred. Semantics didn't get under his skin. "Nineteen ninety-five! Best year ever." The silence was deafening as Trevor and Ethan stood locked in a heated stare, then he motioned to the new arrivals. "Welcome, my friends," Trevor said with a warm smile to Veejay and that fucking Dutch as Ethan turned back to the game without a word.

"Hey, Trevor," Dutch offered a handshake, and set the cigars on the console near the door. "Big day."

Still, Trevor took his hand willingly, knowing that it killed Dutch to be friendly to him. Then he turned his attention to Veejay for a shake.

"What's up bro?" he said to Veejay with a sneer.

Veejay knew what was up. He did look at him differently than he had all weekend, though. The past two days, Trevor had been able to see the fear on his face, the apprehension that his secret might come out. This time, Veejay's tight smile showed anger and defiance. *Why is he mad at me?* Trevor thought. *You should be mad at your friend Ethan for never telling you that he was dumpster diving on my fat fiancé.*

"A few more hours. Last chance to back out!" Veejay said with a forced smile.

Yes, that was typical guy talk. *Oh no, don't do it! Don't get married!* Why the fake outrage with marriage? That little piece of paper was about to get him the world.

"Why on earth wouldn't I want to get married?" Trevor said to him, his eyes never wavering, reminding him who was in charge. "I read an article about how great marriage is." He looked around the room, pretending to search for something. "It's somewhere around here. I cut it out of a paper from a really long time ago. Those old articles can be so fascinating. Has anyone ever read anything from old newspapers? Old foreign ones are the best." He glared at Veejay. "Things are so different in other cultures."

Trevor saw Veejay shit his pants, then his face hardened, and he totally relaxed. He even put his hand on his heart before he spoke next.

"Really, Trevor. Thanks so much for making me a part of this day. It means the world to me that Fiona is going to be so well taken care of."

That's right. Toe the line.

Veejay was probably dying to get married, but Trevor thought that deep down, he was in love with Emma. *Let it go dude, it's never going to happen.* All of Fiona's friends were utterly beneath him.

Like Dutch? That dude was a train wreck. Poor little rich boy. The notches on Dutch's bedpost had whittled it down to a toothpick, but that man would never be satisfied, even after he'd ruined Kelsey's life. His mother probably didn't hold him enough when he was in diapers—she'd preferred to hold champagne flutes and Cartier boxes when he was younger, and, well, Roger when she was older, needing validation that she wasn't a dried-up little old lady. All Dutch had gotten was a black heart that was unable to settle since he'd turned *their* girlfriend into a vegetable. Trevor even knew about the Oscar-nominated A-lister that Dutch bedded one year at the Cannes Film Festival. *She'd* made the move on *him*! Still. Not good enough.

Well, to hell with these guys. They meant nothing to him, and once Fiona found out what they were all hiding, she'd hate them. Of course she'd cling to Trevor, and he'd welcome it with open arms. If she had nothing but him, she'd do whatever it took to keep him happy.

"Score!" Ethan screamed and jumped up from the couch. "Finally got one on the power play!" he exclaimed to no one, then swiveled his head to the right. It was the first time he'd even acknowledged that his friends had arrived. He fist-pumped the air, then spun and high-fived Dutch and Veejay. And then smiled and high-fived Trevor.

Good boy.

"Hey, let's get some video to remember this day," Trevor said. "You know, just guys being guys. Like when we were golfing yesterday." Trevor looked at his watch. "Our photographer will be here shortly. Dutch, why don't you turn your iPhone to video? You can direct. I heard you liked that."

Dutch shifted his weight from one foot to the other. "Shouldn't I be in it? As a groomsman?"

Trevor didn't feel the need to see Dutch in any videos any more than he had to. "Oh, come on Dutch. Aren't you in enough videos? Always hogging the spotlight, am I right?"

All Dutch heard in the silence was the clap of skates on ice and the voice of Sam Rosen commenting on the game. But he immediately retrieved his phone from his jacket pocket and turned it to video. With his shaking hand, he pointed to Trevor. "Action!"

Good boy. See? I'm untouchable.

37

EMMA

The Wedding Day, 5:00 p.m.

Emma craned her neck from one side of the outdoor bar where they all waited, to the end, past the pool, where the trellis was set up on the beach. Trevor stood waiting for his bride, flanked by Ethan, Vee, and Dutch. They all looked extremely uncomfortable in the heat and kept wiping their heads with handkerchiefs.

All their guests were seated, half of them looking anxiously backward, wanting to get the ceremony finished so they could head inside to cocktail hour. Alcohol and air conditioning were clearly first on the menu. The other half looked far past the aisle, the good-looking groomsmen, Trevor, and the sea, all the way to the black cloud that was barreling toward shore.

In Emma's estimation, the storm was at least fifty miles offshore, but that didn't make it any less ominous. Every few minutes, the clouds would go from black to gray, and back to black as the lightning inside did its thing. Ethan had mentioned that there was supposed to be a storm of epic proportions that would take away the humidity, thank God, but it wasn't scheduled to get in until later tonight. It was early, as if it also wanted to stop the wedding. Emma was no meteorologist, and she didn't know how fast storms tended to travel, but that cloud was making its way to the shore like it was an invited guest.

The music that softly played from the surrounding speakers shifted, and that's when Emma knew it was time. She took a deep breath and turned behind her to look at Allie with wide eyes. Allie smiled at her, urging her to walk forward. She plastered on a fake, Barbie-doll-like grin and began down the aisle. The butterflies started immediately when her eyes locked with Ethan's, and he smiled at her with tears in his eyes the way he did on their wedding day. That was the moment when her resentment left her—up, up, up, and away, like a helium balloon. She was going to make sure Trevor died today, and it was going to be worth it for that man, whom she loved more than anyone. Aware of the cameras on her, she dropped her fake smile and settled into a natural, glowing one, to match how she felt inside.

Once settled in her spot, Allie walked down, and she glowed as well. She smiled at Dutch and Vee as she took her place beside Emma. The wedding march came on, and everyone stood. Right before Fiona appeared, Emma looked to her left and Ethan was staring at only her. When he mouthed, *I love you*, she knew he meant every syllable.

Emma finally pulled her gaze from her husband and her upper lip twitched as her eyes landed on Trevor, who smiled as Uncle John kissed Fiona's hand and then joined her hand to Trevor's.

Emma's mind was on autopilot as they said their vows, and the wind began to pick up. It started to speak its own whistle along with them, and Allie's dress and her own began to stir. Women in the crowd began to *Oh, dear!* as they attempted to protect their hair, and men next to them offered jackets as temporary shelter when the first raindrops hit. As "you may now kiss the bride" was uttered by the Justice, the thunder clapped, and the sky opened its blessing on the couple, a horrific downpour of ocean droplets that made its disapproval of the union crystal clear. Trevor took off his jacket and put it over Fiona's head as they were declared Mr. and Mrs. Trevor and Fiona Vaughn, and then sprinted back up the aisle and stood underneath the pavilion in the center of the concrete outdoor area. It was where they were due to take pictures with a beautiful blue ocean behind them, not an opaque sky with panicked guests running for cover.

Allie's head tore back with laughter as Vee took her right arm and Dutch took her left, the rain not bothering her one bit, and they followed Fiona and Trevor into the pavilion. Emma didn't pick up her pace at all as Ethan held out his arm and she hooked her elbow into his. She leaned her head on his shoulder as they made their way toward the rest of their friends.

All the guests had rushed inside, most now wet, as an assistant held a huge umbrella over the photographer, who was getting some great candid shots of their group while they attempted to dry off. Allie's blond hair was matted down, and Emma's bouncy side pony looked like a small dog that'd had a bath.

Trevor's arm was out, waving to the chaos in front of him. *Poor little Type-A Trevor, not getting his way*, Emma thought. The rain pounded down in sheets with the wind forcing unbound pool furniture past them from left to right like they were on a conveyor belt. Umbrellas were bent, tablecloths were blown off, and the trays of champagne glasses they'd had ready for a toast were destroyed.

Everything was wrecked, including Emma's plans. The rain wanted to wash her sins away, not realizing how many sins she'd packed into her life before this day. All of her murderous intentions were washed away with the storm.

"This came out of nowhere," Trevor said, then looked from the approaching black cloud back to Fiona. "We have to get you inside before the center of the storm reaches the shore. These are just the outer rain bands. Is everyone ready to run?"

There was an indiscernible pause, and then Allie took off out of the pavilion without waiting for anyone else to answer. She screamed once the rain began to pelt on her, but then she stopped and faced them all and laughed, the rain spattering on her and around her. Like a defiant child, she tossed her bouquet into the sky and laughed again as it plunged down into a puddle. Her hands were still in the air as she jumped up and down, making a complete and total mess of her hair, her face, and her dress.

But, she looked *so* happy, for just one moment, the rain was washing away her father's cancer. Her eyes were closed as she faced the storm head on, not moving; her arms spread like someone had nailed her to a cross.

"Screw it," Dutch said.

He took off his jacket and pushed the collar to the tip of his index finger and spun the jacket like a lasso as he joined Allie. He let the jacket go as the wind took it and slammed it into the wall of the outdoor bar, covering it with sand and salt water. He shook his head back and forth as his hair got wetter, like a dog shaking itself free of water after a bath, and he howled. They joined hands and jumped up and down, together, them against the storm. Them against the world. Then, he picked her up like she was a sleeping Disney princess as she draped her arms around his neck, and they shared a moment as they stared into each other's eyes. Snapping out of it, he started to run toward the doors, and Allie fit comfortably in his arms like a jigsaw puzzle piece. His maniacal run wasn't in a panic—it was tender, and it was the first time Emma had been able to see them as a couple and wondered why it'd never happened.

Emma needed to push for a way to get them inside, because she had to dose Trevor again, and fast. The rain had washed off the peanut oil in her hair, and on her arms and legs. The powder she'd sprinkled on herself and even on Fiona when she'd pretended to smooth out her dress lines was gone. She had to get inside and start over. She needed it to be sprinkling down on them in the air around him.

"The glitter bin is going to be a hoot now!" Emma exclaimed. "We're all soaked. It's going to stick everywhere. We should have them start with that song by Kool and the Gang. Let's make this a day to remember!"

"Well, we have to get through cocktail hour first, but I think we can arrange that," Fiona said. "Come on, let's get inside and have a drink. I think we all deserve it."

38

ETHAN

The Wedding Day, 6:00 p.m.

Ethan was soaked to the bone as was his jacket, which Emma had draped over herself for the run into the hotel. One photographer caught all the hilariousness on video, the other continued to snap candid shots, as he had from the first raindrop, now capturing their dramatic entrance into the cocktail hour.

They all got a standing ovation after running from the pavilion to the upstairs room that hosted the cocktail hour. They took a bow and scattered like cockroaches—the boys to the bar, the girls to say hello to some other friends before they would inevitably go and "fix" themselves, not realizing how beautiful they looked when they were happy and natural. *Women.*

Ethan rushed to the bar and got a beer next to Vee and Dutch. They clanked the bottles at the neck as they all drank with relief. Ethan patted himself down, looking for his cigarettes, when he remembered that Emma still had his jacket, and they were in the left breast pocket.

"I'll be right back," he said to his friends.

He spotted Emma with Allie and a couple of other girls from college that he didn't even know they were still friendly with. He forgot their names—he was never any good at remembering names. They were both drenched, their dresses clinging to their wet skin, their makeup rubbed off onto the back of their palms as they talked. Emma had his jacket carelessly in her left hand, the bottom dragging on the floor. He made a beeline toward her when he was stopped by Trevor.

"Hey, Ethan!" he said with a smile, clamping his arm around his neck. "Smile!"

They turned toward someone clicking at a camera, someone Ethan didn't know. Probably one of Trevor's wretched family members. It didn't seem like he had many friends. Ethan could've figured that out without a detective kit. He smiled the obligatory smile for the stranger, and even made a peace sign with his right hand. *So happy to be here!*

"Where are you rushing off to?" Trevor asked, then took a dramatic turn toward Dutch and Vee at the bar, guiding Ethan with him.

"What's up, man?" Dutch asked.

"How about grabbing those Cubans?" Trevor asked.

"Oh. Sure." Dutch's expression went blank. "Shit. I left them in the groom suite. Right on the table by the door. I meant to grab them and bring them down earlier, but I was distracted."

"Right. I bet you were." Trevor started at Dutch, who didn't make a move. "Well?"

He set his beer bottle on the bar. "I forgot a cutter."

"I have a cutter," Ethan interrupted, grabbing a glass of champagne off a nearby tray. He handed it to Dutch. "Do you have a key to the suite? I'll get the cutter and grab the cigars on my way."

Dutch felt around his body and then pounded his fist on the bar in front of him. "Dammit. My phone and my key were in my jacket." He pointed at the window. "Out there, when I swung it. Shit."

Ethan held up a hand. "Don't worry. I'll go get it." He wanted nothing more than extra time away from Trevor. "That champagne is getting warm."

Ethan took off. He went down the spiral staircase to the main floor and out the back door. The rain had let up by at least ninety percent and had sputtered to a light drizzle. It smelled like the ocean had come right up to and in the hotel; the sand covered the concrete pathway which made it lopsided beneath his feet. The storm had created a mini surge which pelted the entire outdoor area with the Atlantic floor. He was surprised there weren't fish gasping for life all around him—the rest of the outdoor area looked like Armageddon.

He saw the pavilion in his view and the bar where Dutch's coat had landed. Luckily, the wind didn't take it and it was still on the ground in a crumpled mess. He lifted it up, now twice its weight with water, and wrung it out. He fished out the room key and Dutch's phone, pressing the home button to make sure the thing still worked—he didn't want to have to go into the kitchen and ask them for a bag of rice—and luckily it turned on.

Then, he spied Allie's thrown bouquet, soaked with half of the petals missing, but he knew it was an important part of the whole wedding thing. Emma had agonized for months on the size, the colors, what would be in season, what would look good against the dresses and still complement the scenery for the pictures and align with the table settings—it drove him crazy, but he knew it was important to women. So, he picked it up to bring inside.

He stuck Dutch's phone in his pocket and headed to get the cigars.

Once he retrieved the cigars, he went to his room to search for the cutter. It was there somewhere. For Christmas last year, Emma had gotten him a whole mini-man's set—an engraved flask, a cigar holder and cutter, and a windproof lighter. He had checked everything at the airport, so he searched his golf bag, confident that they were tucked away in one of the pockets. He was right.

Considering the mess that the night had already become, he didn't want to lose one of his precious gifts, so he cut six cigars right there in the room, assuming Trevor's father and Uncle John would join. He'd noticed that Dutch had gotten one with a special ring that said "groom" for that fuckwad. A special cigar, just for him, that he would know was his. Because, of course, he was superior.

He left Dutch's soaked jacket on a chair by the desk to dry out, grabbed an extra pack of cigarettes that he found in his luggage, and did one more thing before he headed out.

39

ALLIE

The Wedding Day, 6:10 p.m.

Allie, Emma, and Fiona were again in the salon for a quick redo. Back in the fluffy robes from earlier in the day, their dresses were being hand-dried by a team with multiple hair dryers and paper towels. Unfortunately, that horrific C was paid for the day as a touch-up artist and was right there waiting to recreate everyone's earlier look, eradicated by the rain disaster. Allie felt warm and fuzzy inside because C had to basically start from scratch, since she'd danced with Dutch under the pounding storm.

"Remember, no Pamela Anderson sharpie liner," Allie said, just to mess with C.

C answered by not answering at all. She dabbed a moisturizing oil over Allie's fair skin before she applied primer and foundation. At the same time, a stylist had braided her wet hair into a million thin braids (okay, around twenty) and then blasted it with a hot dryer and diffuser.

"You're like an A-lister," Emma said to Fiona a few chairs away. "A whole team on call."

"Well," Fiona said while being pampered herself, "Trevor wanted to make sure the pictures were nice all the time. We got the beauty package that came with an additional eight hours of artists. You know my hair tends to get frizzy, and with the humidity it was worse. Plus, my face gets greasy. I didn't want to look like a disco ball in the wedding album."

"They have airbrushing for that," Allie said as she took a selfie while being worked on by two people. Instagram upload, *#ThreeDaysOfFun #A-Lister #MyBeautyRoutine*. Of course, the upload came *after* her filter. Airbrushing and all.

"I'm thinking about changing into my other dress, considering all this," Fiona said.

"What other dress?" Emma asked.

"Remember I sent you guys pictures of two dresses? I have that more casual one that I was going to change into for later in the reception anyway. I think this one got too soaked from the rain. It's not falling on me the right way."

"Oh. I didn't know you were changing dresses," Emma said. "Let me help you change. You know, finger-press the lines in the front and the back again."

"That would be terrific. Thanks."

Allie had little to no interest in helping Fiona change. It wasn't that she didn't want to be a good bridesmaid and friend, it was that she wanted to get back and mingle. With everyone. With Dutch.

When he joined her in the rain, she got giddy inside, and when he swooped her up in his arms, there was nowhere else she wanted to be. The look he gave her had her trembling, and she was sure if they didn't have a wedding to attend, he would've carried her right up to his suite where they'd stay for the rest of the night.

When the team unbraided Allie's hair and shook out the wavy curls left behind, she looked like a goddess. Her makeup was again (reluctantly) perfectly applied by C, and she couldn't wait to get back into her dress and see Dutch. She was the first one ready to leave since Emma was going to hang back and help Fiona. Allie needed a prosecco and some food in her stomach.

"I'll be in the cocktail room. I need to eat something," she said.

"Okay. We shouldn't be far behind," Emma said. "I just have to help her with her dress. We'll be out in about fifteen minutes. Can you give Ethan his jacket back? Tell him I'm almost done if you see him."

Allie grabbed it off a chair and gave a salute. "Aye aye, captain."

She glided down the corridor downstairs, through the lobby, and up the spiral staircase. The huge wall of glass that looked out to the ocean showed a mess out on the deck, like a mini hurricane had passed through. The torrential rain had stopped, and she swore the sun was begging to be let out to play behind a sea of gray skies. Close to the room that held cocktail hour, she decided to call her father first, and was thankful when he answered.

"Daddy!" she exclaimed.

"Hello, my Good Girl." His voice was hoarse as he called her the affectionate nickname. "Aren't you in the Miami?"

She smiled. Everything with him always had "the" in front of it. She'd always rolled her eyes at him when she was a teenager because of it, but she was going to miss it. Immensely.

"Yes, they just got married. There was a storm, and the wedding was outside. Me and the girls just fixed ourselves. I'm about to go into the cocktail hour and it'll be a late night, so I wanted to call you before you went to bed."

ı never need to fix yourself. You're always beau-

ıe had to hold the phone against her chest for a
moment so he wouldn't hear her blubbering. As quickly
as she put it there, she recovered and continued.

"Awww, thanks Daddy. Hey, I'm going to come by
tomorrow night after I land. I'll stay for a while."

"Really? I would love that."

She saw his smile through the phone, which was good,
because then he started a hacking cough that lasted a full
minute.

"Yes, really. I miss you."

"I miss you too." More coughing. "You have fun in the
Florida. Text me when you board tomorrow so I know
you're safe."

"I will. I love you Daddy."

"I love you too. I'll see you tomorrow, my Good Girl."

He made a kissy sound, and then hung up. It took her
a moment to get herself together before she was able to
proceed with her duties for the evening.

At the door to the cocktail room, there was light
music playing, and she heard indistinct conversations on
the other side. She swiveled her head from left to right,
looking for her friends, but she didn't see them.

She craned her neck toward the bar, at least expecting
to see Ethan, but he wasn't there, which was a miracle in
and of itself. She weaved through the people to search the
terrace when she saw Dutch speaking to Vanessa and Lillie
from college—former sorority sisters. They didn't keep in
touch other than Instagram and Facebook, and Allie didn't
really pay attention to what was going on in the lives of
people she didn't see regularly. They'd comment on her
posts every now and again—the ones labeled *I just wanted*

to go skiing! while she stood at the foot of the Alps, and the *What? I wanted a croissant!* from a café in Paris.

Having briefly spoken to them earlier, when she first got in from the storm and looked like a drowned rat, she knew that Vanessa Pashley was a married mother of one toddler, a cherub-faced little boy named August, and was about to publish her third novel. Smart, tall, and put-together, she was a grown up in every sense of the word. Her Ivy League education certainly paid off.

Allie's degree was wasted now.

Lillie Girard, however, had barely moved past college. She'd gotten her degree in criminal justice but didn't get into law school because her LSATs were terrible. She kept *meaning* to retake them, but her *so very busy* day job of working the donation counter at the Met and weekend job as a bartender at a club on the Lower East Side didn't afford her the proper time she'd need to study. That, and that it was beyond noticeable that she'd spent her law school money on implants, which had the stitches at the top of her too tight and too short red dress clinging for dear life. Her very single hand was on Dutch's arm, cradling his elbow—way too familiar. Not only that, when she talked, he listened intently. Allie hung back to observe as he dazzled Lillie with his smile, laughed at her stories, and offered her a drink from the nearby tray.

Vanessa had gone off to speak to someone else with her husband, but Dutch stayed with Lillie, barely noticing Allie's absence. Allie wondered selfishly why he wasn't looking for her—hell, she'd only been gone a half an hour. Only thirty minutes since he'd scooped her up in his strong arms and almost kissed her in front of all their friends. She thought he was exhibiting self-control, but maybe he'd already forgotten about last night.

"Hey, there you are," a voice said from behind her. Vee. "Stunning as usual." He smiled.

"Hey," she said, turning her full attention to him, pretending she didn't notice Dutch talking to that skank. "Where is everyone?"

"Ethan went to grab cigars that Dutch brought for all of us. He should be back soon, I think. And Dutch is over there." He pointed to Dutch and that little hussy, then laughed. "I talked to Lillie a bit in the lobby bar when you girls were all getting ready. She asked about his situation, so I told her he was ready and willing."

That wasn't Vee's fault, but she was still miffed. Allie clenched her fists together at her side, her manicured nails digging into her palms. She took Vee's hand and strolled over as Dutch casually laughed at yet another hilarious thing that the walking flotation device had to say. Upon their approach, Dutch's expression changed. His light eyes pierced into hers as he turned away from Lillie's conversation.

"Hey, there you are," Dutch said, giving Allie his full attention.

Immediately, she knew things were back to normal. He gave her a very quick smirk, a slight nod of the head, a widening of the eyes—all things that Vee wouldn't notice, and it went right over the bimbo's head as well. Allie almost couldn't decipher it, but she did—it was his unspoken plea to her.

"I was wondering what was taking you so long. But now I know. They were making you utterly gorgeous." Dutch lifted her hand and kissed the top.

Her anxiety about people knowing what happened between them must've bubbled to the surface, because immediately Dutch took Vee's hand and kissed the top as well.

"And don't you look smashing," he said with a laugh.

"Why thank you, Sir Dietrich," Vee said with a bow.

"So anyway," Lillie interrupted, like they hadn't made an appearance at all, "then she got all 'well I got stuck cutting up the lemons and the limes' and I was all like 'really, that wasn't my fault.' Like, maybe if she came in on time on Friday, she wouldn't have been stuck wasting time on a Saturday."

"Wow. That sounds like massive work drama," Allie interrupted with a twitch. She could barely contain her laughter at Lillie's cluelessness and had to turn and hide her face in Vee's chest. She felt it sputter against her cheek as if he were stifling his laughter as well. His grip tightened around her shoulders as if he could squeeze the funny out of both of them.

"So, like, are you guys a thing?" Lillie asked, pointing between Vee and Allie. "I can totally see it."

"Sometimes," Vee said, still riding the joke. "What happens in Miami stays in Miami."

"So true," said Allie. "So, so true."

"Hey." Dutch looked at his watch. "Don't we have that wedding party thing?" He looked over the top of her head. "See. Ethan has your bouquet. We should go."

She swiveled her head and saw Ethan, then decided to let Dutch off the hook. "Yeah. We came to get you, but I got enthralled in Lillie's story."

Dutch shot her a look, and she could see him holding his laughter in as well. He turned to Lillie. "I guess I'll see you later?"

"I'm here all night," Lillie said with a wink.

Vee and Allie were in hysterics ten feet ahead of Dutch when he caught up to them, and Allie clung onto Vee's arm to keep from falling.

"*I'm here all night,*" Allie mocked in a high-pitched voice.

"Come on. Leave him alone," Vee said loudly, so Dutch could hear, trying to keep a straight face. "He might have a cocktail emergency later."

"This is true. He likes to pop bottles."

"At least the garnishes will be covered. She seems very skilled in that arena."

"Hardy har. You guys having fun?" Dutch asked once they got to Ethan.

Ethan reached into his pocket and retrieved Dutch's phone and keycard. "Here you go. I left your jacket in my room. It was toast." He said with a chuckle, then yanked the half-wrecked bouquet from under his arm and handed it to Allie. "And I thought you might be missing this."

"Thanks Ethan." She meant it. She handed him his jacket in return. "Your timing is perfect. Lillie Girard cornered Dutch."

He shrugged. "Well at least she's a slam dunk tonight. Wedding sex. Awesome."

Dutch looked back where they were just standing, where Lillie had all but propositioned him for a night of no-strings-attached sex. Even Allie had to admit she was hot; she had that really shiny, thick hair that hung perfectly on her angular face. Sure, she was plastic, but as far as Allie knew, Dutch didn't discriminate when it came to sex.

Dutch crunkled his nose and twisted his face. "Nah. I want to call the girl I met last night."

"Woah. This is news. Dutch likes a girl!" Vee sang the last part.

He shrugged. "Kind of took me by surprise too. We'll see what happens."

And now Allie had more than one reason to get this wedding over with.

40

VEEJAY

The Wedding Day, 6:40 p.m.

Vee grabbed Emma as soon as she came back into the cocktail room.

"Hey. I need to talk to you," he said.

"Don't worry. I know Fiona changed. I took care of it; she's covered in the stuff. And I have enough left to pour into the glitter bin. It's almost over."

"It flippin' better be," Vee said, his voice somewhat threatening. He didn't mean to be.

He impatiently looked around the room and saw Trevor, with Fiona wrapped around him like ivy. Her mother, Uncle John, Jesse, Hector, and Mr. and Mrs. Vaughn were all huddled together with them, so proud, so loving. From the distance, he looked like a doting new husband.

Closeness. Fiona was all over him.

"Why isn't he reacting?" Vee asked Emma.

She pushed her eyebrows together. "What do you mean?"

"If Fiona is covered in peanut powder—why nothing? That time at lunch he went down convulsing, in seconds." He wiped his brow. "What if it's not enough?"

"It's going to be fine, Vee. I promise." Emma looked past him and shook her head. "We can't do this now. Ethan's on his way back. Listen. You have to trust me."

"Trust. Well. Sorry if that's a little hard for me right now."

"Wow." Tears sprang to her eyes. "This is what I was afraid of. Losing you anyway. But please, Vee, I'm begging you. If you ever cared anything about me, anything at all—please don't let me lose Ethan too."

Everything was always about Ethan. Sometimes, in the past, that bothered Vee. He was always there for Emma. Not that it wasn't reciprocated—she'd always been there for him too.

In fact, the longest "relationship" Vee'd had was with a girl named Jessica. It was for almost a year, and they'd only recently broken up when he'd slept with Emma. He'd rationalized their night of passion—of *baby making*—in his head: he was lonely, Emma was lonely, and they were both completely heartbroken. Add alcohol and common misery, and it was a recipe for the disaster he'd recently found out his life had become.

He'd rationalized it because he had to. It wasn't at all because he was in love with her. Nope.

Sometimes, he'd convinced himself of that fact so deeply that he thought he could have an actual relationship with Jessica back then. Well, that was doomed from jump street. He didn't even realize at the time how much the three of them went out together. How he'd blown Jessica off because Emma was sad about Ethan and needed him. He'd told himself she was like a sister, and that he was just being a good friend.

The whole truth was, back then, he'd do anything for her. *Anything.* Was that love? Devotion?

Utter stupidity?

He may have even carried that torch as he stood up next to Ethan at their wedding. He may have pushed it down when he helped her move in with Ethan after they got back from their honeymoon. He kept it away from the surface at all their get-togethers. And he may have even brought the feeling with him to Miami and felt it right until she ripped his flippin' heart out that morning.

As much as he *did* still care about her, until his own problem was taken care of, he didn't have time for her worries. He couldn't put her first—not anymore. It had gotten him nowhere, except in the dark. Sure, she'd said she didn't want to lose him, and he really wanted to believe that. To be honest, he wasn't going to pretend that he knew what it was like to be a woman—a woman in love with one man and pregnant with another's baby.

But part of him was needled that she'd slept with Trevor to further her own agenda. Sex, with that *asshole*. With her friend's fiancé. She was married!

Maybe he didn't know Emma at all. Maybe he never did, because now she was about to kill someone and never look back.

He ran his hand over his hair. "Yeah, I know. Everything is for Ethan and fuck my feelings." His words bubbled to two hundred degrees, just shy of boiling. He'd used that word again.

"What's gotten into you, Vee?"

"How dare you," he whispered, with a soft shake of his downtrodden head. "How dare you ask me that."

Ethan showed up to their standoff with a bottle of water for Emma. "Uh, is everything okay here?" he asked, sensing the tension.

"Yes," Emma said, slipping her arm around his waist. "I just want this wedding over with already. I just want to go home. I wish we'd never come here."

His face fell. "Babe, if this is still about the picture—"

"I think Emma's just being emotional," Vee cut him off, diffusing another awkward situation. "Maybe she is still sore about the picture. Let's just try to get through the next couple hours. We all get to go home tomorrow."

Vee had made a promise to Emma, and he was already waist-high in bull crap. He was the one who got her the peanuts. He was an accessory to what was about to happen.

"Hey, Ethan, where are those cigars?"

41

DUTCH

The Wedding Day, 6:55 p.m.

Outside on the terrace of the main reception room, Dutch stood with Vee, Ethan, and Trevor. Uncle John and Harrison Vaughn had declined the cigars, so it was just the four of them again.

Trevor and Fiona had already been introduced and had their first dance. She danced with her uncle to something by Christina Aguilera, and he danced with his mother to "Mr. Wonderful." What a douchebag. People still ambled about getting drinks, and there was going to be some light dancing before the speeches and the start of dinner.

When Dutch spoke to Ethan and Vee about giving a speech, they'd mutually agreed to say a few words each, and keep it generic. All the lies of *Fiona is so lucky to have found you*, and *Congratulations to the new Mr. and Mrs.!* in lieu of one long, drawn out speech by any of them. Plus, none of them even knew him well enough to say anything deep—there were no memories of them as children, as high school pals, as college buddies, and adults navigating their way through careers.

They were all strangers to Trevor.

Trevor held his left hand up, where his ring glistened off the overhead light. "I'm a married man. Can't get rid of me now!" he said with a chuckle.

"We don't mind. We'll keep you," Dutch said, still hoping for a way out of his mess.

Ethan held up the cut cigars. "This one is especially for you. It's got the groom ring on it." He handed it to Trevor.

"Thanks, buddy," he said, looking at Ethan, then switched his glance over to Dutch. "Actually, I should be thanking you. You're the one who got them for us. What a guy," he said, clapping Dutch on the shoulder, which still made him cringe. "God, I'm starving. All this socializing, I haven't been able to eat."

Ethan produced a windproof lighter and shoved it in front of the cigar at Trevor's mouth. He took a couple of deep puffs as Ethan stared. "Good?"

"Excellent," Trevor said with a cough.

The rest of them lit their cigars and got a couple of puffs in before the door opened, and Fiona appeared.

"Trevor, come on! They're doing Kool and the Gang now. You know I have the glitter bin set up for the Instagram video! Let's go!"

He looked back at the boys, coughed, held his throat for a moment as he crinkled his nose, and then raised his eyebrows. "Happy wife, happy life, am I right?"

They all placed the cigars in an ashtray outside and followed him in.

The unmistakable first notes of the song started to play, and everyone got on the dance floor. At the far end, there was a huge box filled to the brim with glitter—pink, silver, gold, purple, and blue. Everyone screamed as they threw it into the air, jumping up and down along with the song, and the videographer documented everyone dancing with glitter falling about the dance floor, glistening off the disco ball, and onto the ground. Everyone's clothes and hair were covered.

Dutch and his friends all danced together. It was the first really fun time he'd had all weekend. Well, the second, after his night with Allie. She looked so beautiful, like an angel, twirling around, smiling, glitter making the pink of her dress stand out against the blond of her hair. At one point, Dutch grabbed her hand and they jumped up and down together. She widened her eyes and then winked at him and grabbed Emma's hand with her other. She had Ethan's hand, who grabbed Vee, who grabbed Fiona, who grabbed Dutch. Just the six of them dancing the night away, like back in college. Even though Trevor hovered near them.

"This was a great idea!" Allie screamed above the loud music. "This is going to look awesome on Instagram! I bet you go viral!"

"Did you hear that, Trevor?" Fiona said to her new husband. "How cool!"

She was all smiles, but Trevor wasn't. *Typical*, Dutch thought. As a matter of fact, Dutch thought he looked disgusted as his lips curled, and he turned red. He coughed, then loosened his bowtie.

"Is he okay?" Dutch asked.

Something happened. Trevor was most certainly *not* okay, and he fell to the ground, convulsing.

"Trevor?" Fiona yelled, looking at him on the ground. "Trevor!" she screamed to no one. "Help!"

A crowd gathered around him, some still laughing, thinking he was doing some updated version of break dancing as he shuddered on the ground.

"What happened?" his mother Margot asked, looking on in fear.

"What's going on?" said one guest.

"Give him some room!" said another.

"Back up!"

"Help him!"

"Trevor!"

"What's happening?"

"Where's his EpiPen?" Fiona wailed, her face tear streaked. "Someone get my bag on the table!"

"I'll get it!" Allie shouted.

She ran over in such a panic that she knocked over the plates of cheese and glasses of champagne that were on the table and everything shattered on the ground. When she got back to Fiona, she emptied the bag next to her.

"Where the hell is his EpiPen?" Fiona screamed. "Someone help me!"

Dutch and his friends didn't know what to do. When they got closer, other guests told them to stay away and let him breathe, but that wasn't helping. Trevor's leg was shaking, and his lips blew up to twice their size. His mouth was wide open, gasping for air that never came as he clutched his throat. His eyes were bloodshot, full of fear, and Fiona slapped him on the face as he stopped moving.

"Is there a doctor here?" Fiona cried out through her tears. "Trevor! Wake up. Wake up, please wake up!"

Dutch didn't know if Trevor's face was red from the constant slapping or the fact that he hadn't had oxygen in minutes.

The DJ had finally cut the music, which made Fiona's voice ring through the hall like nails on a chalkboard. It went on for about three or four more minutes, and after a CPR attempt by one guest, the banquet manager for the hotel found their emergency EpiPen—but Trevor had stopped breathing quite some time ago. The EpiPen plunged into his leg for ten seconds, and then out, but it was no use jamming it into a cadaver. Fiona was on the floor, Trevor's head in her lap, and she panicked when he didn't respond to the injection.

"What's going on? Why won't he wake up?" Fiona screamed and cried, inconsolable, as he lay motionless.

Everyone stood and watched the chaotic scene. There were kitchen attendants cleaning up the glass mess that Allie left behind at the sweetheart table, there were people huddled and screaming, there were people crying, and some were taking pictures and video, because if it wasn't documented for social media, did it really happen? The wedding director ushered everyone out of the room as the paramedics came in. Fiona stayed behind with her family and Trevor's parents. All the guests were told to go wait in the lobby bar.

Dutch couldn't believe what he'd just witnessed. How horrific. How devastating.

How perfect.

He felt bad for thinking that. Not really, though.

They all gathered at the bar where Dutch gave a very quick explanation to the bartender on duty and asked for an entire bottle of vodka, quickly, and to charge whatever anyone wanted to his room.

Bottle in hand, Dutch went to one of the cocktail tables where his friends stood and placed the bottle there, then went back to retrieve an armful of shot glasses. He poured nine shots of vodka and offered them to anyone around them.

"I can't believe this just happened," Dutch said, slinging back a shot.

"Poor Fiona," Vee said, and then did his shot.

Ethan had his shot, and then poured another. Emma looked at the shot glass of vodka in front of her, surely contemplating her pregnancy, and then decided she needed it. No one said a word as she took her drink. Allie followed Ethan's lead by pouring another immediately after her first.

Another medic with a stretcher rolled by the lobby bar very quickly, into the ballroom. It was less than five minutes later when screams echoed and pressed against the closed doors.

"Oh my God," Dutch said. "Do you think…"

He didn't finish the question. There was no need. All heads sank low and turned away as the stretcher came out, body bag on top, and he was lifted into the waiting ambulance.

Trevor's grief-stricken parents got into the ambulance with the body to make an official identification and likely schedule an autopsy. Fiona's mother and Uncle John escorted her out of the ballroom, her makeup streaked all over her face. Her hair was destroyed, again, as they passed the lobby bar to take her up to the honeymoon suite. Two police officers walked behind them.

"Jesus." Fiona's brother Jesse was by their side, and helped himself to a vodka shot. "What the hell just happened?"

"My God. Was it an allergic reaction?" Allie asked.

"It had to be. He was allergic to peanuts, if I'm not mistaken," Emma said.

Jesse shook his head back and forth. "Nope. *Tree* nuts. Not peanuts," Jesse said, then poured himself another shot from the bottle on the table. "It's not the same thing at all. He was able to eat peanuts. I have no idea what happened."

Part Three

42

EMMA

The Wedding Day, 7:30 p.m.

"I think I'm going to be sick," Emma said. "I haven't had alcohol in a while. I never should've had that shot." It was the truth, but that wasn't the reason she wanted to be sick all over the bar floor. She put her hand over her mouth and turned toward the bathroom.

"Hey, wait. I'll come with you," Allie said.

"No. I don't want you to hear me retching. I'm going to be sick. Please, just stay here. Maybe have some water waiting for me when I get out. Thanks."

Emma's heels clanked against the marble floor as she rushed to the ladies' room. *I didn't kill him. He's not allergic to peanuts. It wasn't me and Vee.*

Who was it? What was it that killed him?

Who else wanted him dead?

Inside the bathroom, she didn't recognize the reflection that stared back at her. There was going to be an investigation. What if someone found out she'd *tried* to kill him? What if she really did, with Vee's help? What if his allergy changed, and suddenly peanuts were on the no-can-do list? It had been known to happen. What if, what if, what if… she could go on all night with what-ifs. But then, the really bad ones crept their way into her consciousness.

What if an investigation revealed that she'd slept with Trevor two months prior? What if an investigation found all the stuff that he had on her and Vee? What if, in an attempt to keep it all a secret, it was going to be exposed anyway?

She had to tell someone. Someone she could trust.

Allie. She had to tell Allie everything, from the beginning. Sleeping with Vee, the baby, sleeping with Trevor. God, just thinking about it made her sound like such a slut. Why didn't she just try to jump on Dutch later that night? A superfecta of fuck! Her stomach turned and twisted, like it was trying to squeeze the murderer out. She swung a metal stall door open and landed on her knees, clutching around the bottom of the toilet bowl. The vodka came up with the rest of the pickings she'd had at cocktail hour.

After exiting the stall, she rinsed her mouth out with water and used some of the mouthwash that was on the counter for patrons. She blew her nose, washed her hands, and then opened the door to spill the rest of her guts to Allie.

Of course, Vee was waiting.

"Are you okay?" he asked.

"We didn't do it. It wasn't us, Vee."

"I know." He looked past her, into the lobby bar and the sea of people waiting around in shock. Anyone passing wouldn't be able to tell if it was a wedding or a fancy funeral. Half the people were crying, the other half were drinking. All dressed up and nowhere to go. "But someone did it. I wonder if he was blackmailing anyone else."

That thought hadn't occurred to Emma. And why didn't it? Good grief, he probably had a file on everyone invited. It was probably why he had no friends.

Friends.

Trevor certainly had information on her and Vee. But, did he have files on her friends?

"Vee, I was thinking about telling Allie. About everything."

"No, Emma. You can't."

"What if he was blackmailing everyone? What if Dutch and Ethan were as happy to be a groomsman as you were?" Emma thought back. "Ethan has never explicitly said how much he liked Trevor. Usually I just got 'he's an okay guy' and stuff like that. He was happy for Fiona, and he seemed taken with the fact that you and Dutch were so eager to be in the wedding."

"But I wasn't."

Emma paused. "Maybe Ethan and Dutch weren't either."

They both turned their heads and looked into the bar. Dutch and Allie stood alone, smiling at each other, their fingers almost touching on the cocktail able. Emma stared at her two friends, deep in conversation, like no one else was there, like there wasn't just a death. It was two people she'd known for almost fifteen years, and it was the first time she sensed heat between them. "Wow. If I didn't know any better, I'd think those two were playing us. They look like they're in love or something." She turned her attention back to Vee. "But you're right. I can't tell Allie. I'm just afraid all this is going to come out anyway. After everything."

Ethan came back from the bar with more glasses, interrupting Allie and Dutch. From afar, Emma was able to see what Ethan couldn't. The way they jumped away from each other, the way they looked at each other and smiled behind his back when he poured another drink, the way she poked him in his arm when Ethan went to the bar to get some limes.

She'd ask Allie about it later. Right now, there were more pressing issues at stake. "Come on. We have to get back."

She took Vee's arm, a move that once felt so natural to her, and she felt him repel her. Of course, to the naked eye, everything was fine, and once back in the bar no one seemed to think that she and Vee were anything but the best of friends. She noticed a glass of water garnished with a lemon and took a sip. The hint of lemon refreshed her, but all she wanted was more alcohol.

"Thanks Allie," she said. "I feel much better already."

"Should we go up and check on her?" Allie asked.

"I don't think that's a good idea," Ethan said, returning to their table with a scotch.

"I think we should just go up. Maybe just me and Emma. We're bridesmaids," Allie said. "And her best friends. We should be there."

"Should we go wait in the groom's suite?" Dutch asked and when he saw Ethan's horrified face, he added, "Full bar up there. And I don't want to be around these people. They keep consoling me like Trevor was my best friend and I don't even know what to say to them anymore. You still have the key, right?"

Ethan softly nodded. "Maybe we should."

"Good luck," Vee said to Emma and Allie. "Take care of our girl. Just remember all the nice things about Trevor with her."

Emma took that as a warning to keep her mouth shut.

43

ALLIE

The Wedding Day, 7:45 p.m.

In the elevator, Allie pushed the wrong button.

"Shit. I pushed my floor. Not the honeymoon suite," she said as a second button lit up underneath her index finger. "Butterfingers today."

"Yeah," Emma said. "So, you and Dutch looked cozy."

She shrugged. "And? So did you and Vee. What's that supposed to mean?"

Point taken.

"I can't believe he's—" Emma had trouble saying the word. "I can't believe Trevor is dead."

Once off the elevator, the heaves and the wails could be heard from down the hall. They both took small steps, neither knowing what to say or do when they got there. Their arms were linked as they walked in tandem. Stopped at the door, neither knocked, waiting for the other to do it.

Finally, Allie took a deep breath, let it out with an audible sigh, and rapped on the door.

"Who's that?" someone said. Allie thought it was Fiona's uncle.

"Don't let anyone else in," a female voice said. Could've been Fiona's, but it was hard to tell. Probably her mother.

There was movement at the door, then a muffled whisper. The door opened, the chain still secured in place.

"Hi girls. Fiona doesn't feel like having company," her uncle said. "Can you come back later?"

"We just wanted to see if we can help," Emma said, then moved her face closer to the door and raised her voice. "Fiona, it's just me and Allie. Please let us in."

"She's talking to the cops," Uncle John said.

"Actually, maybe they can help," a deep voice said from inside.

Uncle John closed the door. The chain jingled and scraped, and then he opened it.

"Don't upset her," he whispered. "It's been a harrowing evening, as I'm sure you know." He looked back at his niece; someone he'd practically raised as his own. "We all really liked Trevor."

Allie detected something robotic in his voice that said he liked Trevor as much as she did. She'd been detecting a lot of that of late.

Allie and Emma looked toward the couch in the main room, and Fiona was there, in a heap, leaning on her mother's shoulder. She still had her second dress on, but her hair was out of the former updo, now twice its size, and her face looked like an artist's palette. A kindergartener's outside-the-lines mess, really. Her mother, Susan, sat on one side of the couch, with a T-shirt thrown over her gown and her hair let out of the swirled updo it had been in earlier. A cop was on the other side, unsure of what to say.

"Hi. I'm Allie Whitton," Allie said, hand out for a shake, taking charge and introducing herself to cop number one, the one who was standing just off the entryway.

He shook her hand, wrote something down on a notepad, and nodded. "Detective Morris. That's Gomez," his deep voice boomed as he gestured toward the other gentleman on the couch. Then he looked curiously at Emma.

"Emma Pierce," she said, and shook his hand. "What can we do to help?"

Allie sized up Detective Morris. He was very tall, almost Dutch's height, and his buzz cut gave away his career choice before anyone had to ask. He was in plain clothes, black pants and a black polo, his shield worn on his belt buckle. His eyes were a soft brown like Vee's, but his hair was almost the same shade of platinum that she currently sported against her will. He was tan and fit, and probably hadn't hit forty yet, but was close.

No wedding ring. Of course, that was just a reflex. So was reapplying her lip gloss, which she did in front of everyone.

"Well, first let me say how sorry I am that you lost your friend," he said.

Allie rubbed her newly shined lips together, but other than that, she and Emma were like stone, and his eyes shifted between them.

"Right. Thanks," Allie said, quick to diffuse the mood. Then she pushed a tear out and dramatically wiped it away. "It's been a hard evening. Poor Fiona."

"How well did you know the deceased?"

This guy was all business, and Allie had to convince him she had no ill will toward Trevor. She certainly didn't need a detective looking into her past. Thankful as she was that Trevor had dropped dead, she'd hate to think her friends would find out the truth anyway.

She couldn't let her father find out. That's all she cared about.

"To be honest, not all that well. They didn't date for very long before she moved to Miami with him so none of us ever really got to know him," Allie offered.

"Huh." More writing in the notepad. "But weren't his groomsmen friends of yours from college?" He flipped back a few pages. "Dietrich Von Ryan? Veejay Rahna? Ethan Pierce?" He looked at Emma curiously. "Yours?"

"Yes. Ethan is my husband," she said, and put her hand on her abdomen. "We're pregnant with our first."

Strange thing to say, Allie thought.

"Congratulations." The detective raised his eyebrows. "So, the guys knew him enough?"

"Oh, we can't answer for them. I think everyone just wanted to support Fiona," Allie said.

Allie took a hard look at Fiona—a shell of her former self, which was already a shell of her former self. God, she didn't know what to do. The detective seemed hell-bent on getting information, but there was nothing to give. No one had any information to give him. Trevor's death was a fluke. Right?

"There was a bit of an altercation last night, I heard," he said, then looked at Emma. "Some commotion at the rehearsal dinner?"

Emma turned white but recovered quickly. "I overreacted to something. It was stupid girl stuff."

This time he raised one eyebrow. "That's not what it sounded like."

Emma made a gesture toward Fiona and then nodded her head to the corner of the room, and he followed her. Allie did for good measure as well. She had no idea what Emma was going to say to him.

"Look," she whispered. "Everyone was drinking, and I found out that my husband hooked up with her when we were broken up. It was a hundred years ago, and I don't even care. I just overreacted. She's one of my best friends. She's *still* one of my best friends. It was just the pregnancy hormones rearing their ugly head."

"Can we sit with Fiona for a bit?" Allie interrupted. "We really came up here to be with her. She just lost her husband a few hours after her wedding. She needs us."

"Of course," he said, his face softening, remembering why they were there. "Do you know where I can find the groomsmen?"

"Yeah, they're either in the bar downstairs, or in the groom's suite on the other side of the hotel."

"Gotcha."

His notebook snapped closed with a popping sound, and then he whistled softly over to Gomez, who stood. Detective Gomez had that quintessential detective look to himself as well. He wore the same outfit as Detective Morris, but his pants were navy, and his polo was white. His shield hung on a chain around his neck, and his hair was cropped to a buzz. Dark-framed, rectangular glasses bookended his brown eyes. When he caught Detective Morris's stare, he gave Fiona a soft pat on her shoulder and then slipped past her and her mother. He nodded to Allie and Emma before he and Detective Morris closed the door behind them.

Allie and Emma awkwardly stood a few feet from the couch, no one speaking a word. Fiona's mother looked up at them through tears, her heart obviously broken for her daughter, already knowing what it was like to lose a husband.

"Come on, Sue. Let's grab a coffee," Uncle John said. "Give the girls some time alone."

"Are you all right, pumpkin?" Susan asked Fiona.

Her head lifted from Susan's shoulder, with the left side's eyelash strip clinging for dear life from her undone upper lid. Her face was tear streaked, her nose red and puffy. There were at least twenty used tissues piled on the table in front of her, with a few more scattered on the ground around the couch.

"Yeah. At least my friends are here," she said, grabbing another tissue.

Her mother stood and then bent to kiss her on the head and held her face under her chin. "I'll be right back. I guess John and I should talk to some people downstairs."

"Don't let anyone else come up," she said with a sniffle. "Please. Just tell everyone to go home."

Susan and John exchanged a pitiful glance, and Susan put her hand on Allie's forearm as she strode past.

"Thanks for coming up," she whispered. "She's a mess. I can't believe it myself. It's too much," she said, distressed, looking back at Fiona one more time. "I mean, after losing my husband—her father—it's just so…"

"I know. It's okay," Allie whispered back, not wanting to hear any more about death. After all, her father was on his deathbed, and she'd be in the same position soon. Mourning. It was too much to think about. Too much tragedy. "Go take a break with your brother-in-law. We'll take care of her."

"Thank you."

Susan looked at herself in the mirror next to the door and rubbed at the black liner that had collected under her eyes like a raccoon. She licked her index finger on its side and then rubbed again until her circles became peach. She smoothed her wispy, light hair back before they exited the suite, clearly not caring that she had a cat T-shirt on over her gown. There were more important things to attend to.

Allie plunked on one side of Fiona and Emma on the other. The three of them cried together, and even though Allie hated Trevor, she'd never wanted her friend to be in this kind of pain. Even though she helped cause it. Why didn't she just come clean to Fiona in the first place?

Right. Her father.

"I'm so sorry," Emma said. "I feel like an asshole saying that, but I really don't know what else to say. This is so tragic."

"I know," Allie said, wrapping her arms around Fiona, a move that Emma followed. "It's crazy. I can't believe he's—"

"Don't say it," Fiona warned. "I just don't understand," she said, separating from the two of them and grabbing another tissue. "He was dancing. What could it have been? His reaction is usually pretty immediate. I don't understand." She blew her nose in a squeaky, stuffy, old-man-with-a-handkerchief way.

Emma looked at Allie and widened her eyes, then she got up and went into the bathroom, eventually returning with two more boxes of tissues.

"Can you guys stay here tonight, with me?" Fiona asked. "I don't know how I'm going to sleep alone on my wedding night. We didn't even get to—consummate. Am I even really married?" She began to cry again, heavily, before she realized her bluff. "Actually, I'm not married. I'm a widow. Already."

Allie tugged a tissue out of the dispenser that was on Fiona's lap and handed it to her. Yes, she had to stay with Fiona—it meant she couldn't stay with Dutch. Whatever happened between them would have to be taken back to New York.

Fiona stunned her with her next statement. "This whole thing makes me wonder. He had some bad information on my Uncle John. Something from a long time ago, when he was in college. I saw some papers once when I was cleaning Trevor's office. You don't think my uncle had anything to do with this, do you?"

"Your uncle?" Emma said, rather unsurprised. "What was it?"

"Shit," Fiona said, and tears fell again. "Don't tell anyone, guys. You have to swear to keep this a secret."

Allie raised her hand to God, one over her heart, while Emma nodded.

"He and a couple of friends were caught in a cheating ring. Running it, really. And he was still able to graduate with honors. My grandfather—he had power at that school." Her head shook slowly. "I don't know how Trevor got the information since everything was sealed. You know all about his political aspirations, and Uncle John seemed to do whatever he said. It always made me wonder who was the powerful one in the room."

Allie gulped. "That's all you saw? Papers about your uncle?"

"Yeah. Trevor came into the office, and I pretended I was dusting around it. I never asked him about it, and I never saw them again. Ignorance is bliss, I guess." She wiped her nose on her arm and sniffled. "What if he was blackmailing him?"

"No," Emma went on. "Trevor and your uncle got along so well. And your uncle never would've let you marry him if he did that. You're his brother's daughter." Then she chuckled. "Blackmail. This isn't a movie."

A light bulb went off in Allie's brain. Emma seemed to be talking Fiona out of telling the cops anything about blackmail. Like she didn't want the authorities to look into anything that had to do with Trevor. Truth was, it did sound fishy. Uncle John certainly had enough power. But Emma persisted. *It was just a freak accident! Nothing to see here!*

Allie was thankful, but couldn't help but wonder—did that mean that Trevor had something on Emma as well? Something she didn't want found out?

44

ETHAN

The Wedding Day, 8:00 p.m.

Ethan swiped his keycard at the door to the groom suite and Dutch and Vee followed him in. They all tossed their jackets onto a chair near the door and let out a sigh. Ethan grabbed a beer for himself from the mini fridge and then tossed one to Vee and one to Dutch. He put a cigarette in his mouth and motioned outside. They nodded.

The open door let in a wonderful breeze—it was amazing how the storm brought the change in the weather. Before the reception everything was too hot and muggy and awful, and now that it was over, everything was perfect again.

Trevor was oppressive heat, thunder, lightning, gale-force winds, and torrential rain.

And now he was gone.

Ethan sucked the smoke into his lungs and closed his eyes for a moment, savoring the light-headedness, and then blew it out. He was going to miss smoking.

"I'm quitting, you know," Ethan said. "As soon as this trip is over. I have to do it for Emma and the baby."

"It's disgusting. You should do it anyway," Vee said. "No matter what happens."

Ethan scraped a chair back and sat down and motioned for the guys to do the same. "We should relax while we can. The night isn't over."

Ethan guessed that in minutes, the suite would be stormed by cops. Which is why he made sure Dutch and Vee were comfortable. He knew Fiona's diary, or proof of what was in it, was somewhere inside the suite, and he had to find it and destroy it. If Trevor *died* and the rest of it came out anyway, he would be beside himself with grief. He'd never want Emma to know that there were feelings involved, no matter how fleeting—or long gone—they were. Looking back, they didn't even matter. Emma mattered. They weren't even his feelings.

Ethan sucked his beer down quickly, giving him a slight buzz after the shots he'd inhaled downstairs. He smashed his cigarette in the ashtray.

"I have to take a leak, and I'll bring back more beers. Stay here. I'll be right back."

Ethan slid the door closed behind him, grateful that Dutch and Vee didn't move—they were enjoying the peace that came with Trevor's death. They'd barely reacted either, which made Ethan curious—but not curious enough to bring it up. He had a mission.

In the bedroom, he went right for the closet and found the safe locked. Shit. What could the code be? He didn't want to get caught putting in one wrong combination after another, so he tried to think. His wedding date? Ethan punched in 1-2-1-4. Nothing. Of course not— Trevor had no heart. He had to think like Trevor.

"Nineteen ninety-five! Best year ever."

The Devils' first Stanley Cup year. *Please, please, please work*. With a shaking hand, he hit the buttons.

1—

9—
9—
5—

The wheels turned, and the safe popped open. Inside were a bunch of thumb drives, all labeled.

"John Hawthorne"—Uncle John? Holy shit. *"Cameron Trivett"*—who? *"Gregory Hanson"*—who? *"Brandon Weatherly." "Beth Brooks." "Caleb Jackson."* Who, who, and who?

And then one that made his heart stop.

"The Bridal party."

Fuck.

There was no physical diary, but maybe he was right earlier, and Trevor had the digital copy on the thumb drive. Ethan tucked it in his pocket and locked the safe back up—1—9—9—5. Then he found an undershirt on the floor of the closet and wiped down the buttons. No fingerprints.

He headed to the bathroom, sweat beading at his forehead, and he splashed water on his face. What else was on that thumb drive? Was he threatening everyone?

Did Ethan want to know what was on there? *Emma.*

His phone dinged near the door—he'd had it in his jacket. There was a text from Emma.

Where are you? The cops are looking for you guys.

Ah, crap. It was starting. He tapped back.

We're in the suite. Have them come up here.

She wrote back: *I told them to check the bar and then the suite. Hey, if they ask about last night, I told them I found out you hooked up with Fiona a hundred years ago and I overreacted. So don't lie to them. Don't cause an issue where there isn't one.*

Shit. He took the thumb drive out of his pocket and stuck it in his sock, at the bottom of his foot, and put his shoe back on. He tried to walk normally back out to the terrace.

"Hey, guys," he said to them through the open door. "Emma texted me. She said the cops were going to the bar to look for us, and then they were going to come up here."

"I don't know what information they think *we* have," Dutch said.

"Exactly. But let's show them there's nothing to see here. When are they coming?" Vee asked.

And then there was a knock on the door.

45

VEEJAY

The Wedding Day, 8:15 p.m.

Vee stood up. "Well, how's that for timing?"

Ethan lit another cigarette and slid into a chair, rooting himself outside. "I'm not answering it."

Vee looked at Dutch, who looked at the ocean.

"I'll get it," Vee said, rolling his eyes.

He knew the cops were on the other side, but he also knew he didn't do anything wrong. Right? Just act natural, he told himself as he looked through the peephole and indeed, there were two detectives standing there—one had his shield around his neck. Vee opened the door.

"Hey," he said, opening the door wide and gesturing for them to come in. "I'm Veejay Rahna."

"I'm Detective Morris, this is Gomez," he said, pointing over to the shorter one with a pen that he'd already produced in one hand while a notebook was in the other.

Vee shook Gomez's hand, since Morris's were both occupied as he flipped back a couple of pages.

"Is there an Ethan Pierce and a Dietrich Von Ryan here?"

"Yeah, they're out on the terrace. Do you want to come out?"

"I'd rather have them come in. It's dark out."

He wanted to read their faces.

"Sure, I'll get them." Walking at a regular pace, he made his way to the terrace door and opened it, then stuck his head outside. "Hey, guys, there are a couple of detectives here. Come on inside."

He turned back, and Morris and Gomez were each already sitting on a couch. Vee grabbed all three of their tux jackets from the chair by the door and placed them on the sideboard near the bar; he skidded the chair to the sitting area and sat down. Dutch and Ethan entered the room.

"Ethan Pierce," he said, and shook their hands.

"Dutch. Dietrich. Von Ryan," Dutch said, getting confused by his own name as he shook their hands.

Dutch sat next to Morris, and Ethan sat next to Gomez.

"A real tragedy tonight, huh?" Morris said, looking between all three of them.

"It was unbelievable," Vee said, shaking his head. He had an awful itch on his neck, but he didn't dare attempt to scratch it. "Horrible."

"Right. Poor Fiona," Ethan said.

"What the hell even happened?" Dutch asked.

"Well, that's what we're trying to figure out. It was probably his allergy, but we want to cover our bases. We spoke with the girls, with your wife." Morris looked at Ethan. "She said you guys didn't know him all that well?"

"Well," Vee interrupted, "he—Trevor—he asked us to be groomsmen when we were all at a brunch together. All

263

of us, and Allie and Emma and Fiona. It was the day he proposed. It was really nice."

Detective Morris must be writing shorthand because there was no way he otherwise got all of that in the three seconds before he looked up. "He proposed in front of all of you?"

"Yeah. She'd moved to Miami with him about a month before that and they were up for a visit. I guess he wanted her friends involved in the proposal since she missed us so much."

"Ah," he said. "Did you know he was going to propose that day?"

"Nope," Vee said quickly. "Total surprise."

"Any of you know?" Morris looked at Ethan and Dutch, who both shook their heads.

"I ordered a bottle of champagne and we celebrated once he was okay," Dutch said.

"What do you mean?"

"Oh. He had an allergic reaction. It was quick—Fiona had an EpiPen. He was treated at the scene, and he was fine. I mean, they took him to the hospital for observation, but he lived."

"Yeah," Ethan said. "A guy at work is allergic to peanuts too. I didn't think it could actually kill you. I wonder if Trevor knew what was happening. Poor guy. Jesus."

"Except he wasn't allergic to peanuts," Morris said. "You had a bit of history with the bride, yes?"

All eyes flew to Ethan, and he closed his eyes and held up a hand, nodding in a self-deprecating way. "Yeah, yeah. We hooked up once. Emma and I were broken up. It was years ago. At least five. Maybe more."

"Mmm hmm," he said, jotting down notes. "Any lingering feelings?"

"For Fiona?" Ethan almost said it as a laugh. "No feelings to linger. It was a one-time bad call with a familiar face on five shots of tequila."

"Fiona's EpiPen went missing," Gomez said. "She said she had it in her purse before the ceremony."

Vee tried not to squirm. He remembered that Emma said she'd take care of it, and she'd clearly kept her word. It probably had been easier in the bedlam after the rain—Fiona was completely frazzled with getting her hair and makeup redone and changing her dress. He made sure his expression didn't change. Wait, were they looking for that? Should he scratch his neck now? Cough? Do jumping jacks?

"Right. She said it wasn't there when he first went down. But she *did* open her bag and dump it out everywhere. Could it have skidded away in the chaos? Maybe it's under a table or something?" Vee made sure they knew he was being helpful.

"We've reviewed the video of when it happened. The blond—Allie Whitton—brought the bag over and Fiona opened and emptied it immediately. Ms. Whitton getting the bag and Fiona turning it inside out is all in video. It didn't skid away. It was never in there," Morris said, then reached into his back pocket and took out three cards and set them on the table. "Well, if you can think of anything else, please call me. And I'm very sorry about your friend."

"Thanks," they all muttered in their own grave way.

They all shook hands and then the two detectives left. That was it. Home free. Ethan stood by the door with his right eye trained on the peephole and turned back into the room when the detectives got on the elevator.

"Okay guys, we need to talk," Ethan said.

"About what?" Vee asked.

"I need to know something."

Ethan's stare was intense. He looked back and forth between them both like it was the first time he'd seen them, but he didn't say anything.

"Well, don't keep us in suspense, man," Dutch said. "What is it?"

Ethan leaned over and took off his shoe, then his sock, and shook it until something fell out onto the carpet. It was small, made of metal and plastic. Vee recognized it immediately as a thumb drive.

"What's that?" he asked.

"I need to know something," Ethan said again, then picked it up and held it up. "How did you guys really feel about Trevor?"

He knows! Vee thought.

The whole scheme of the last five months was all coming crashing down. Vee must've turned lily white imagining that Ethan knew about his accident. About him and Emma. And Ethan saw it on him, sniffed it out like a shark sensing blood in the water from a mile away.

"Do you want to go first, Vee?" Ethan asked with a direct stare.

"What is that, Ethan?" he asked instead of giving himself up immediately.

"Honestly, I don't know. I just know it's about us. *All* of us."

The fear lifted immediately. Not only did Ethan *not* know about his accident, but he also didn't know about him and Emma. And the baby.

"Where did you get it? What's going on?"

"Don't worry about that. I just know we're all in some sort of trouble, and it all revolves around Trevor."

Dutch shifted uncomfortably, and Vee wanted to make sure they were all together when the truth came out. Safety in numbers.

"Do you know what I really think? I think we need Emma and Allie here before we start," Vee said. "If it's really about all of us, we should *all* be here."

46

EMMA

The Wedding Day, 8:30 p.m.

> Me and Vee and Dutch need you and Allie
> to come to the groom's suite. ASAP, babe.
> It's an emergency. Don't tell Fiona.

That's what Emma's text from Ethan said, and she panicked. What had the detectives said to them? She didn't want to say anything out loud. As it was, the last hour had been her and Allie listening to Fiona cry.

First, they'd gotten her to change into a T-shirt and track pants, and they used makeup wipes to erase the colors that had dripped down her face. Allie spritzed her with an Evian mist that she'd gotten at Sephora to keep her skin dewy and hydrated, and then they'd pulled her hair back into a ponytail. Fiona looked so tiny and frail, as if in the last two hours her clothes had outgrown her.

She seemed to feel a tad bit better, enough to grab a bottle of champagne to drink away the pain. But as soon as they popped the top off, her crying resumed, saying it was supposed to be their wedding night champagne and she couldn't drink it without Trevor.

Allie clearly didn't have that problem and slugged it down, glass after glass. When Allie was distracted by Fiona, Emma snuck sips where she could. She almost didn't care if they caught her and chastised her about drinking while pregnant. She wasn't pregnant, and she didn't feel like she could stay sober any longer during this chaos.

When Ethan's text came in, Emma widened her eyes at Allie and held her index finger to her lips in a *shhh* gesture, then nodded at her phone. She held it up behind Fiona's head and Allie read it. She mouthed *what the fuck*, then turned her attention back to Fiona and raised her shoulders at Emma, like, *what are we going to do?*

Emma tapped back, *We'll try. Her mom should be back any second. We can't leave her alone.*

He wrote back immediately. *The sooner the better.*

Emma's eyes welled up because she could only imagine what he wanted. She prayed he hadn't found out about her and Vee. The sickness churned in her stomach until she couldn't take it anymore, and she excused herself to the bathroom, where she was sure Allie and Fiona heard her throw up, again, for the second time that day. She rinsed with Fiona's mouthwash and then went back to join them on the couch.

"Hey, can you text your mom and see when she's coming back?" Emma asked. "Since we're having a slumber party, I want to go change into my nightclothes and wash the day off my face. I'm sure Allie feels the same way."

"Yeah, that's a good idea," Allie said.

"Why don't you go now, and Allie can go when you come back?" Fiona said.

"Oh. Okay. Sure." *Shit.* She widened her eyes at Allie again, who returned the expression.

Like a gift from God himself, the lock on the front door turned and Susan and Uncle John came back in with coffees and a tray of cookies and assorted desserts.

Susan placed them on the table. "We got these from downstairs in case you guys were hungry," she said. "We had a Venetian hour after—for after. I didn't want to cut the cake. I don't know what—I thought—I know it's all junk, but I thought—"

"Thank you, Mrs. Hawthorne," Emma said. "I'm actually starving. We're going to stay here tonight, so Allie and I are going to change, and we'll be back shortly." She grabbed a cookie. "Thanks so much for this. I can't wait to dig in when we get back. Allie?"

"Yeah, thanks so much. Let's get going. The faster we leave, the faster we can get back."

When the door clicked closed behind them, Emma texted Ethan that they were on their way.

"What do you think is going on?" Allie asked. "Are the cops still there? Do they know something?"

"I don't know," Emma said. "All I know is that they want us there. I'm a little freaked out."

"Why? You didn't do anything."

"Allie—" She stopped. "Allie, I'm afraid of something."

"What? What's wrong?"

"Trevor—he—" Emma shook her head back and forth, like she was shaking the lies out of her skull. She didn't want to betray Vee, but self-preservation got the best of her. Again. "He knows something about me. Something that no one else knows."

Allie stopped and grabbed Emma's arm. "What?"

Emma's eyes watered as Allie looked at her with concern. "I don't know what to do. I'm going to lose Ethan."

"What did you—you know what? Don't tell me." Allie had her hand up in defiance. "I don't care what you did. It's not my business. But I want you to answer a question honestly. Can you do that?"

"Yes. I'm tired of lies."

"Did Trevor ask you to push this wedding on Fiona in order to keep whatever it is a secret?"

Emma's eyes went wide with recognition. "You too?"

Allie nodded. "Me too. And I don't care what you did. But I'll be damned if you're going to lose your husband because of that asshole. Let's go."

47

DUTCH

The Wedding Day, 8:45 p.m.

Ethan reentered the room after having a cigarette, waving his phone in front of his face. "The girls are on their way. Emma just texted me," he said and slid the door closed behind him.

Dutch's eyes were trained on the flash drive. He knew what was on there—a file of him, acting like an obnoxious prick and practically murdering his old love. Trevor's old love.

Even worse: What *else* was on that flash drive? Ethan said it was all of them. Was there something worse than pictures of Ethan with Fiona? What else did he do? And Vee? And Emma?

And Allie?

Was he about to get involved in something he couldn't handle? He still didn't know where he stood with her. They couldn't exactly talk about it tonight.

"Hey. Should we look at it?" Dutch asked.

"At this?" Ethan held it up. "No way. Wait until the girls get here. I think we all need to talk about Trevor."

And just like that, there was a knock at the door. Ethan opened it to his wife and Allie.

272

"Hey," he said, and pecked Emma on the forehead.

"What's going on?" she asked. "What's the emergency?"

"Sit down," Ethan demanded of them both.

Dutch was surprised to see them follow his command. Emma sat next to Vee, who hadn't said much all night and barely looked in Emma's direction. Allie sat next to Dutch. Ethan stayed standing, the man in charge, his hands in his pockets, pacing back and forth. The flash drive was in one of his hands, hidden from all of them.

Where did he even get it?

"Okay," Ethan began. "We all need to talk, and we all need to be honest. Vee and Dutch, I'm going to ask you something first, and I need total honesty." His demand was answered with silence, which he probably took as compliance. "Why did you agree to be a groomsman today?"

No one spoke. Emma started to cry, and Vee held her hand. Emma's reaction let Dutch know that she was knee-deep as well.

"Anyone?" he asked again.

"I'll go." Vee raised his hand. He took a deep breath. "I was forced to. I flippin' hated Trevor."

Everyone let out a scoff at the same time. It was a mixture of relief and anger.

"Listen to me!" Vee said loudly. "Yes, he badgered me into doing this. He knows things. I thought it would be easy, like, shut up and do what he says, and it'll all be over. But that was easier said than done." He paused, leaned forward, and twiddled his thumbs. He never looked directly at his friends. *Shame.* "He threatened me five months ago, right before they got engaged. His relationship was falling apart. He wanted to marry into her family. And he told me to talk her into it."

Silence fell upon the room. No one asked why he agreed to the nonsense. They didn't have to. They all did the same thing.

"I think he had something on all of us." Ethan removed the flash drive from his pocket. "This was in the safe."

"What do you mean? What is it?" Allie asked.

"When did you even find that?" Dutch asked nervously, recognizing it. *Don't look at it.*

Ethan looked at Dutch. "Just before. When we all got here. After he died." Pause. "So, what does this all mean?"

"How did you get in the safe, man?"

Ethan pinched the top of his nose. "I figured out the code. He was as one dimensional as he seemed. And this wasn't the only one in there. He had dirt on so many other people." He shook his head back and forth in disbelief. "I left the rest of them in there. They're not our business."

"But why?" Emma asked him. "Why did you break into his safe? What were you even looking for?"

He blew enough air out of his lungs that he had to have lost two pounds. "Because he threatened me five months ago too and told me that I'd better be in the wedding to show how much I liked him, because he wanted Fiona to think that anything bad about him was in her head. And he threatened me with *this* all weekend. The Fiona stuff." He waved the thumb drive around in the air. "And now I'm sure he was doing it to all of you too," he said, pointing at his friends and his wife. "Look, we all need to be on the same page here. Someone better start talking." He looked at Vee. "Someone else, anyway."

"He threatened me," Allie offered in a whisper.

He did? Dutch thought. What did Allie do?

Ethan closed his eyes. "With what?"

Allie turned defiant. "What did he threaten *you* with? Or *you*?" She looked at Vee, who put both of his hands up in defense. "What does it matter? Apparently, we all suck."

"Hey! Let's not turn on each other!" Emma shouted. She looked at Dutch. "Well?"

What could he do? He didn't want to say it out loud, so he nodded.

Ethan looked at his wife. "And you too?"

Her head hung low. "Yes." Her voice was barely audible.

Tears fell over Ethan's eyes, and Dutch knew the thought of someone like Trevor threatening his wife made him see red, but at the same time, he knew Ethan wanted to know the truth. Emma was a saint. What could she possibly have done that merited *blackmail*?

Ethan immediately went to his wife and leaned over and took her hands. "With what, babe? What did you do?"

"Guys!" Dutch shouted. He couldn't take it anymore. No one needed to know what Emma did; it was irrelevant. "Look man, does it really matter what any of us did?" The guilt had been ripping him apart the entire weekend, and he was sure everyone else had the same feeling. "Roger was the only one who stood up to Trevor, and we didn't. We let that asshole control us, and we repaid our only friend with morals by ditching him." The shame ate at him, enough so that he started not to care what happened between Roger and his mother. Mostly.

He'd fix it with Roger—he vowed to—but still, he couldn't let them find out what he did to Kelsey. That

Kelsey was involved with Trevor. That Trevor black-mailing all of them was because of Dutch. Everyone remained quiet, contemplating their involvement in the sham of a marriage, their own hidden demons, and, of course, Roger.

Ethan was vulnerable as he sat by Emma, and Dutch knew that. In one fell swoop, Dutch was up and off the couch and in record time had the flash drive in his hand. "You know what I think of this?" He held it up for everyone to see. "This is nothing but trouble."

And just like that, he dumped it in a glass of water that sat on the table.

"Jesus Christ, Dutch!" Ethan made a move for it and Dutch blocked him.

"Leave it alone, man."

Dutch's eyes backed up his words. Then he looked at it plunking to the bottom of the glass and thought maybe someone would end up sticking it in a bag of rice and fixing it like they do with iPhones. No way. He took it out, took off his shoe and smashed it with the heel into clanking shards which flew in every direction. Emma and Allie both shrieked and covered their faces. Ethan lurched and Vee stood up between his two friends.

"Pick up the pieces," Allie said, not missing a beat, immediately on her hands and knees. "Flush them down the toilet."

"Has everyone gone insane?" Ethan asked. "What was so bad that we all sold Fiona out? I feel like an asshole."

Dutch sympathetically put a hand on Ethan's shoulder. "Leave it alone, man," he said again.

Dutch didn't want to leave Allie alone on the floor, so he bent next to her and picked up the silver metal pieces and placed them on the table as Ethan, Emma, and Vee watched in silence. When they were confident that they got them all, Dutch swept them into his left hand and headed to the bathroom. Allie followed him.

"Dutch?" she said when they were alone.

He turned to look at her, defeat all over his face. Now she knew there was something wrong with him, something worth blackmail. Well, it was fun while it lasted.

One more kiss, though.

He placed the broken pieces of the thumb drive on the counter, grasped her face in his hands, and pressed his lips to hers quickly. It was a panicked, desperate kiss. When he pulled back, she tugged at the front of his shirt and went for one more, this time more passionate.

"We have to stop," Dutch whispered into her lips. "Everyone is over there." He nodded with his head. "And I have to get rid of this."

She pressed her lips together and backed away.

It took four flushes to get everything down, but it was gone. All the evidence of their bad deeds, gone.

But it wasn't over—it couldn't be over, not when Trevor had threatened other people. It was a reason for their secrets to be discovered. What if one of the other people talked after the evidence was found? He knew what had to be done.

Dutch and Allie reemerged from the bathroom. "Get the rest of them," Dutch said to Ethan. "We have to destroy everything."

"No way. It has nothing to do with us," he said.

"You want the detectives to find them tomorrow, then? And have a reason to look into anyone? What if there are more files on his computer? Of us? Let's not give them a reason to search for anything." Dutch stood his ground.

"Let them think it was the allergy. If they start looking into him, we're all fucked."

"He's right," Vee said.

"I agree," Allie said, still next to Dutch.

Ethan looked at Emma for support, but she just looked at her feet before she spoke. "You know they're right."

"What happened to Trevor?" No one answered Ethan, because deep down, Dutch knew they were all relieved. "So then tonight was just an unfortunate accident?"

"It was, if we get rid of the rest of them," Dutch said. "Open the safe."

Ethan huffed, but it was four against one. They all followed him into the bedroom closet. He punched in the code, and next to Trevor's passport and some cash, were six additional thumb drives. They all stared at the open safe, then Dutch took control and took them all out in a handful. The rest of his friends followed him out into the living room, and they watched as he smashed each one with the heel of his shoe, just like he did on the first one. They all helped pick up the pieces, and the girls flushed some of the parts in the half bathroom while the guys flushed the rest in the full.

Multiple flushes later, everything was a memory. The safe was locked back up, wiped clean, and it was time for them to go on with their lives, as if the day had never happened, as if they never knew that there were deadly secrets between them.

As if one of them hadn't killed Trevor.

48

EMMA

The Wedding Day, 9:15 p.m.

"I'm going to change into comfy clothes. I'm spending the night in Fiona's suite. We both are," Emma said to no one.

"I'll walk you back," Ethan said, and then turned to Vee and Dutch. "Let's meet back at the bar. Act natural."

"I don't even know what that means anymore," Vee said.

"Allie, I'll pick you up at your room in about fifteen minutes," Emma said.

"Okay." She shot a quick glance toward Dutch. "Make it a half hour, I think I need a face mask. Take your time."

"I'll text you when I'm on my way." Emma grabbed Ethan's hand. "Come on." When the door clicked closed behind them, Emma's stomach lurched.

Their clutched hands swung in tandem beside them as they walked in silence to the elevator. Her husband knew that she'd done something awful. Something that made her sell out one of her best friends. But he didn't know what it was.

Emma knew that it was going to come up. The rest of the lies between everyone—the secrets—whatever you want to call them, didn't matter. Ethan didn't care what Vee or Dutch or Allie had done. He cared what his wife did.

People from the wedding were still in the lobby bar as Ethan and Emma walked past. Some approached them, looking for information, but Ethan held up a hand and shook his head, playing the hurt friend. Ethan and Emma still stayed silent as they walked to the other end of the hotel, into that elevator bank, and then into their room. Emma immediately went into the bathroom and started the faucet, and then thought washing away her sins would require more than a sink, so she shut it off and turned the shower on. As she closed the door, Ethan sat on the bed, his head in his hands.

Stepping into the glass stall, she let the water wash over her head and run down her face. She hadn't bothered to remove her makeup the correct way, so she scrubbed hotel soap onto her face with her palms, detaching the false eyelashes and surely taking some of her own along with it. Her skin felt tight even as the steam got hotter around her, and she poured half of the tiny bottle of shampoo over her head and lathered it until she washed away the storm, and any residual peanut oil. After a coating of conditioner and body wash, she turned off the water and stepped out.

On the counter, she found her moisturizer and let it sink into her skin, relieving it of the tightness and transforming it into peaches and cream. A wide tooth comb trailed through her hair and then she wound it up into a tight bun at the nape of her neck. She dropped the towel and put on the hotel robe to rummage through her clothes in the room.

Ethan had changed into jeans and a T-shirt and his Rangers hat, and he stared blankly at the television with the remote control in his hand. CNN was on, but she knew he wasn't paying attention, as he hadn't reacted to anything they'd said. It was as if he was looking at a kaleidoscope, mesmerized by the colorful images in front of him as they changed.

In a drawer, she pulled out a pair of track pants and a tank top, then quickly dressed. When she turned around to find her flip-flops, her heart stopped. The small bottle of peanut oil was front and center on the table by the door. She knew she didn't leave it out in the open—she remembered putting it on her hair and her legs in the bathroom as Ethan slept earlier in the day.

How did it get there?

"Ethan?" she asked.

He swiveled his head to his wife, and she was holding the peanut oil. His face showed recognition, then guilt.

"Oh. Yeah. I used some of that earlier. Sorry."

"On what?"

He didn't answer, and instead said, "Emma, what did you do?" He shook his head back and forth slowly, with tears in his eyes. "The not knowing—it's killing me."

She had already decided that she was going to tell him the whole truth—the good, the bad, and the ugly—just not now, and not without Vee. But she had to tell him something that would satisfy his curiosity, that he'd understand would make her do what she did. She sat next to him on the couch and muted the television and looked into his eyes.

That face. She loved his face, his cheekbones, his dark hair and light eyes and fair skin. She'd never loved anyone as much as she loved him. Not even little Mikey Miller in fifth grade, when she'd stayed up all night making him a Valentine and planning their wedding and their children, enacting it with her dolls. She swore one day she'd marry Mikey, and that he was the only one she'd ever love.

Kids are funny like that.

"Ethan, you know I love you, right?"

He nodded. "And I love you more than anything. I'm so sorry about the Fiona thing. I'd rather kill myself than ever let anything hurt you ever again."

"I never wanted you to hurt either. That's why I never told you."

He nodded and looked away, then back to her with tear-filled rims. "Just tell me."

She took a deep breath. "One of the times we were broken up—I slept with someone else. Trevor found out. I don't know how, but he did. I'm sorry. It didn't mean anything. It was only once when I was upset. And I missed you. I just needed something."

She saw the hurt in his face—he knew he was no longer the prize, the only one who'd ever had her.

But he had her now. And that was what should count. They had each other now, even if he had once had Fiona, too.

He pressed his forehead to hers and held the back of her neck. "I have to tell you something."

"Go ahead."

Her eyes were closed and filling with tears, which leapt out of her lids and down her face. She'd never wanted to hurt Ethan, and she knew she'd gutted him with her last declaration. He was going to say something just to hurt her back; she knew it. That was the price she was going to have to pay—their relationship would become tit for tat, bitter and angry and jealous.

She deserved it. She deserved to be hurt.

"I never wanted you to be hurt, Emma. It's the last thing I'd ever want. And Trevor was threatening me all weekend—he had more stuff about me and Fiona. He wanted to break us up. So," he paused and took a deep breath. "The peanut oil. I put it on his cigar. I wanted to kill him. I thought I did. And I did it for you."

49

ALLIE

The Wedding Day, 9:45 p.m.

When Allie's text beeped, it was Emma saying she'd be there in three minutes.

"Dutch, you have to go. Emma's going to be here any second."

When he had offered to see her back to her room, she gladly accepted. She knew there wouldn't be time for sex, but she wanted him there. Of course, once they got into her room, their clothes came off in a rush for a quickie. They'd both needed a release.

She quickly tossed on her long silk nightgown to Dutch's delight.

"You expect me to leave you now?" he said and drew her in closer as he sat under her sheets.

She'd forgotten that she wasn't actually going to bed. To bed, with this beautiful man. "Bad idea. I can't walk through the hallway in this," she said as she pulled it off over her head.

His blue eyes took in her nakedness as she tugged on yoga pants and a T-shirt to his dismay. She ran a brush through her hair quickly and found her sneakers.

"I have to go meet the guys in the bar," he said, standing, and it was her turn to take in his body.

It was like looking at a carved marble statue from Italy—she knew he'd been raised on sports and discipline and karate, and he volunteered as a big brother and played hoops with the guys, but he was sculpted more than she'd even realized the night before. She saw every muscle as he bent over to pull on his boxers and pants, and as he buttoned his shirt, she envisioned ripping it open and kissing his chest.

"Hey. What are you doing tomorrow night?" His head whipped up, leaving a wayward platinum curl near his icy blue eye. "When we land? Did you want to grab a drink?"

Yes.

"I can't," she said solemnly. "I'm having Ahmed take me straight to Connecticut to see my father. He's not doing so well."

"Oh. Shit. I'm sorry, Allie."

She shrugged, even though the thought of losing him killed her inside. It wasn't that Dutch didn't know, or even that she wouldn't confide in him—she just didn't want to, yet. There was a line—relationship on one side, caring for her father on the other. Allie didn't think they could coexist.

"I've been preparing for the last few months, but his nurse Val called today and—" her voice cracked, and she stopped talking.

Dutch approached her, his arms open, and she fell into them. They didn't say anything else. In fact, they lost track of time, and before they knew it there was a knock on the door.

"Shit. It's Emma. I have to go," she said, and held her finger to her lips. "You can let yourself out. I'll see you tomorrow morning. I don't even know if the brunch is still happening, but I assume we'd all go together anyway. I'll text you once I know more."

He nodded. She didn't kiss him again but reapplied her lip gloss before she slipped out the door.

"Hey," she said to Emma and jiggled the handle behind her to make sure it was locked.

Emma was clean and fresh and ironed and dewy, yet she looked downright defeated. Allie was sure she'd had it out with Ethan again. What a terrible weekend it had turned into. Allie never thought she'd be rooting for Emma and Ethan to make it, but she wouldn't let Trevor win. Even though he'd already lost.

Although curious, she never asked Emma what she was hiding—what secrets Trevor had on her. If Emma wanted to tell her, she would. It was hard to picture her having any sort of sordid past—she was practically a nun. Then again, looks were deceiving. Allie wouldn't voluntarily offer up her side hustle, even if she did see it fading into a past life, puddling with the rest of the terrible things she'd done. All she wanted was to move forward. Possibly with Dutch. If that was what he wanted.

"Everything okay?" Allie asked instead.

Emma smiled and nodded. "I just want to go home."

"Me too."

"Anything else from Val?"

"No. I talked to my dad earlier though. I'm going out there tomorrow night, as soon as we get in."

"That's a good idea." Emma paused and drew in a deep breath. "You know if you ever need anything—"

"I know. Thanks."

When they knocked on Fiona's door, her mother answered. She had also changed out of her wedding attire and into a long nightshirt, a pink one with "Live, Laugh, Love" on the front. It was likely Fiona's. Allie wondered how she felt about the saying now.

"Hi girls. Come in," she whispered as she moved aside. "Try to be quiet. She's sleeping. I gave her a Xanax. I didn't know what else to do." She craned her neck over to the hallway where the bedroom was located, and the door was shut. "I canceled my flight home. I'm going to stay here until we settle this. Then—then I think she might come home. She has no place being down here in Miami. She never did."

"We didn't think so either," Emma said.

Allie had to remember that it was business as usual. However, she didn't need to sit with Fiona's mother all night when there was something else she'd rather be doing. She raised her arms over her head in a yoga stretch and yawned.

"What a day. Since Fiona is passed out, I think I'm going to do the same in my own bed. Should we assume the brunch is canceled?"

Susan looked at her watch. "That's okay. My nieces are coming here soon, once they put the younger kids to bed with some of the older cousins watching them. My brother-in-law might come back in a bit too. And brunch is already paid for, so you might as well eat something before you get on the plane."

"Thanks Mrs. Hawthorne," Allie said as she stood, then looked at Emma. "I bet Ethan is waiting for you."

"Yeah. I should get going too," she said.

"Thanks girls." Susan gave both of them a hug and ushered them to the door. "Try to get some sleep." The heavy door snapped closed behind them.

In the hallway, Allie exhaled. "Thank God," she whispered. "I just want to go back to my room."

"Yeah. Me too," Emma said, and pulled out her phone, presumably texting Ethan. They walked in silence to the elevator when Emma's phone pinged. "Ethan said they're all wiped out too. They're finishing their drinks and then going to bed."

Allie certainly hoped so. She quickly texted Dutch that she was going back to her room, and he was welcome to join. She just wanted to wake up, with or without Dutch, and have it be the day that they all went home.

50

VEEJAY

The day after the wedding, 9:00 a.m.

Vee had forgotten to shut the blackout shades and burned his retinas as soon as he opened his eyes in the morning. The misery of yesterday's storm was gone, and the sun shone bright into his room, through the wispy white drapes, as if it were a spotlight on the hotel.

Hungover, he didn't want to move, didn't want to get up out of his comfortable bed, didn't want to face the rest of the world as he knew it now—as a father. To a daughter. That he never knew about. He didn't know how he would ever reconcile his feelings about it.

But last night, he knew what to do. Apparently, Fiona had passed out, so Ethan went to Emma, and after one more drink Dutch insisted it was bedtime. Which was good because Vee wanted to be alone.

"What time is it?" Lillie asked from under the covers next to him, where they were both stark naked. "My flight is at noon."

Thank God, Vee thought.

"It's just past nine. You should probably start to hustle," Vee said.

He thought maybe Dutch was planning to make a move on her, but he was nowhere to be found as Vee drank alone in the bar, contemplating his life, the day, Trevor, Emma, Bianca, Fiona, peanut dust—one drink turned into another and another. There were so many people from the wedding approaching him and trying to sympathize with him for losing his friend—he couldn't take the lies anymore. But instead of engaging with them, he just let them buy him drinks to the wee hours of the night. He didn't even remember asking Lillie back to his room. He couldn't remember if he made the first move or if she did.

But there she was. The professional bartender he'd made fun of the day before.

Okay, so he was a jerk. He felt entitled to be at the moment.

Lillie stood and grabbed a towel that was on the floor and wrapped it around herself as she silently gathered her clothes and went into the bathroom. When Vee heard the sink running, he jumped up and grabbed a pair of track shorts to put on and retrieved a bottle of water from the minibar fridge. After a long sip, he opened the balcony door and stepped outside. If he didn't know any better, he'd think there was almost a chill in the morning air.

What a difference a day makes.

He leaned his arms on the railing in front of him and took a deep breath, his eyes closed. The palm trees swayed in the wind, the scent of coconut and ocean in his nostrils. When he stopped his brain from moving for at least a few seconds, he forgot about the chaos that his life had become. Just three days ago, he was at the airport with his four best friends en route to paradise. The journey to the airport later in the afternoon would certainly be a different one.

"Do you have extra toothpaste?"

Lillie's voice cracked through his headache, and he went inside to get an aspirin. In the bathroom, she was back in her tight red dress and her hair was brushed back into a short ponytail, and she was gargling mouthwash. Vee entered and dug around in his vanity bag until he found toothpaste, which she put on her finger and smeared onto her teeth after she spit and rinsed. Following her lead, he grabbed his toothbrush and did the same, silently. He didn't want to make small talk with her. It was awkward enough, and he didn't want to make fake plans to see her again. He didn't want to see her again.

She left the bathroom while he was still brushing, but he saw through the mirror that she was sitting on the bed, waiting. So, he took his time.

"I have to go, Veejay," she shouted to him.

He *really* wanted to give her a peace sign with his free hand, but he just wasn't that type of guy. Exhaling loudly, he rinsed his mouth out and then popped two aspirin and turned back into the room. She didn't say anything, so he gave her a crooked smile.

"Well, that was fun?" he said, unsure of what else to say.

"Yeah," she said softly. "Sorry I got so aggressive. And thanks for stopping it before it got too far. You were right, I was too drunk." She looked directly at him. "You're one of the good ones. Maybe you can call me once we're back in the city?"

Oh. So, he didn't get laid. *Good*. The last thing he needed added to the heap of shit that his life had become was to be a #MeToo poster boy. Vee supposed it was in his bones to always do the right thing.

She stood, holding her heels, and they had a quick embrace. "Sure, Lillie. I'll call you."

"Okay. I left my number on the desk."

"Great."

He walked her to the door and pecked her on the cheek, then closed the door behind him. His phone pinged, and it was Ethan.

> We're all meeting downstairs at ten-thirty for brunch. The limo is coming to get us at one.

Their flight was shortly before three, and he'd be home by seven p.m. If going to brunch would facilitate the process that much faster, then that's what he'd do. Because once he was home, he could spend the time thinking about his daughter, and if he'd be able to repair his relationship with Emma. He hoped so.

He also had to rehearse what to say to Allie. In his alcohol induced state the night before, he'd decided he was going to come clean. Even if she never spoke to him again—which would kill him—he needed to know that there were no more secrets. He'd also have to talk to Emma about telling Ethan about their past. It probably wouldn't happen immediately, but he had to convince her it was the right thing to do. There was a long road ahead.

He also wanted to know if last night was truly an accident. If it wasn't—then who killed Trevor?

51

EMMA

The day after the wedding, 10:30 a.m.

When Emma and Ethan got to the private brunch room, her heart sank. It must've been decorated the night before, with pink and white and silver balloons in the shape of hearts and flowers of the same colors on each numbered table. Even worse, there was an enormous picture, probably three feet by four feet, of Fiona and Trevor. It was one of their engagement photos, the one of them on the beach at sunset. His left hand held her right hand. She wore a lacy white strapless dress and beige wedges on the sand. She was smiling, or laughing even, with her eyes squinted, her cheeks up to the top of her face. Trevor had his right hand in the pocket of his black pants, and he was staring at her with a look of pride. It was framed with poster board, and everyone was supposed to write well wishes for their marriage on it and sign it.

Now, the marker hung loosely at its base, as no one dared go near it. Emma carefully approached and took a last look at Trevor.

His expression in the photo was one Emma had never seen before.

What if there was a side of Trevor that wasn't an asshole? What if he actually loved Fiona, and wanted to create a life with her, and he'd resorted to those ridiculous threats because he was scared of losing her? Emma couldn't picture it. Or maybe she'd actively not pictured it. Guilt fired up in her belly that she'd tried to kill him.

Emma needed a moment with Ethan last night, after he'd told her that he put peanut oil on Trevor's cigar. He was vulnerable, shaking as he told her, how he'd said that he'd do anything for her. Emma believed him, and the disgust and shame she'd had about her sins and faking the pregnancy were about to come out, so instead, she told him that she purposely wore the peanut oil to try to get a reaction out of him, too. That way, Ethan wasn't alone, and it was something they'd done together—attempted murder. That was something new they could put on their Christmas cards.

Because, she'd kill for Ethan too. She wanted him to know that. She needed him to know. Overnight, their relationship went to a different place, and Emma liked it. A more secure one. It was obvious what they'd both do for the other. Because of that, Emma decided she needed a long talk with Vee. They'd already planned to have dinner back in the city tomorrow night, and she had to convince him that they should tell Ethan the truth. No one would ever hold this over her—or Vee—ever again.

Thankfully, the brunch wasn't yet crowded. It was a buffet style and Dutch was already there, sitting alone at table four and scrolling through his phone. Vee followed a few minutes after Emma and Ethan. Allie, of course, was last, all fluffed hair and glossed lips and stared at Emma by the picture. Emma picked up the marker.

We love you, Fiona.

She signed her name, all loops and exaggerations. Allie followed with *We're always here for you*, and a bunch of hearts. The guys appeared behind her and took their turn, with Ethan writing *We're so sorry*, Dutch writing *Hang in their kid, xoxo* and Vee writing truest statement of them all, *At least we're all still best friends. Forever.*

They all filled their plates and used eating as an excuse not to talk. Dutch dove into a plate of waffles, while Ethan and Vee piled theirs with eggs, bacon, sausage, and French toast. Emma and Allie stuck to fruit and yogurt. Emma couldn't even bother with the omelet station.

Everyone's eyes were nervously trained at the entrance, waiting for Fiona to arrive. When she finally walked in with her mother and uncle, the air of the room changed. No one knew whether to look at her or look away.

Table four stared at their coffee cups. They didn't even look at each other. The clanking of silverware and the slurping of drinks did nothing for anyone, as Fiona may as well have been a pink elephant.

"We have to tell her," Dutch said, breaking the silence. "We owe it to her. Not now, but once we all get home, we have to tell her," he repeated.

"Tell her what? That she married a monster?" Allie interjected. "And that her so-called friends sold her out and that we're probably worse than he is? *Was*?"

Dutch shook his head back and forth. "She needs to know Trevor was blackmailing us. It's my fault. I'll put it all on me. But she deserves to know. I can't believe we did this. Look at her."

While Emma knew what he meant, *we did this*, she knew it wasn't her. Whatever happened to Trevor that caused his death wasn't her, and it wasn't Vee. It wasn't even Ethan, tried as he might've. But Fiona did deserve to know what he was really like. What they were all really like. What they did. Emma was ready to face all the consequences of her actions.

"Yes," Emma said, nodding. "Dutch is right. We're her friends. She needs to know."

"Hey," Ethan said as he squeezed Emma's hand. "Do you mind if I—" He nodded in Fiona's direction.

"No. Go ahead, *meu amor*." She meant it.

Ethan wiped his mouth with his napkin and got up and approached her. They spoke for about ten seconds before Fiona fell into his arms for comfort, and Emma didn't even feel a pang of jealousy. That part was over. Dutch looked around the table, then stood next, followed by Vee. Emma and Allie exchanged a glance and decided to get it over with as well.

They all embraced in a hug as everyone else stared. *Oh God, it's the bridal party without the seventh musketeer!*

"Are you okay?" Emma asked Fiona.

"No. But I will be. I'm so glad you guys are still here," she said.

"We tried to stay with you last night, but you were passed out," Allie said. "You know we wouldn't just ditch you."

"I know. You all meant so much to Trevor. He talked about you guys all the time."

I bet. Emma's guilt bubbled, but she knew that Trevor had to make them all seem like angels to Fiona, so it would hurt her even more if he needed to tear them down. Emma still agreed with Dutch that getting the truth out was going to be the right thing to do, even if it fractured everything and everyone in the beginning.

"My mom is staying in Miami for a while. Just until I get everything settled with—with the situation," Fiona said. "Then I guess I'll be coming home."

Home. New York. All of them, together. As it should've been.

"Do they know what happened?" Emma asked.

"Yeah, they know. They said it was an accident. They found almond residue on his teeth and in his throat. We don't know how, and we don't know why my EpiPen was gone. There was too much chaos yesterday with the storm." She wiped her nose on the back of her hand. "I'm afraid it's my fault. If only I paid closer attention—I should've been looking for it."

"No, Fiona, don't do that to yourself. It was an accident."

Emma knew that now. It was an accident.

It was serendipity.

52

ETHAN

The day after the wedding, 12:30 p.m.

Saying goodbye to Fiona was hard, but Ethan just wanted to go home. As he packed after brunch, he grappled with the idea that he tried to murder Trevor—and that Trevor ended up dead anyway. It didn't matter. All he wanted out of this weekend was for Emma to feel like the only one. Even if *he* wasn't the only one for her anymore. It killed him.

As Emma closed her suitcase next to him, he moved behind her and kissed the back of her neck, then placed his hands over her abdomen, gently rubbing his baby.

"Careful," Emma said. "I've been feeling really crampy lately."

"It's probably just nerves," he said into her hair. "This wasn't exactly the relaxing weekend we had planned."

"No, it wasn't," she said softly. "I hope it doesn't affect the pregnancy."

"Hey," Ethan said as he turned her around to face him. "I love you."

He meant it more than he'd ever meant anything.

"I love you too." She looked toward the bathroom. "The peanut oil is still in there. I want to get rid of it.

Even though we're going to tell her that Trevor was a shit, I don't want it here. She can know the bad things we did, but she can't know that you and I tried to take him out." She left Vee out of it. Ethan didn't need to know she was working with him yesterday.

"Oh. Right."

He retrieved it from the counter and wrapped it in toilet paper and was about to drop it in the trash can, then had a better idea. He looked at his to-go coffee cup, took off the top, poured out the coffee in the sink, and placed the small bottle inside and put the top back on.

"Better safe than sorry. No one will know there's a bottle in here. I'll get rid of it downstairs in a public can. Let's go."

In the lobby, Dutch was already waiting for the limo with Allie and Vee. Ethan pretended to take a last sip of coffee and threw the cup in a nearby trash can with all the other random cups and bags and sunscreen bottles, wishing for it to be taken away with his previous intent to kill. It was necessary at the time, but he never wanted to feel like that again.

He left Emma with them and stepped outside and lit a cigarette, one of only three left in his pack. The dawn of a new day was coming, one where he'd be a nonsmoker. And a father. What could be better than that? He'd just lit the cigarette when the limo pulled up, the same Hummer style that had taken them there. Dutch came out and spoke to the driver, who then began to load everyone's bags as they piled in, one by one. Ethan was last and as the door shut behind him, he wanted to forget the last three days of fun.

53

DUTCH

The day after the wedding, 2:30 p.m.

Dutch got comfortable in his first-class seat. It was the same seating arrangements as last time. Ethan and Emma were in the row next to him, and Vee was at his side while Allie was diagonal, behind Ethan.

No one had spoken much in the limo. He thought everyone was tired and done with it all. He certainly was. Tired. Much like the rest of the weekend, he didn't get much sleep but instead was with Allie all night. He really wanted to see her later that night, once they were back in New York. Home. But he understood her going to Connecticut. Her father needed her.

She took him by surprise. It felt so natural to be with her, even though on the surface it looked like a bad idea. Like vodka and olives—it just worked. She was a close friend, if anything—he'd even debated telling her that he had Trevor's "groom" cigar specially rolled, with crushed peanuts toward the base.

Dutch thought he'd killed him and didn't bat an eye. It was especially deserved when he found out later in the night that Trevor had been blackmailing all his friends, and a bunch of other poor saps that Dutch didn't know. What a funny coincidence that it ended up *not* being Dutch who killed him. What an opportune occurrence that he ate an almond.

He thought about Roger, and how he—and everyone else—banished him. His heart squeezed at the lost friendship. Roger was a victim of circumstance, just like any of them could've been. Dutch and the rest of the gang needed to get off their high horses. No one was perfect—that much was clear. If anything, Roger was the only one with any integrity. He'd been blackmailed just like the rest of them, and he was the one who stood up for Fiona when no one else did.

The man deserved a medal, not to be cast aside by those who were closest to him.

He deserved forgiveness, no matter how hard it would be. Dutch needed to swallow his own pride and admit his mistake. While he couldn't forget what Roger did, he could forgive him. He knew he could. He was embarrassed at his own behavior for cutting him out, knowing what he'd done himself.

Dutch turned his head and looked at Allie through the stream of people that were still boarding for coach. Her eyes were already closed with a sleep mask perched atop her head, iPad in one hand and her phone in the other.

Vee was quiet next to him, headphones on, enthralled in the book he never got to read while relaxing in Miami. Dutch pulled out his phone and texted Allie.

I miss you.

He heard her rummage from his seat, no doubt waking from the vibration in her hand. He saw the three dots on his phone signaling her reply.

> You're adorable. I just want to get the damn show on the road. The traffic to CT is going to be insane.

Poor Allie just wanted to see her dying father.

> Soon enough xx

Then Dutch texted Pavlov to make arrangements.

Dutch's eyes closed as soon as the plane began to taxi on the runway, and he fell into a deep sleep. His broken airplane dreams consisted of dragons and knives and blood, all signs of betrayal. Him. His friends. His guilt. When his eyes opened at landing, he was back in New York, a new man. Before the plane made it to the jetway, he turned his phone on and scrolled to a number he'd never erased and sent a text message.

> Hey. Long time no see. I miss you bro. Can we talk?

Roger answered immediately.

> I miss you too. Can you talk now?

Dutch smiled as he tapped back.

I'll call you tonight.

It was all going to be okay. Dutch tucked his phone in his shirt pocket before unclasping his seatbelt.

54

ALLIE

The day after the wedding, 5:50 p.m.

Allie stood and stretched the second the soft ding purred from the speakers and seatbelt sign went off. Truthfully, she was happy to be on the ground after such a turbulent flight—it woke her from her initial slumber and she was sure the plane would be struck down, punishing her and all her friends for whatever they'd done. She knew there was nowhere to go until they opened the door, but she was anxious. She tapped her fingers on the back of Ethan's seat as she tried to mush her way into the aisle. She wanted to be the first one off the plane. Her father was waiting.

After they all disembarked and got their luggage, they stood around the conveyor belt awkwardly, all wanting to leave but none making the first move. At the same time, they all drew into a group hug and none wanted to let go. Bonded by friendship and time, heartaches and celebrations, love and disagreements, they were forever a unit—one that now included blackmail.

But she had to go. Allie said goodbye to her friends and took off running, looking for Ahmed's waiting car.

"Hey. Allie. Wait," yelled Dutch. He dragged his golf bag and his suitcase behind him trying to keep up with her. "There was an accident on ninety-five. It's backed up for hours."

Tears sprung to Allie's eyes—how was she going to get to her father now?

"Hey, it's okay," Dutch said with a soft hug. "Follow me."

She did without question, until they reached a private entrance. A man came out, spoke to Dutch who showed him ID, and then another man came and took their bags.

"What's going on?" Allie asked.

"Get your ID out," he said with his amazing smile. "You're hitching a ride on the chopper."

Allie had been on helicopters before with Wharton, for sightseeing tours or quick trips to the Hamptons when they wanted to bypass traffic, like right now. They were both escorted by private car to Dutch's father's helicopter, which was lying in wait. She texted Ahmed, apologized for making him come all the way to LaGuardia, and Venmo'd him twice his charge. Then they got into the helicopter, buckled themselves in as the doors shut, and they were up, up, and away.

Below her, there were miles of cars locked in bumper-to-bumper traffic, and when it sunk in that her father was mere minutes away, not hours, she gripped onto Dutch's hand. How could she ever thank him?

They got clearing to set down at a landing about twenty minutes away from her father, and Dutch had already arranged a black car to be waiting for Allie. As she jumped off the chopper, he followed her and saw her safely into the car.

"Are you going to be okay?" he asked her from the open window as she buckled herself in.

"Dutch, I—I don't know how I can ever repay you for this. It means more to me than you'll ever know."

"I'm sure you can think of a way," he said with a wink. "So, you'll let me know when you get there?"

"Absolutely," she said, and then pulled him in for a lingering kiss; she didn't want to let go. But she did. "Can we get together when I get back?" She knew she looked like she swallowed a frog. "I want to tell you something. About this weekend." If she was going to start something with him, she wanted to tell him what Trevor knew.

"Definitely. I'll be waiting. And hey—I want to talk to you about this weekend too. Not just us. Some other stuff that I think you deserve to know."

"Okay. I don't know how long I'll be here, though."

"Don't worry. I'll wait." His head tilted down, then his eyes met hers. "I texted Roger earlier. I'm going to talk to him tonight. We all need to forgive, Allie."

A knowing smile broke out on Allie's lips as she nodded. She wanted that too. Roger was part of their family, and she felt terrible for the way things ended with all of them. Especially now. They were an imperfect little family, Roger being the only one with a pair of balls, the one who had told Trevor to fuck off when it mattered. She hated that it took all this to see it.

Dutch smiled as she raised the car window, and she watched as he boarded the helicopter and lifted off to go back to the city.

The car pulled out smoothly onto the country road that would take her to her father, the only one that mattered. She texted him that she landed safely and would be there shortly. The tires crunched on the gravel as she reached into her bag and finished off the last of her trail mix, happy again that he'd never have to know anything bad about her.

About her crimes.

About her divorce.

And about how she stuffed an almond from her trail mix into Trevor's cheddar cheese cube as he was smoking a cigar.

Allie knew that as soon as the Instagram live video started, Trevor would be distracted. When he passed her and Fiona on his way to smoke, he demanded food be waiting for him upon his return. Allie volunteered for the task when another guest stole Fiona's attention. That was her first stroke of luck. If she controlled the food, Trevor couldn't control her anymore.

In her bag, she nonchalantly reached for two dimpled nuts. Most people were milling about, exiting the cocktail room for the reception room. No one paid her any attention. She smushed an almond into the cheese cube, then into another, and molded both back into shape. She put some assorted meats and vegetables on the plate but kept the cheese on top—she knew he'd go for that first. She set it on the sweetheart table and walked away.

Before being dragged onto the dance floor, he passed by the plate, and he looked pleased as he grabbed a handful of the cheese on top. With all the commotion surrounding the start of the video, he probably didn't notice the crunch when he bit into it. When his face turned red, and his throat closed and he couldn't breathe, she knew she'd succeeded.

When she volunteered to get Fiona's bag, she'd purposely knocked everything over, breaking the glass—she wanted all evidence swept away, which was exactly what happened. The EpiPen was missing—that was her second stroke of luck. She pretended to fuss as he lay dying, but there was a moment between her and her tormentor. He looked right at her. She smiled and mouthed *Fuck you*.

He knew it was her, before he took his last breath. He took all her secrets with him when he hit the ground, and she hoped the last thing he ever felt was regret for fucking with her and everyone she loved.

It was over, and she'd gotten away with it, and no one was the wiser. She was safely in Connecticut, with Miami and that past sin over a thousand miles away.

Allie's phone pinged from her bag while she was in the back of the car. It was her father.

> I'm glad you're okay. I can't wait to see you, my Good Girl.

Acknowledgments

Special thanks again to my agent, Anne Tibbets, for always being a partner to me in this crazy game called publishing. Just because you make it look easy doesn't mean it is, and I'm forever grateful to have you in my corner.

To my remarkable editor, Luisa Smith—well, this one was a labor of love, am I right? Thank you for believing in me a second time. Your ideas on how to turn this book amazing were top notch. All the challenges you had from beginning to end were handled with mercy (I know this one was a bear, so thank you!), and I truly love how our little baby turned out. I can't wait to work with you again! Thank you to my publishers Otto Penzler and Charles Perry, and my publicist Jacob Shapiro for all you continue to do. Thanks to those assisting the team: Linda Biagi, Kathy Strickman, and Charles Brock.

To Vanessa Lillie, Jennifer Pashley, and Danielle Girard— our Rhody Writer's Retreat text thread is still a daily godsend and I love getting to commiserate and celebrate everything with you girls. To authors Mary Keliikoa and Jessica Payne, having you both in my life as critique partners and friends is something I treasure, and you've both already made book three so much better. Cheers to the May releases!

I've gotten blurbs through two books now from authors that I idolize. Michele Campbell, Samantha

Bailey, Mary Kubica, Jeneva Rose, Robyn Harding, Wendy Walker, and Aggie Blum Thompson—your extraordinary books continue to make me strive to be better.

Bookstagram: You *all* rule. I got to know so many of you during the last year. I continue to be in awe of the clever ways you display books and work assiduously to get reviews out. All authors appreciate you! A few in particular I want to shout out: @firepitandbooks, @thriller_chick, @gareindeedreads, @darkthrillsandchills, @jayme_reads, @blondethriller-booklover, @whatshesees, @the_reading_beauty, and @bonechillingbooks.

Florida crew—I'd like to thank the amazing, tireless staff at The Deck Bar and Grille for always knowing when to refill my Sauvy B: Cedric, Laura, John, Sadie, Kris, Sanela, and Jay. I'm happy to spend more time with Jamie and Keflin, Steve and Sachi, Amon and Lee, Michelle and Tom, and my new Bayway neighbors who welcomed us from day one. Don't worry Lauren and David, you haven't been replaced.

To my family and friends previously mentioned in *Finding Tessa*, I love you all. There's one addition to the family this year that gets a special mention: welcome to the world, beautiful Mia Juliette Slininger. You are loved beyond comprehension!

Always, special thanks to my parents Hank and Geri Sbordone, my best friend Ann Marie DePaulis, and my supportive husband John, because you guys are always there for everything. John, there's no one I'd rather spend two straight days in a car with every six weeks going back and forth from NJ to FL. Well, Cosmo too.

To the readers: you make the world go 'round.